THE WIFE UPSTAIRS

THE WIFE UPSTAIRS

RACHEL HAWKINS

LARGE PRINT PRESS
A part of Gale, a Cengage Company

Copyright © 2020 by Rachel Hawkins.
Large Print Press, a part of Gale, a Cengage Company.

LIBRARY OF CONGRESS CIP DATA ON FILE.
CATALOGUING IN PUBLICATION FOR THIS BOOK
IS AVAILABLE FROM THE LIBRARY OF CONGRESS.

ISBN-13: 978-1-4328-9431-3 (paperback alk. paper)

Published in 2022 by arrangement with St. Martin's Publishing Group.

Printed in the United States of America
1 2 3 4 5   25 24 23 22 21

*For Mama, who is thankfully
nothing like the mothers in this book*

There are always two deaths, the real one and the one people know about.

— Jean Rhys, *Wide Sargasso Sea*

■ ■ ■ ■

PART I
JANE

■ ■ ■ ■

1

February

It is the absolute shittiest day for a walk.

Rain has been pouring down all morning, making my drive from Center Point out here to Mountain Brook a nightmare, soaking the hem of my jeans as I get out of the car in the Reeds' driveway, making my sneakers squelch on the marble floors of the foyer.

But Mrs. Reed is holding her dog Bear's leash, making a face at me, this frown of exaggerated sympathy that's supposed to let me know how bad she feels about sending me out in the rain on this Monday morning.

That's the important thing — that I know that she feels bad.

She still expects me to do it, though.

I've been walking dogs in the Thornfield Estates subdivision for almost a month now, and if there's one thing I've definitely figured out, it's that what matters most is how everything *looks.*

Mrs. Reed *looks* sympathetic. She *looks* like she absolutely hates that I have to walk her collie, Bear, on a cold and stormy day in mid-February.

She *looks* like she actually gives a fuck about me as a person.

She doesn't, though, which is fine, really.

It's not like I give a fuck about her, either.

So I smile, tugging at the bottom of my army-green raincoat. "Came prepared," I tell her, taking Bear's leash. We're standing in the front foyer of the Reed home. To my left is a giant framed mirror propped against the wall, reflecting me, Mrs. Reed, and Bear, already straining toward the door. There's also a distressed wood table holding a bowl of potpourri as well as a pair of diamond hoop earrings, flung carelessly when Mrs. Reed came in last night from whatever charity function she'd been attending.

Charity functions are big around here, I've noticed, although I never can figure out what they're actually raising money for. The invitations I see lying on end tables or fastened to refrigerator doors with magnets are a word salad of virtue signaling. *Children, battered women, homeless, underprivileged:*

various euphemisms that all mean "poor."

No telling what Mrs. Reed was supporting last night, really, but that's another thing I don't actually care about.

And I don't let my eyes linger on the earrings.

Bear's leash is smooth in my hand as I give Mrs. Reed a little wave and head out onto the wide front porch. It's painted cement, slick in the damp, and my ancient sneakers nearly skid across it.

I hear the door close behind me, and wonder what Mrs. Reed will do this morning while I'm off walking her dog. Have another cup of coffee? Chase it with a Xanax? Plan some other charity function?

Maybe a brunch to raise money for kids who don't know how to yacht.

The rain has tapered off some, but the morning is still cold, and I wish I'd brought gloves. My hands look raw and chapped, the knuckles an angry red. There's still a light pink burn mark splashing across my skin between the thumb and forefinger of my right hand, a trophy from the last day I worked at Roasted, a coffee shop in Mountain Brook Village.

I remind myself that walking dogs sucks, but at least it doesn't carry the threat of second-degree burns.

Bear tugs on his leash, sniffing every mailbox we come to, and I let him pull me along behind him, my mind more on the houses, the neighborhood, than on my charge. Behind every one of these McMansions is a bright green backyard, so it makes no sense that anyone would even need a dog-walker. But *need* is not a word people like this think of. Everything with them is *want.*

That's what all these houses are about.

Mrs. Reed and her husband live alone on Magnolia Court in eight bathrooms and seven bedrooms, a formal living room and a family den, an upstairs lounge and a "gentleman's study." Every house in Thornfield Estates is like that from what I can tell. I've been in four of them so far because of course once one neighbor has a dog-walker, everyone else needs — *wants* — one. I work for the Reeds, walking Bear, and now for the McLaren family on Primrose Lane, walking their dalmatian, Mary-Beth. Then there's the Clarks on Oakwood with their shih tzus, Major and Colonel, and Tripp Ingraham on Maple Way just hired me to walk his late wife's Labrador, Harper.

All in all, it's a good gig, certainly better than working at Roasted. Here, people actually look me in the eye because they want to be the kind of people who tell themselves they're not assholes if they actually call "the help" by their first name. "Jane is like family," Mrs. Reed probably says to the other ladies at the country club, and they all make simpering sounds of agreement and have another Bloody Mary.

My sneakers squeak as I walk down the sidewalk, and I think of my apartment, how it's probably leaking in that one spot in the kitchen again, the ceiling a darker, dingy gray against the rest of the dingy gray. The apartment is cheap and not in a terrible part of town, but sometimes it feels like living in a little concrete box, and no matter how much I try to dress it up with posters from Target or pretty blankets I've picked up from thrift stores, the gray fights back.

There isn't any dingy gray in Thornfield Estates.

Here, the grass is green no matter the time of year, and every house has flowerpots or window boxes, or huge bushes covered in colorful flowers. The shutters are bright yellow, navy blue, deep red, emerald green. If there's any gray at all, it's soft and elegant — dove gray, I heard Mrs. Reed call it. There's a constant hum of activity from lawn services, carpet cleaners, and housekeeping vans going in and out of driveways, even on a rainy day like today.

Bear stops to pee against a curb, and I use my free hand to push the hood back from my head, cold rainwater slithering down my neck as I do. The rain jacket is old, and the seam on the left side is torn, but I can't bring myself to buy a new one. It's an expense that doesn't seem quite worth it, and sometimes I wonder if anyone around here would notice if an older raincoat went missing.

Too big a risk, I remind myself, but I still spend a solid two minutes imagining walking through this neighborhood in something sleek and pretty, something that doesn't leak cold rainwater all over me. Something like the Burberry jacket Mrs. Clark had hanging up by the door last week.

Don't even think about it.

So instead, I think about the diamond earrings at Mrs. Reed's, how if both went missing, well, that looks suspicious, but one? One could've fallen off the table. Could be pressed into the carpet at the country club. Could be loose in a pocket somewhere.

Bear stops to smell another mailbox, but I pull him on, making my way toward my favorite house.

It's at the end of a dead-end street, set back farther from the road than the others, and it's one of the few that doesn't seem to have a steady stream of people going in and out. The yard is just as green as the other lawns in the neighborhood, but shaggier, and the pretty purple bushes that bloom out front have climbed too high, blocking off windows on the first floor.

It's the biggest house in the neighborhood, rising taller, two massive wings sprouting off either side, two oak trees climbing high on the front lawn. It was clearly older than the other homes in the neighborhood, probably the first house ever built here.

The sameness of Thornfield Estates means that eventually, all the houses blur together. I like that — a beautiful blur is better than the depressing monotony of my part of town — but there's something about this house, all alone at the end of a cul-de-sac, that draws me back every time.

I step off the sidewalk, and into the center of the road, to get a closer look.

This part of the neighborhood is always so quiet that it doesn't even occur to me that standing in the street might not be the safest thing to do.

I hear the car before I see it, but even then, I don't move, and later, I'd look back at that moment and wonder if I somehow knew what was going to happen. If everything in my life had been leading me to that one spot, to that one house.

To him.

2

Almost all of the cars in Thornfield Estates are the same, some version of luxury SUV. They're basically movable versions of the houses — notably expensive, bigger than could ever be necessary. I barely notice them anymore, just register them as champagne or midnight-blue tanks that roll through the streets regularly.

The car that comes flying out of the driveway of my favorite house isn't an SUV, though. It's a sports car, an older one with a growling engine, and candy-apple red, bright as a wound against the gray day.

Bear barks, dancing on his back legs, and I try to move out of the way, my fingers getting tangled in the leash as the car's bumper rushes toward us.

The asphalt is slick with rain, and maybe that's what saves me because as I step back, my foot skids and I fall, landing hard enough to rattle my teeth. My hood drops over my face, so I can't see anything except army-green vinyl, but I hear the squeal of brakes, then the soft crunch of metal. Bear is barking and barking and barking, moving nervously, and the leather leash bites into my wrist, making me wince.

"Jesus Christ," I hear a man say, and I finally manage to push the hood back.

The back half of that gorgeous car now rests against one of the fancy streetlights that line the road. He hadn't been going all that fast, but the car was so lightweight that the metal had crumpled like paper, and my mouth suddenly goes dry, heart pounding heavily in my chest.

Shit, shit, shit.

A car like that is worth more than most people make in a year. It would take me ages at the coffee shop to even afford a down payment on something like that, and now it's seriously fucked up because I've been gaping at this guy's house from the middle of the street.

The driver's door is open, and I finally make myself look at the man standing there, one arm slung across the top of the door.

He doesn't look like the other men I've seen in Thornfield Estates. They wear polo shirts and khakis, and even the ones who are young and in good shape have a sort of softness to them. Weak chins or bellies that sag slightly over their expensive leather belts.

There's nothing weak or sagging in this man. He's wearing jeans and boots that are meant to look lived-in, but I know are expensive. Everything about him looks expensive, even his rumpled white button-down.

"Are you alright?" he asks, stepping toward me. Even though it's raining, he's wearing a pair of aviator sunglasses, and I can see myself reflected in them, the pale oval of my face against the dark green of my hood.

And when he takes off the glasses, hooking them in the collar of his shirt, his eyes are very blue. A trio of wrinkles pop up over the bridge of his nose as he looks down at me.

It had been a long time since anyone looked at me like they were actually worried about me, and that's almost more attractive than the nice clothes, the gorgeous car, the perfect bone structure.

I nod at him as I push myself to my feet, yanking on Bear's leash to bring the dog closer.

"Fine," I tell him. "I shouldn't have been standing in the street."

One corner of his mouth kicks up, revealing a dimple in his cheek. "I shouldn't have been pulling out of the driveway like a bat out of hell."

He leans down then, giving Bear a quick scratch between the ears. The dog twists into his touch, tongue lolling out.

"I'm guessing you're the new dog-walker everyone's so excited about," the man says, and I clear my throat, cheeks suddenly hot.

"Yeah, I am," I say, and he keeps watching me, waiting. "Jane," I blurt out. "That's . . . my name is Jane."

"Jane," he repeats. "Don't see many Janes around lately."

I don't tell him that it's not even my real name, but the name of a dead girl I knew in a dead life. My real name is equally boring, but it's one he might hear more often than Jane.

"I'm Eddie," he tells me, offering his hand, and I shake it, painfully aware of how clammy my palm must feel and the grit of the road still embedded in the meaty place just below my thumb.

"Don't see many Eddies around lately, either," I say, and he laughs at that. It's a rich, warm sound that makes something at the base of my spine tingle.

And maybe that's why when he asks if I

want to come in for a cup of coffee, I say yes.

3

Up close, the house is even more impressive than it is from the street. The front door towers over us, curving into an arch. It's a defining feature in all these houses, these massive doors. At the Reeds', the bathroom doors are at least eight feet tall, making even the smallest rooms feel grand and important.

Eddie ushers me and Bear inside, and the dog immediately shakes himself, sending droplets of water to the marble floor.

"Bear!" I say sharply, tugging on his collar, but Eddie only shrugs.

"Floors will dry faster than you, huh, big guy?" He gives the dog another pat, then gestures for me to follow him down the hall.

There's a heavy table just to the right — more marble, more wrought iron — holding an elaborate flower arrangement, and when I pass by, I let one finger trail over the nearest blossom.

It feels cool and silky, slightly damp under my finger, so I know the flowers are real, and I wonder if he — or his wife, let's be real — have new ones brought in every day.

The hallway leads to a massive living room with high ceilings. I'd expected something like the Reeds' house again, a sea of neutrals, but the furniture in this room is bright and looks comfortable. There's a pair of sofas in a deep cranberry, plus three wingback chairs with bold prints that don't match, but manage to go together. The floors are light hardwood, and I spot a few rugs, also in bright colors.

Two tall lamps throw warm pools of golden light on the floor, and the fireplace is framed by built-in bookshelves.

"You have books," I say, and Eddie stops, turning to me with his hands in his pockets, his eyebrows raised.

I nod at the shelves, which are crammed full of hardbacks. "Just . . . a lot of these houses have that shelving, but I usually don't see books."

The Reeds have a few framed photos, some weird-looking vases, and a whole bunch of blank space on their built-ins. The Clarks prefer china plates on little stands with the odd silver bowl.

Eddie's still watching me, and I can't read

his expression. Finally, he says, "You're observant."

I'm not sure if that was supposed to be a compliment or not, and I suddenly wish I hadn't said anything at all.

I turn my attention to the wall of windows looking out onto the backyard. Like the front, it's a little shaggier than the other yards in the neighborhood, the grass higher, the bushes not as uniform, but it's prettier than those other cookie-cutter lawns, too. This property backs up to woods, tall trees stretching out toward the gray sky.

Eddie follows my gaze. "We bought the land behind this plot so that we'd never have to look at the back of another house," he said. He's still holding his car keys, and they jangle in his hand, a nervous tic that doesn't seem to fit the rest of him.

I think about what he just said — *we.*

It's stupid to be disappointed. Of course, a man like this has a wife. There are no single men in Thornfield Estates except for Tripp Ingraham, and he's a widower. Single men don't live in places like this.

"It's pretty," I tell Eddie now. "Private."

Lonely, I also think, but don't say.

Clearing his throat, Eddie turns from the window and walks into the kitchen. I follow behind, Bear still trudging in my wake, my

26

coat dripping on the floor.

The kitchen is as grand as the rest of the house with a massive stainless-steel refrigerator, a dark granite island, and beautiful cream-colored cabinets. Everything seems to gleam, even the man standing in front of the Keurig, loading up a coffee pod.

"How do you take it?" he asks me, his back still to me, and I perch on the edge of a stool, Bear's leash in one hand.

"Black," I reply. The truth is, I don't really like black coffee, but it's always the cheapest thing at any café, so it's become a habit.

"I see, you're tough, then."

Eddie smiles at me over his shoulder, his eyes very blue, and my face goes hot again.

Married, I remind myself.

But when he hands me the cup of coffee, I glance down at his hands. Fine-fingered, manicured, a smattering of dark hair over his knuckles.

And no ring.

"So, tell me about yourself, Jane the Dog-Walker," he says, turning back to make his own cup of coffee. "Are you from Birmingham?"

"No." I blow across the surface of my coffee cup. "I was born in Arizona, lived mostly out West until last year."

True, but vague: my preferred way of

explaining my background to new people.

Eddie takes his mug from the Keurig machine and faces me, leaning back against the counter. "How'd you end up down here?"

"I was looking for something new, and a friend from school lived here, offered me a room."

There's a trick to spinning lies. You have to embed the truth in there, just a glimmer of it. That's the part that will catch people, and it's what makes the rest of your lies sound like truth, too.

I was looking for something new. I was. Because I was running from something old.

A friend from school. A guy I met in a group home after my last foster situation ended badly.

Nodding, Eddie takes a sip of his coffee, and I fight the urge to squirm in my seat, to ask why the hell he brought me into his house to make small talk, where his wife is, why he isn't at work or wherever it was he was going in such a hurry this morning.

But he seems happy to just sit there in the kitchen with me, drinking coffee and looking at me like I'm a puzzle he's working out.

I can't help but feel like I cracked my head on the road this morning and dropped into some alternate universe where rich, handsome men seem interested in me.

"What about you?" I ask. "Are you from Birmingham originally?"

"My wife was."

Was. I hold that word, that tense, in my mind.

"She, uh. She grew up around here, wanted to move back," he goes on, and his fingers are drumming on the side of his mug, that same gesture I'd noticed earlier in the street. Then he puts the mug down and leans on the island in front of him, arms crossed.

"You're staying in Mountain Brook?" he asks, and I raise my eyebrows, making him laugh. "Is this creepy? The third-degree thing?"

It maybe should be, but instead, it's nice to have someone actually interested in me — not the fake, feigned interest of Mrs. Reed, but something genuine, real. Plus, I'd rather sit here talking and drinking coffee in his gorgeous kitchen than walk Bear in the rain.

I let my fingers trace a vein in the marble as I say, "Only mildly creepy. Tier One on the creep meter."

He smiles again, and something tingles at the base of my spine. "I can deal with Tier One."

I smile back, relaxing a little. "And no, I'm not staying in Mountain Brook. My friend's place is in Center Point."

Center Point is an ugly little town about twenty miles away, once part of the suburban sprawl of Birmingham, now a haven of strip malls and fast-food joints. There are still nice neighborhoods tucked in and around it, but on the whole, it feels like another planet compared to Thornfield Estates, and Eddie's expression reflects that.

"Shit," he says, straightening up. "That's quite a hike from here."

It is, and my crappy car probably can't take it much longer, but it's worth it to me, leaving behind all that ugliness for this place with its manicured lawns and brick houses. I knew it would've been smarter to find work in Center Point, like John, but as soon as I'd moved in, the first thing I'd done was look for ways to escape.

So, I didn't mind the drive.

"There wasn't much work in Center Point," I tell him, which is another half-truth. There were jobs — cashier at the Dollar General, checkout girl at Winn-Dixie, cleaner at the "Fit Not Fat!" gym that used to be a Blockbuster Video — but they weren't jobs that I wanted. That would get me any closer to the type of person I wanted to be. "And my friend knew someone who worked at Roasted in the village, and that's where I met Mrs. Reed. Well, I met Bear first, I guess."

At the sound of his name, the dog wags his tail, thumping against the base of my stool, a reminder that I should probably get going. But Eddie is still watching me, and I can't seem to stop talking. "He was tied up outside, and I brought him some water. Apparently, I was the first person he hadn't growled at since Mrs. Reed got him, and she asked if I ever did any dog-walking, so now . . ."

"So now here you are," Eddie finishes up, lifting one shoulder in a shrug. The movement is elegant despite his wrinkled clothes, and I like how his lips are caught somewhere halfway between a smile and a smirk.

"Here I am," I say, and for a moment, he holds my gaze. His eyes are very blue, but they're rimmed in red, and his stubble is dark against his pale skin.

The house is well taken care of and clean, but something about the feeling of emptiness inside of it — and the emptiness in Eddie's eyes — reminds me of Tripp Ingraham. I hate walking his dog because then I have to go into that stuffy, shut-up house where it's as if the pause button was hit the second his wife died.

And then I remember that Tripp's wife didn't die alone. She and her best friend were both killed in a boating accident just six months back. I never registered the friend's name because to be honest, I hadn't really cared about old gossip, but now I wish I had.

Was. He'd said *was.*

"And I've kept you from your work by nearly running you over, then forcing you to make small talk with me," Eddie says, and I smile, turning my mug around in my hands.

"I like the small talk. Could've done without the near-death experience."

He laughs again, and I suddenly wish I didn't have anywhere else to be, that I could sit here talking with him the rest of the day.

"Another cup?" he asks, and even though I still have half my coffee left, I push the mug away.

"No, I should probably get going. Let Bear finish up his walk."

Eddie puts his own mug in the smaller sink there by the coffeemaker. All the houses have that because god forbid rich people have to walk the extra three feet to use the main sink, I guess.

"How many dogs are you walking in the

neighborhood?" he asks as I slide off the stool, reaching for Bear's leash.

"Four right now," I tell him. "Well, five, the Clarks have two. So five dogs, four families."

"Could you squeeze in a sixth?"

I pause as Bear pushes himself to his feet, stretching.

"You have a dog?" I ask.

He smiles at me again, a real smile this time, and my heart turns a neat flip in my chest.

"I'm going to get one."

4

"Since when does Eddie Rochester have a dog?"

Mrs. Clark — Emily, I'm actually supposed to call her by her first name — is smiling.

She's always smiling, probably to show off those perfect veneers that must have cost a fortune. Emily is just as thin as Mrs. Reed and just as rich, but rather than Mrs. Reed's cute sweater sets, Emily is always wearing expensive athletic wear. I'm not sure if she actually goes to the gym, but she spends every second looking like she's waiting for a yoga class to break out. She's holding a monogrammed coffee thermos now, the *E* printed in bold pink on a floral background, and even with that smile, I don't miss the hard look in her eyes. One thing growing up in the foster system taught me was to watch people's eyes more than you listened to what they said. Mouths were good at lying, but eyes usually told the truth.

"He just got her," I reply. "Last week, I think."

I knew it had been last week because Eddie had been as good as his word. He'd adopted the Irish setter puppy, Adele, the day after we met. I'd started walking her the next day, and apparently Emily had seen me because her first question this morning had been, "Whose dog were you walking yesterday?"

Emily sighs and shakes her head, one fist propped on a narrow hip. Her rings catch the light, sending sprays of little rainbows over her white cabinets. She has a lot of those rings, so many she can't wear them all.

So many she hasn't noticed that one, a ruby solitaire, went missing two weeks ago.

"Maybe that'll help," she says, and then she leans in a little closer, like she's sharing a secret.

"His wife died, you know," she says, the words almost a whisper. Her voice drops to nearly inaudible on *died,* like just saying the word out loud will bring death knocking at her door or something. "Or at least, we presume. She's been missing for six months, so it's not looking good."

"I heard that," I say, nonchalant, like I

hadn't gone home last night and googled Blanche Ingraham, like I hadn't sat in the dark of my bedroom and read the words, *Also missing and presumed dead is Bea Rochester, founder of the Southern Manors retail empire.*

And that I hadn't then looked up Bea Rochester's husband.

Edward.

Eddie.

The joy that had bloomed in my chest reading that article had been a dark and ugly thing, the sort of emotion I knew I wasn't supposed to feel, but I couldn't really make myself care. He's free, she's gone, and now I have an excuse to see him every week. An excuse to be in that gorgeous home in this gorgeous neighborhood.

"It was *so. Sad,*" Emily drawls, apparently determined to hash out the entire thing for me. Her eyes are bright now. Gossip is currency in this neighborhood, and she's clearly about to make it rain.

"Bea and Blanche were like *this.*" Twisting her index and middle finger together, she holds them up to my face. "They'd been best friends forever, too. Since they were, like, little bitty."

I nod, as if I have any idea what it's like to have a best friend. Or to have known someone since I was *little bitty.*

"Eddie and Bea had a place down at Smith Lake, and Blanche and Tripp used to go down there with them all the time. But the boys weren't there when it happened."

The boys. Like they're seventh graders and not men in their thirties.

"I don't even know why they took the boat out because Bea didn't really like it. That was always Eddie's thing, but I bet he never gets on a boat again."

She's watching me again, her dark eyes narrowed a little, and I know she wants me to say something, or to look shocked or maybe even eager. It's no fun to spill gossip if the recipient seems bored, so that's why I keep my face completely neutral, no more interest than if we were talking about the weather.

It's satisfying, watching her strive to get a reaction out of me.

"That all sounds really awful," I offer up.

Lowering her voice, Emily leans in even closer. "They still don't even really know what happened. The boat was found out in the middle of the lake, no lights on. Blanche's and Bea's things were all still inside the house. Police think they must've had too much to drink and decided to take the boat out, but then fallen overboard. Or one fell and the other tried to help her."

Another head shake. "Just real, real sad."

"Right," I say, and this time, it's a little harder to fake not caring. There's something about that image, the boat in the dark water, one woman scrabbling against the side of the boat, the other leaning down to help her only to fall in, too . . .

But it must not show on my face because Emily's smile is more a grimace now, and there's something a little robotic in her shrug as she says, "Well, it was tough on all of us, really. A blow to the whole neighborhood. Tripp is just a *mess,* but I guess you know that."

Again, I don't say anything. *Mess* does not even begin to describe Tripp. Just the other day, he asked if I'd start packing up some of his wife's things for him, since he can't bring himself to do it. I was going to refuse because spending any more time in that house seems like a fucking nightmare, but he's offered to pay me double, so I'm thinking about it.

Now I just watch Emily with a bland expression. Finally, she sighs and says, "Anyway, if Eddie's getting a dog, maybe that's a sign that he's moving on. He didn't seem to take it as hard as Tripp did, but then he didn't depend on Bea like Tripp did on Blanche. I swear, that boy couldn't go to the bathroom before asking Blanche if she thought that was a good idea. Eddie wasn't like that with Bea, but god, he was broken up."

Her dark hair brushes her shoulder blades as she swings her head to look at me again. "He was crazy about her. We all were."

I fight down the bitter swell in my chest, thinking back to the one photo I pulled up of Bea Rochester on my laptop. She was strikingly beautiful, but Eddie is handsome, more so than most of the husbands around here, so it's not a surprise that they were a matched set.

"I'm sure it was a really big loss," I say, and finally, Emily waves me and the dogs away with one hand.

"I'll probably be gone when you get back, so just put them in the crate in the garage."

I take Major and Colonel for their walk, and sure enough, Emily's SUV is missing when we return. Their little fluffy bodies tremble with excitement as I settle them in the crate. Major and Colonel are the smallest of all the dogs I walk, and the ones who seem to least enjoy the exercise.

"I know how you feel, dudes," I tell them as I close the latch, watching Major sink into a dog bed that costs more than I make in a couple of weeks.

Which is why I don't feel all that bad taking the sterling silver dog tag from his collar and slipping it into my pocket.

5

"You're late on your half of the rent."

I look up from my spot on the couch. I've only been home for ten minutes and had hoped I might miss John this afternoon. He's an office assistant at a local church, plus he works with the Youth Music Ministry, whatever that actually means — I've never been a big churchgoer — and his hours are never as set as I'd like. This is hardly the first time I've come home to find him standing in the kitchen, his hip propped against the counter, one of my yogurts in his hand.

He always eats my food, no matter how many times I put my name on it, or where I try to hide it in our admittedly tiny kitchen. It's like nothing in this apartment belongs to me since it was John's place first, and he's letting me live here. He opens my bedroom door without knocking, he uses my shampoo, he eats my food, he "borrows" my laptop. He's skinny and short, a wisp of a guy, really, but sometimes it feels like he sucks up all the space in our shared 700 square feet.

Another reason I want to get out.

Living with John was only ever supposed to be a temporary thing. It was risky, going back to someone who knew my past, but I'd figured it would just be a place to land for a month, maybe six weeks, while I figured out what to do next.

But that was six months ago, and I'm still here.

Lifting my feet off the coffee table, I stand, digging into my pocket for the wad of twenties I shoved in there after my visit to the pawnshop this afternoon.

I don't always get rid of the stuff I take. The money has never been the point, after all. It's the *having* I've always enjoyed, plus knowing they'll never notice anything is missing. It makes me feel like I've won something.

But dog-walking isn't bringing in enough to cover everything yet, so today, I'd plucked Mrs. Reed's lone diamond earring from the pile of treasures on my dresser, and while I didn't get nearly what it was worth, it's enough to cover my half of this shitty concrete box.

I shove it into John's free hand, pretending I don't notice the way his fingers try to slide against mine, searching for even a few seconds of extra contact. I'm another thing in this apartment that John would consume if he could, but we both pretend we don't know that.

"How's the whole dog-walking thing going?" John asks as I cross back over to our sad couch. He's got a bit of yogurt stuck to the corner of his mouth, but I don't bother pointing it out. It'll probably stay there all day, too, forming a crust that'll creep out some girl down at the Student Baptist Center where John volunteers a few nights a week.

I already feel solidarity with her, this unknown girl, my sister in Vague Disgust for John Rivers.

Maybe that's what makes me smile as I sit back down, yanking the ancient afghan blanket out from under me. "Great, actually. Have a few new clients now, so it keeps me pretty busy."

John's spoon scrapes against the plastic tub of yogurt — *my* yogurt — and he watches me, his dark hair hanging limply over one eye.

"Clients," he snorts. "Makes you sound like a hooker."

Only John could try to shame a girl for something as wholesome as dog-walking, but I brush it off. If things keep going as well as they're going, soon I won't have to live here with him anymore. Soon I can get my own place with my own stuff and my own fucking yogurt that I'll actually get to eat.

"Maybe I am a hooker," I reply, picking up the remote off the coffee table. "Maybe that's what I'm actually doing, and I'm just telling you I walk dogs."

I twist on the couch to look at him.

He's still standing by the fridge, but his head is ducked even lower now, his eyes wary as he watches me.

It makes me want to go even further, so I do.

"That could be blowjob money in your pocket now, John. What would the Baptists think about that?"

John flinches from my words, his hand going to his pocket, either to touch the money or to try to hide the boner he probably popped at hearing me say *blowjob*.

Eddie wouldn't cringe at a joke like that, I suddenly think.

Eddie would laugh. His eyes would do that thing where they seem brighter, bluer, all because you've surprised him.

Like he did when you noticed the books.

"You ought to come to church with me," he says. "You could come this afternoon."

"You work in the office," I say, "not the actual church. Not sure what good it would do me watching you file old newsletters."

I'm not normally this openly rude to him, aware that he could kick me out since this place is technically all his, but I can't seem to help myself. It's something about that day in Eddie's kitchen. I've known enough new beginnings to recognize when something is clicking into place, and I think — *know* — that my time in this shitty box with this shitty human is ticking down.

"You're a bitch, Jane," John mutters sullenly, but he throws away the empty yogurt and gathers his things, slinking out the door without another word.

Once he's gone, I hunt through the cabinets for any food he hasn't taken. Luckily, I still have two things of Easy Mac left, and I heat them both up, dumping them into one bowl before hunkering down with my laptop and pulling up my search on Bea Rochester.

I don't spend much time on the articles about her death. I've heard the gossip, and honestly, it seems pretty basic to me — two ladies got too drunk at their fancy beach house, got on their fancy boat, and then succumbed to a very fancy death. Sad, but not exactly a tragedy.

No, what I want to know about is Bea Rochester's *life.* What it was that made a man like Eddie want her. Who she was, what their relationship might have looked like.

The first thing I pull up is her company's website.

Southern Manors.

"Nothing says Fortune 500 company like a bad pun," I mutter, stabbing another bite of macaroni with my fork.

There's a letter on the first page of the site, and my eyes immediately scan down to see if Eddie wrote it.

He didn't. There's another name there, Susan, apparently Bea's second-in-command. It's full of the usual stuff you'd expect when the founder of a company dies suddenly. How sad they are, what a loss, how the company will continue on, burnishing her legacy, etc., etc.

I wonder what kind of a legacy it is, really, selling overpriced cutesy shit.

Clicking from page to page, I take in expensive Mason jars, five-hundred-dollar sweaters with HEY, Y'ALL! stitched discreetly in the left corner, silver salad tongs whose handles are shaped like bees.

There's so much gingham it's like Dorothy Gale exploded on this website, but I can't stop looking, can't keep from clicking one item, then another.

The monogrammed dog leashes.

The hammered-tin watering cans.

A giant glass bowl in the shape of an apple someone has just taken a bite out of.

It's all expensive but useless crap, the kind of stuff lining the gift tables at every high-society wedding in Birmingham, and I finally click away from the orgy of pricey/cutesy, going back to the main page to look at Bea Rochester's picture again.

She's standing in front of a dining room table made of warm, worn-looking wood. Even though I haven't been in the dining room at the Rochester mansion, I know immediately that this is theirs, that if I looked a little deeper into the house, I would find this room. It has the same vibe as the living room — nothing matches exactly, but it somehow goes together, from the floral velvet seat covers on the eight chairs to the orange-and-teal centerpiece that pops against the eggplant-colored drapes.

Bea pops, too, her dark hair swinging just above her shoulders in a glossy long bob. She has her arms crossed, her head slightly tilted to one side as she smiles at the camera, her lipstick the prettiest shade of

47

red I think I've ever seen.

She's wearing a navy sweater, a thin gold belt around her waist, and a navy-and-white gingham pencil skirt that manages to be cute and sexy at the same time, and I almost immediately hate her.

And also want to know everything about her.

More googling, the Easy Mac congealing in its bowl on John's scratched and water-ringed coffee table, my fingers moving quickly, my eyes and my mind filling up with Bea Rochester.

There's not as much as I'd want, though. She wasn't famous, really. It's the company people seem to care about, the stuff they can buy, while Bea seemed to keep herself out of the spotlight.

There's only one interview I can find — with *Southern Living,* of course, big surprise. In the accompanying photo, Bea sits at another dining room table — seriously, did this woman exist in any other rooms of a house? — wearing yellow this time, a crystal bowl of lemons on her elbow, an enamel coffee cup printed with daisies casually held in one hand.

The profile is a total puff piece. Bea grew up in Alabama, one of her ancestors was a senator in the 1800s, and they'd had a gor-

48

geous home in some place called Calera that had burned down a few years ago. Her mother had sadly passed away not long after Bea started Southern Manors, and she "did everything in memory of her."

My eyes keep scanning past the details I already know — the Randolph-Macon degree, the move back to Birmingham, the growth of her business — until I finally snag on Eddie's name.

Three years ago, Bea Mason met Edward Rochester on vacation in Hawaii. "I was definitely not looking for a relationship," she laughs. "I just wanted some downtime to read a few books and drink ridiculous frozen drinks. But when Eddie showed up . . ."

She trails off and shakes her head slightly with a becoming blush. "The whole thing was such a whirlwind, but I always say marrying Eddie was the only impulsive decision I've ever made. Luckily, it ended up being the *best* decision I ever made, too."

Sighing, I sit back from my laptop, my back protesting, my legs slightly numb from how long I've had them folded up under me. The throw over my thighs smells like cheap detergent, and I push it away, wrinkling my nose.

Hawaii.

Why does that make it worse for some reason? Why did I want them to have met at church or the country club or one of the other five thousand boring and safe locations around here?

Because I wanted it not to be special, I think. *I wanted* her *not to be special.*

But she is. Beautiful and smart and a millionaire. A woman who built something all her own, even if she did come from money and the kind of background that made achieving shit a hell of a lot easier than it did for someone like me.

I stare at that picture some more, wondering what her voice sounded like, how tall she was, what she and Eddie looked like together.

Gorgeous, obviously. Hot. But did they smile at each other? Did they touch each other easily, his arm around her waist, her hand on his shoulder? Were there furtive caresses, brushings of hands under tables, secret signals only they knew?

There must've been. Marriage was like that, even though most of the ones I'd seen hadn't seemed worth the effort.

So, Bea Rochester had been perfect. The

perfect mogul, the perfect woman, the perfect wife. Probably had never even heard of Easy Mac or seen the inside of a pawnshop.

But I had one thing over her. I was still alive.

6

Eddie isn't there when I walk Adele the next morning. His car is missing from the garage, and I tell myself I'm not disappointed when I take the puppy from the backyard and out for her walk.

Thornfield Estates is just up the hill from Mountain Brook Village where I used to work, so this morning, I take Adele there, her little legs trotting happily as we turn out of the neighborhood. I tell myself it's because I'm bored with the same streets, but really, it's because I want people to see us. I want people who don't know I'm the dog-walker to see me with Eddie's dog. Which means, in their heads, I'm linked with Eddie.

It makes me hold my head up higher as I walk past Roasted, past the little boutique selling things that I now recognize as knock-offs of Southern Manors. I pass three stores with brightly patterned quilted bags in the windows, and I think how many of those bags are probably tucked away in closets in Thornfield Estates.

What would it feel like to be the kind of woman who spent $250 on an ugly bag just because you could?

At my side, Adele trots along, her nails clicking on the sidewalk, and I'm just about to turn by the bookstore when I hear, "Jane?"

It's Mrs. McLaren. I walk her dalmatian, Mary-Beth, every Wednesday, and now she's standing in front of me, a Roasted cup in hand. Like Emily Clark, she wears fancy yoga clothes half the time, but she's smaller and curvier than Emily or Mrs. Reed, her hair about four different shades of blond as it curls around her face.

"What are you two doing all the way down here?" She asks it with a smile, but my face suddenly flames hot, like I've been caught at something.

"Change of scenery," I reply with a sheepish shrug, hoping Mrs. McLaren will just let this go, but now she's stepping closer, her gaze falling to Adele.

"Sweetheart, it's probably not safe to have the dogs out of the neighborhood." The words are cooed, sugar-sweet, a cotton candy chastisement, and I hate her for them.

Like I'm a child. Or, worse, a servant who wandered out of her gated yard.

"We're not far from home," I say, and at my side, Adele whines, straining on her leash, her tail brushing back and forth.

Home.

There's a shopping bag dangling from Mrs. McLaren's wrist as she steps closer. It's imprinted with the logo of one of those little boutiques I just passed, and I wonder what's in it, wanting to catch a glimpse of the item inside, so that when I see it lying around her house later, I can take it. A stupid, petty reaction, lashing out, I know that, but there it is, an insistent pulse under my skin.

Whatever this bitch bought today, she's not going to keep it, not after making me feel this small.

"Okay, well, maybe run on back there, then?" The uptick, making it a question. "And sweetie, please don't ever take Mary-Beth out of the neighborhood, okay? She gets so excitable, and I'd hate for her to be out in all this . . ." she waves a hand, the bag still dangling from her wrist. "Rigma-role."

I've seen maybe three cars this morning, and the only *rigmarole* currently happening is Mrs. McLaren stopping me like I'm some kind of criminal for daring to walk a dog outside Thornfield's gates.

But I nod.

I smile.

I bite back the venom flooding my mouth because I have practice at that, and I walk back to Thornfield Estates and to Eddie's house.

It's cool and quiet as I let myself in, and I lean down to unclip Adele's leash. Her claws skitter across the marble, then the hardwood as she makes her way to the sliding glass doors, and I follow, opening them to let her out into the yard.

This is the part where I'm supposed to hang up her leash on the hook by the front door, maybe leave a note for Eddie saying that I came by and that Adele is outside, and then leave. Go back to the concrete box on St. Pierre Street, think again about taking the GRE, maybe sort through the various treasures I've picked up on dressers, on bathroom counters, beside nightstands.

Instead, I walk back into the living room with that bright pinkish-red couch and floral chairs, the shelves with all those books, and I look around.

For once, I'm not looking for something to take. I don't know what it says about me, about Eddie, or how I might feel about Eddie that I don't want to take anything from him, but I don't. I just want to *know* him. To learn something.

Actually, if I'm being honest with myself, I want to see pictures of him with Bea.

There aren't any in the living room, but I can see spaces on the wall where photographs must have hung. And the mantel is weirdly bare, which makes me think it once held more than just a pair of silver candlesticks.

I wander down the hall, sneakers squeaking, and there's more emptiness.

Upstairs.

The hardwood is smooth underfoot, and there are no blank spaces here, only tasteful pieces of art.

On the landing, there's a table with that glass bowl I recognize from Southern Manors, the one shaped like an apple, and I let my fingers drift over it before moving on, up the shorter flight of stairs to the second floor.

It's dim up here, the lights off, and the morning sun not yet high enough to reach through the windows. There are doors on either side, but I don't try to open any of them.

Instead, I make my way to a small wooden table under a round stained-glass window, there at the end of the hall.

There's only one thing on it, a silver-framed photograph, and it's both exactly what I wanted to see, and something I wish I'd never seen at all.

I had wondered what Bea and Eddie looked like together, and now I know.

They're beautiful.

But it's more than just that. Lots of people are beautiful, especially in this neighborhood where everyone can afford the upkeep, so it's not her perfect hair and flawless figure, her bright smile and designer bathing suit. It's that they look like they *fit*. Both of them, standing on that gorgeous beach, her smiling at the camera, Eddie smiling at her.

They'd found the person for them. That thing most of us look for and never find, that thing I always assumed didn't exist, because in this whole wide world, how could there ever be one person who was just right for you?

But Bea was right for Eddie, I can see that now, and I suddenly feel so stupid and small. Sure, he'd flirted with me, but he was probably one of those guys for whom it was second nature. He'd had *this*. He certainly didn't want me.

"That was in Hawaii."

I whirl around, the keys falling from my suddenly numb fingers.

Eddie is standing in the hallway, just at the top of the stairs, leaning against the wall with one ankle crossed in front of the other. He's wearing jeans today and a blue button-down, the kind that looks casual, but probably costs more than I'd make in a couple of weeks at the coffee shop or walking dogs. I wonder what that's like, to have so much money that spending someone's rent on one shirt doesn't even register.

His sunglasses dangle from his hand, and he nods at the table. "That picture," he tells me, as if I hadn't known what he was referring to. "That's me and Bea in Hawaii last year. We met there, actually."

I swallow hard, shoving my hands into the back pockets of my jeans, straightening my shoulders. "I was just looking for the bathroom," I tell him, and he smiles a little.

"Of course you were," he says, pushing off from the wall and walking closer. The hall is wide and bright, filled with light from the inset window above us, but it feels smaller, closer, as he moves nearer.

"It was the one picture I couldn't bring myself to get rid of," he says now, and I'm very aware of him standing right next to me, his elbow nearly brushing my side.

"The rest were mostly shots of our wedding, a few pictures of when we were building this house. But that one . . ." Trailing off, he picks up the frame, studying the image. "I don't know. I just couldn't throw it out."

"You threw the rest of them away?" I ask. "Even your wedding pictures?"

He sets the frame back on the table with a soft clunk. "Burned them, actually. In the backyard three days after the accident."

"I'm so sorry," I say quietly, trying not to imagine Eddie standing in front of a fire as Bea's face melted.

But then he looks at me, his blue eyes narrowing just a little bit. "I don't think you are, Jane," he says, and my mouth is dry, my heart hammering. I wish I'd never come upstairs into this hallway, and I am so glad I came into this hallway because if I hadn't, we wouldn't be standing here right now, and he wouldn't be looking at me like that.

"What happened was awful," I try again, and he nods, but his hand is already coming up to cup my elbow. His fingers fold around the sharp point, and I stare down at where he's touching me, at the sight of that hand on my skin.

"Awful," he echoes. "But you're not sorry, because her not being here means that you can be here. With me."

I want to protest, because what a horrible thing to think about me. What a horrible thing for me to *be.*

But he's right — I'm glad that Bea Rochester was on that boat with Blanche Ingraham that night. I'm glad because it means Eddie is alone.

Free.

The fact that he sees that in me should make me feel ashamed, but it only makes me giddy.

"I'm not *with* you," I say to him, though, because that's the truth. We may be standing here, his hand on my arm, but we're not together. There's still a big fucking canyon between the Eddie Rochesters of the world and me.

But then he smiles, that slow smile that only lifts one corner of his mouth and makes him look younger and more charming.

"Have dinner with me tonight," he says.

I like that. How it's not a question. "Yes," I hear myself say, and it's that easy.

It's like walking through a door.

7

I don't let him pick me up.

I'd be insane to let Eddie see where I really live, and the thought of him and John crossing paths is enough to make me shudder. No, I want to exist only in Eddie's world, like I'd sprung from somewhere else, fully formed, unknowable.

It's true enough, really.

So, I meet him in English Village, a part of Mountain Brook I've never been to, although I'd heard Emily mention it. There are lots of "villages" in Mountain Brook: Cahaba Village, Overton Village, and Mountain Brook Village itself. It seemed silly to me, using a word like *village* to mean *different part of the same community* — just use *neighborhood,* you pretentious assholes, we don't live in the English countryside — but what did I know?

I park far away from the French bistro where Eddie made a reservation, praying he won't ask to walk me to my car later, and meet him under the gold-and-black-striped awning of the restaurant.

He's wearing charcoal slacks and a white shirt, a nice complement to the deep eggplant of my dress, and his hand is warm on my lower back when the maître d' shows us to our table.

Low lights, white tablecloths, a bottle of wine. That's the part that stands out to me most, how casually he orders an entire bottle of wine while I was still looking at the by-the-glass prices, wondering what would sound sophisticated, but wouldn't be too expensive.

The bottle he selects is over a hundred dollars, and my cheeks flush at knowing I'm worth an expensive bottle of wine to him. After that, I put the menu away entirely, happy to let him order for me.

"What if I pick something you don't like?" he asks, but he's smiling, His skin doesn't seem as pale as it did that first day. His blue eyes are no longer rimmed with red, and I wonder if I've made him happy. It's a heady thought, even more intoxicating than the wine.

"I like everything," I reply. I don't mean for the words to sound sexy, but they do, and when the dimple in his cheek deepens,

I wonder what else I can say that will make him look at me like that.

Then his eyes drop lower.

At first, I think he's looking at the low neckline of my dress, but then he says, "That necklace."

Fuck.

It had been stupid to wear it. Reckless, something I very rarely was, but when I'd looked in the mirror before leaving, I'd looked so plain with no jewelry. The chain I'd taken from Mrs. McLaren wasn't anything fancy, no diamonds or jewels, just a simple silver chain with a little gold-and-silver charm on it.

A bee, I now realize, and my stomach sinks, fingers twisting in my napkin.

"A friend gave it to me," I say, striving for lightness, but I'm already touching the charm, feeling it warm against my chest.

"It's pretty," he says, then glances down. "My late wife's company makes one similar, so . . ."

Eddie trails off, and his fingers start that drumming on the table again.

"I'm sorry," I say. "I . . . I heard about Southern Manors, and it's —"

"Let's not talk about it. Her." His head shoots up, his smile fixed in place, but it's not real, and I want to reach across the table and take his hands, but we're not there yet, are we? I want to ask him everything about Bea, and forget she existed, all at the same time.

I want.

I want.

As the waiter approaches with our expensive wine, I smile at Eddie. "Then let's talk about you."

He raises his eyebrows, leaning back in his seat. "What do you want to know?" he asks.

I wait until the server has finished pouring a sample of the wine into Eddie's glass, then wait for Eddie to take a sip, nod, and gesture for our glasses to be filled, a thing I've only ever seen happen in movies or on reality shows about rich housewives. And now it's happening to me. Now I'm one of the people who has those kinds of dinners.

Once we have full glasses, I mimic Eddie's posture, sitting back. "Where did you grow up?"

"Maine," he answers easily, "little town called Searsport. My mom still lives there; so does my brother. I got out as soon as I could, though. Went to college in Bangor." Eddie sips his wine, looking at me. "Have you ever been to Maine?"

I shake my head. "No. But I read a lot of

Stephen King as a teenager, so I feel like I have a good idea of what it's like."

That makes him laugh, like I'd hoped it would. "Well, fewer pet cemeteries and killer clowns, but yeah, basically."

Leaning forward, I fold my arms on the table, not missing the way his gaze drifts from my face to the neckline of my dress. It's a fleeting glance, one I'm used to getting from men, but coming from him, it doesn't feel creepy or unwanted. I actually like him looking at me.

Another novelty. "Living here must be a big change," I say, and he shrugs.

"I moved around a lot after college. Worked with a friend flipping houses all over the Midwest. Settled in California for a bit. That's where I first got my contractor's license. Thought I'd stay there forever, but then I went on vacation, and . . ."

He trails off, and I jump in, not wanting another loaded silence.

"Have you ever thought of going back?"

Surprised, he pours himself a little more wine. "To Maine?"

I shrug. "Or California." I wonder why he stays in a place that must have so many bad memories for him, a place in which he seems to stick out, just the slightest bit, to be set apart, even with all his money and nice clothes.

"Well, Southern Manors is based here," he replies. "I could run the contracting business from somewhere else, but Bea was really set on Southern Manors being an Alabama company. It would feel . . . I don't know. Like a betrayal, I guess. Moving it somewhere else. Or selling it."

His expression softens a little. "It's her legacy, and I feel a responsibility to protect it."

I nod, glad our food arrives just at that moment so that this conversation can die a natural death. I already know how important Southern Manors is to him. In my Google stalking, I found several articles about how just a few months after Bea went missing, Eddie fought for a court order to have her declared legally dead. It had something to do with Southern Manors, and there was a lot of business and legal jargon in it I hadn't understood, but I'd gotten the gist — Bea had to be dead on paper for Eddie to take over and run the company the way she would've wanted it to be run.

I wondered how that had made him feel, declaring his wife's death in such a formal, final way.

As he cuts into his steak, he looks up at me, smiling a little. "Enough about me. I want to hear about you."

I provide a few charming anecdotes, painting Jane's life in a flattering light. Some of the stories are real (high school in Arizona), some are half-truths, and some are stolen from friends.

But he seems to enjoy them, smiling and nodding throughout the meal, and by the time the check comes, I'm more relaxed and confident than I'd ever thought I'd be on this date.

And when we leave, he takes my hand, slipping it into the crook of his elbow as we exit the restaurant.

It's ridiculous, I know that. Me, here with him. Me, with my arm linked through his.

Me, in his life.

But here I am, and as we make our way to the sidewalk, I hold my head up higher, stepping closer to him, the edge of my skirt brushing his thighs.

The night is warm and damp, my hair curling around my face, streetlights reflecting in puddles and potholes, and I wonder if he'll kiss me.

If he'll ask me to stay the night.

I'm going to.

He'd ordered a piece of pie to go, and I think about eating it with him in his gorgeous kitchen. Or in his bed. Is that why he'd ordered it?

I think about walking into that house at night, how pretty the recessed lighting will be in the darkness. What the backyard will look like when the sun comes up. What his sheets feel and smell like, what it's like to wake up in that house.

"You're quiet," Eddie says, tucking me closer to his side as we wander, and I tilt my head up to smile at him.

"Can I be honest?"

"Can I stop you?"

I nudge him slightly at that, feeling how solid and warm he is beside me. "I was thinking that it's been a long time since I've been on a date."

"Me, too," he replies.

In the streetlights, he's so handsome it makes my chest ache, and my fingers rub against the softness of his jacket, the material expensive and well-made. Nicer than anything I own.

"I'm —" I start, and he turns his head. I think he might kiss me there, right there on the street in English Village where anyone might see us, but before he can, there's a voice.

"Eddie!"

We turn at almost the same time, facing a man on the sidewalk who looks like Tripp

Ingraham or Matt McLaren or Saul Clark or any of the other pastel guys in Thornfield Estates.

He's got his face screwed up, that expression of sympathy that twists mouths down and eyebrows together. His thinning blond hair looks orange in the streetlights, and when he lifts a hand to shake Eddie's, I catch the glint of a wedding ring.

"Good to see you, man," he says. "And so sorry about Bea."

Eddie's body is stiff against me. "Chris," he says, shaking the man's hand. "Nice to see you, too. And thank you. I really appreciated the flowers."

Chris only shakes his head. He's wearing a light gray suit, and there's a Mercedes parked against the curb just behind him. A woman is still sitting in the passenger seat, watching us, and I feel like her eyes land on me.

I don't tug at the skirt of my dress, the only nice one I have, but my fingers itch at my side.

"Awful thing, just awful," Chris goes on, like Eddie doesn't know that his wife drowning is a bad thing, but Eddie just grimaces and nods.

"Thanks again," he says, because what can you say, I guess, but then Chris's eyes flick briefly to me.

"She was a helluva woman," he adds, and I can feel the questions that are clearly burning a hole in the roof of his mouth.

Who the hell am I, is this a date, is Eddie seriously going to replace Bea with me, this pale-faced plain girl in a dress that's one size too big?

"She was," Eddie replies, and I wait for it, the moment he's going to introduce me.

Chris is waiting for it, too, but it passes with an awkward smile from Eddie and a firm pat on Chris's shoulder. "See you around," he says. "Tell Beth I said hello."

Then we're moving down the sidewalk, and Eddie has not looked at me since Chris appeared, since Bea's name rose up like a ghost between us.

He doesn't ask to walk me to my car.

And he doesn't kiss me good night.

8

Everything in the Ingraham house feels like it's waiting for Blanche to return.

I walk in the next morning, feeling heavy and slow, last night's failed date with Eddie sitting like a rock low in my stomach. It somehow seems fitting that this should be the day I'd agreed to go over and start packing up some of Blanche's stuff for Tripp.

Bea's ghost last night, Blanche's today.

It's been months since she went missing, but one of her handbags is still sitting on the table in the foyer. There's a pile of jewelry there, too, a coiled necklace, a careless pile of rings. I imagine her coming home from a dinner out, taking off all that stuff, tossing it casually against the wide glass base of the lamp, kicking her shoes just under the table.

The pair of pink gingham flats is still lying there, too. It was July when she went missing, and I imagine her wearing them with a matching pink blouse, a pair of white capris. Women here always dress like flowers in the summer, bright splashes of color against the violently green lawns, the blindingly blue sky. It's so different from how things were back East, where I grew up. There, black was always the chicest color. Here, I think people would wear lavender to a funeral. Poppy-red to a wedding.

I've never tried to take anything from Tripp. Trust me, he'd notice.

Unlike Eddie, Tripp has kept all the pictures of Blanche up and in plain sight. I think he might have actually added some. Every available surface seems overcrowded with framed photos.

There are at least five of their wedding day, Blanche smiling and very blond, Tripp looking vaguely like her brother, and nowhere near as paunchy and deflated as he looks now.

He's sitting in the living room when I come in, a plastic tumbler full of ice and an amber-colored liquid that I'm sure is not iced tea.

It's 9:23 A.M.

"Hi, Mr. Ingraham," I call, rattling my keys in my hand just in case he's forgotten that he gave me a key so that I could let myself in. That was back when he still pretended like he might go into work. I'm not even sure what he does, if I'm honest. I thought he was a lawyer, but maybe I just assumed that because he looked like the type. He doesn't seem to own any other clothes besides polo shirts and khakis, and there's golf detritus all over the house — a bag of clubs leaning by the front door, multiple pairs of golfing shoes jumbled in a rattan basket just inside the front door, tees dropped as carelessly as his wife's jewelry.

Even the cup he's currently drinking his sad breakfast booze in has some kind of golf club insignia on it.

There's a photo album spread across his lap and as I step farther into the dim living room, Tripp finally looks up at me, his eyes bleary behind designer glasses.

"Jan," he says, and I don't bother to remind him it's Jane. I've already done that a few times, and it never seems to actually penetrate the muck of Woodford Reserve his brain is permanently steeped in.

"You asked me to start on the second guest room today," I tell him, pointing upstairs, and after a beat, he nods.

I head up there, but my mind isn't on Tripp and Blanche.

It's still on Eddie, on our dinner last night. The way he'd just nodded when I had said

I'd walk to my car on my own. How we'd hugged awkwardly on the sidewalk, and how quickly he'd walked away from me.

I'd thought —

Fuck, it doesn't matter. Maybe I'd thought something was happening there, but clearly, I'd been wrong, and the only thing *currently* happening was that I was heading into the "second guest room" at the Ingrahams' house to pack up . . . who knew what.

The bedroom was on the second floor, and it was relatively small, done all in shades of blue and semi-tropical floral patterns. There were boxes and plastic storage containers on the floor, but I had the feeling Tripp hadn't put them there. He had sisters. Maybe they had come to prepare the room for me to pick up, a sort of pre-cleaning to maintain the fiction that Tripp had his shit together.

Which he decidedly did not.

I'd only been up there ten minutes before I heard him coming.

I think that once in his life, Tripp had probably been a lot like John. Not as pathetic, of course, and blonder, handsomer. Less like something that grew in dark places behind the fridge. But there's a similar vibe there, like he'd totally eat food with someone else's name on it, and I bet more than

74

one woman at the University of Alabama had turned around surprised to suddenly find Tripp Ingraham in the doorway, had wondered why someone who looked so innocuous could suddenly feel so scary.

But all the drinking had foiled Tripp on the creeper front. I think he meant to sneak up on me there in the "blue bedroom," but I could hear his tread coming down the hall even though he was moving slowly, and, I think, trying to be quiet.

Maybe don't wear golf shoes on hardwood floors, dumbass, I thought to myself, but I was smiling when I turned to face him there in the doorway.

"Is everything okay?" I asked, and his watery hazel eyes widened a little. There was a sour look on his face, probably because I'd ruined whatever it was he'd hoped for. A girlish shriek maybe, me dropping a box and clasping my hands over my mouth, cheeks gone pink.

He would've liked that, probably. Tripp Ingraham was, I had no doubt, the kind of asshole who had jerked steering wheels, jumped in elevators, pretended to nearly push girlfriends off high ledges.

I knew the type.

"You can pack up everything in here if you want," Tripp says, rattling the glass in his plastic cup. "None of this really meant anything to Blanche."

I can see that. It's a pretty room, but there's something hotel-like about it. Like everything in here has been selected for just how it looks, not any kind of personal taste.

I glance over beside the bed, taking in a lamp meant to look like an old-fashioned tin bucket. The shade is printed in a soft blue-and-green floral pattern, and I could swear I've seen it before. Wouldn't surprise me — all the knickknacks in these houses look the same. Except for in Eddie's house.

It strikes me then that actually, everything in these houses seems to be a pale knockoff of the stuff at Eddie's, a Xerox machine slowly running out of ink so that everything is a little fainter, a little less distinct.

And then I realize where I'd seen that tin bucket lamp.

"That's from Southern Manors, isn't it?" I ask, nodding toward the bedside table. "I was looking at their website the other night, and —"

Tripp cuts me off with a rude noise, then tips the glass to his mouth again. When he lowers it, there's a drop of bourbon clinging to his scraggly mustache, and he licks it away, the pink flash of his tongue making me grimace.

"No, that lamp was *Blanche's*. Think it had been her mom's or something, picked it up at an estate sale, I don't know." He shrugs, belly jiggling under his polo shirt. "Bea Rochester wouldn't have known an original idea if it bit her in her ass. All that shit, that 'Southern Manors' thing. All that was Blanche's."

I put down the half-empty box. "What, like she copied Blanche's style?"

Tripp scoffs at that, walking farther into the room. The tip of his shoe catches an overstuffed trash bag by the door, tearing a tiny hole in it, and I watch as a bit of pink cloth oozes out.

"Copied, stole . . ." he says, waving the cup at me. "They grew up together, you know. Went to school at the same place, Ivy Ridge. I think they were even roommates."

Turning back to the stack of books on the bed, I start placing them in the box at my feet. "I heard they were close," I reply, wondering just how much more info I can get out of Tripp Ingraham. He's the only one so far who hasn't talked about Bea like the sun shone directly from her ass, so I wouldn't mind hearing more of what he has to say. But gossip is tricky, slippery. Pretend to be too interested, and suddenly you look suspicious. Act bored and nonchalant, sometimes the person will clam up totally, but then sometimes they're like Emily Clark, eager to keep sharing, hoping to find the right worm to bait the hook.

I don't know what kind Tripp is, but he sits on the corner of the bed, the mattress dipping with his weight.

"Bea Rochester," he mutters. "Her name was Bertha."

I look up at that, tucking my hair behind my ear, and he's watching me, his eyes bleary, but definitely focused on my face.

"Seriously?" I ask, and he nods. His leg is moving up and down restlessly, his hands twisting the now empty cup around and around.

"She changed it when she went to college, apparently. That's what Blanche said. Came back to Birmingham one day all, 'Call me Bea.' " He sighs again, that leg still jiggling. "And Blanche did. Never even mentioned her real name to people far as I know."

Bertha. The name sits heavily on the tongue, and I think back to those pictures I looked at last night, those red lips, that shiny dark hair. She definitely didn't look like a Bertha, and I couldn't blame her for wanting to change it.

Plus, it was another thing we had in common, another secret tucked against my chest. I hadn't been born "Jane," after all. That other, older name was so far behind me now that whenever I heard it on TV or in a store or on the radio, part of a snatch of conversation as I walked by people, I didn't even flinch or turn my head. I had buried that person somewhere in Arizona, so that name meant nothing to me now.

I was lucky, though. There was no one here who had ever known the other me. Bea Rochester hadn't had that luxury. What was it like, living right down the street from someone who knew how much you needed to change?

Tripp is still talking, but none of the information is useful now. It's just a bourbon-fueled stream of grievances, veering back to Blanche, about how he isn't sure what he's going to do with all her things.

I hear this at least once every time I'm over here, this idea that he's suddenly going to toss all of Blanche's stuff, start fresh, maybe move somewhere smaller, "somewhere near the golf course."

He won't do it, though. He's going to stay right here in this house, which he'll keep as a kind of shrine to her.

The Rochester house isn't a shrine.

I think about this as I leave Tripp's, shutting the door on all that sadness and bitterness. Eddie has just one picture of Bea still, that shot from Hawaii. Does it mean that he's moving on — or wants to move on, at least?

I think he does.

And then, like I'd conjured him into being, suddenly he's there, jogging down the sidewalk. He sees me and stops, his dark hair sweaty against his brow.

"Jane."

"Hi."

We stand there, me clutching my old purse tightly against my body, Eddie in his expensive running gear, and he puts his hands on his hips, breathing hard.

His chest is broad in his T-shirt that's wet with sweat, and suddenly I don't care anymore about last night, or his dead wife, or how many people might be watching us right now.

"Are you working for Tripp?" he asks, a trio of wrinkles appearing in his brow, and I shrug.

"Kind of? I walked his dog for a while, but now I'm mostly helping pack up his wife's stuff."

The frown deepens, his fingers digging into his hip bones, and then he says, "I was an asshole last night."

I shake my head, already denying it, but

he holds up one hand. "No, seriously. I used to work with Chris, and him bringing up Bea . . . it fucking rattled me, and I started thinking it was too soon, or that people might be dicks to you about it, and I just . . ."

He sighs, and hangs his head briefly. When he looks up at me, his hair is falling over his forehead like a little boy's, and it's so charming, so perfect, that my fingers want to smooth it back for him.

"Can I have a take two?" he asks.

Even if he weren't smiling, even if his eyes weren't so blue, even if I didn't want to touch him so badly my jaw ached with it, I would've said yes.

I would've remembered the smell and closeness of Tripp's house.

The way Mrs. McLaren looked at me in the village.

Emily Clark's hard eyes.

Eddie's house and the way it felt to slide my hand into his at dinner.

Yes.

9

April

Whirlwind.

It's hard not to use that word to describe my relationship with Eddie, but every time it comes into my head, I remember Bea, meeting Eddie on vacation.

She called it a whirlwind, too.

But maybe that's just what being with Eddie is like. Maybe every woman who's ever come into his life gets swept up in the same way because once he's decided he wants you, it's the only way he knows how to behave.

I give Eddie the second chance he wanted, but set it on my terms. No dates in Mountain Brook. Neutral territory. He thinks it's because I'm worried about the other people in Thornfield Estates finding out. I don't want them to know about us yet — and I don't want to risk another fuckup like the thing with Chris — but it's not because I'm worried about my job. My dog-walking days are ticking down so steadily I can practically hear the click.

No, I don't want anyone to know yet because I like having this secret. The biggest piece of gossip in the neighborhood, and it's mine.

They'll find out eventually, I know, but I'm determined that when they do, I'll be so deeply entrenched there won't be shit they can do about it.

So as February slides into March, March into April, we go to fancy restaurants with menus I can barely read. We walk through parks, our shoulders and hips touching. We go to movies, and sit in the back, like teenagers. His hand is always on me, resting against my palm, tracing the line of my collarbone, a warm weight on my lower back so that I can feel his touch even when we're apart.

That's the strangest part to me, really. Not the dates, not the idea that someone like Eddie Rochester might want to spend time with me. It's how much I want him, too.

I'm not used to that.

Wanting *things*? Sure. That's been a constant in my life, my eyes catching the sparkle of something expensive on a wrist, around a neck; pictures of dream houses taped to my bedroom wall instead of whatever prepubescent boy girls my age were supposed to be interested in.

But I've been dodging men's hands since I was twelve, so wishing a man would touch me is a novel experience.

I think I like it.

The first time he kissed me, it was beside his car outside a restaurant. His mouth tasted like the red wine we'd shared, and his hands holding my face hadn't made me feel trapped, but . . . safe. And beautiful.

I'd liked the clear disappointment in his eyes when I pulled back. Because, of course, I pulled back. Timing is everything here, and I'm not about to fuck up something this big by being an easy conquest for him.

So, any intimacy is limited to kisses for now and the occasional heated touches, his palms sliding over my upper arms, my thighs, my fingers resting on the hard muscles of his stomach but not going lower.

He hasn't had to wait for anything in a long time, I think, so he can damn well wait for me.

But it isn't just the kissing, the desire I feel for him that has my head spinning. It's how much he notices things. Notices *me*.

On our third date — sandwiches at a place in Vestavia — I pick a bottle of cream soda from the cooler, and before I can stop myself, I'm telling him the story of a foster dad I had early on, when I was ten. He was obsessed with cream soda, bought giant cases of it from Costco, but never let me or the other kid in the house at that time, Jason, touch any of it — which, of course, meant that cream soda was all I ever wanted to drink.

It surprised me, how easily the story poured out. It hadn't been that exact story, of course. I'd left out the foster care part, just saying "my dad," but it was the most truthful I'd been about my past with anyone in years.

And Eddie hadn't pried or looked at me with pity. He'd just squeezed my hand, and when I went to his house the next day, the fridge was stocked with the dark glass bottles.

Not the cheap shit Mr. Leonard bought, but the good stuff they only sell in fancy delis and high-end grocery stores.

I've gone so long trying not to be seen that there's something intoxicating about letting him really *see* me.

John knows something is going on, his beady eyes are even more suspicious than usual as they follow me around the apartment, but even that doesn't bother me now.

I like keeping this secret from him, too, the smug smile I wear, the different hours I'm keeping.

But all of that — kissing Eddie, fucking with John — is nothing compared to how I feel now, crouched in front of Bear's crate as I put him back after his walk, listening to Mrs. Reed on her cell phone.

"Eddie is *dating someone.*"

I allow myself a small smile. I'd been waiting for this, but it's even more satisfying than I'd imagined, the thrill rushing through me similar to how I feel when I swipe a ring or put a watch in my pocket.

Actually, it might even be better.

"I know!" I hear Mrs. Reed exclaim from behind me. There's a pause, and I wonder who's on the other end of the phone. Emily, maybe? They go back and forth between friends and enemies, but this week, they're on the friends' side of things. All it will take is one snide comment about someone's yoga pants being too tight, or a passive-aggressive dig at the lack of kids, and then they'll be feuding again — but for now, they're besties.

And talking about me.

Except they don't know that it's me, and that's the fun part, the part I've been waiting weeks for now.

I smile as I turn back to Mrs. Reed, handing over Bear's leash.

She takes it, then says, "Girl, let me call you back," into the phone. Definitely Emily, then. They do that "girl" thing with each other constantly when they're friends again.

Putting her phone back on the counter, she grins at me. "Jane," she practically purrs, and I know what's coming. She's done this before about Tripp Ingraham, squeezing me for any stray info, anything I've picked up from being around him. It kills me that she thinks she's subtle when she does it.

So when she asks, "Have you noticed anyone new around the Rochester house?" I give her the same bland smile as always and shrug.

"I don't think so."

It's a stupid answer, and I take pleasure in the way Mrs. Reed blinks at me, unsure what to do with it, before moving past her with a wave of my fingers. "See you next week!" I call cheerfully.

There are Chanel sunglasses on a table by the door, plus a neatly folded stack of cash, but I don't even look at them.

Instead, the second I'm on the sidewalk, I pull out my phone to text Eddie.

■ ■ ■ ■

If Eddie was surprised that I actually initiated a date — and that I suggested we "eat at home" — he didn't show it. He had texted me back within minutes, and when I'd shown up at his house at seven that evening, he already had dinner on.

I didn't ask if he'd actually cooked it himself or if he'd picked up something from the little gourmet shop in the village that did that kind of thing, whole rows of half-assed fancy food you could throw in the oven or in some gorgeous copper pot and pass off as your own.

It didn't matter.

What mattered is that he could've just ordered takeout, but instead, he'd put some effort into the night, effort that told me I was right to take the next step.

I wait until after dinner, until we're back in the living room. He's lit a few candles, lamps spilling warm pools of golden light on the hardwood, and he pours me a glass of wine before getting a whiskey for himself. I can taste it on his lips, smoky and expensive, when he kisses me.

I think of that first day we were in here, drinking coffee, dancing around each other.

These new versions of us — dressed nicer (I'm wearing my least faded skinny black jeans and an imitation silk H&M top I found at Goodwill), alcohol instead of coffee, the dancing very different — seem layered over that earlier Jane and Eddie.

Jane and Eddie. I like how it sounds, and I'm going to be Jane forever now, I decide. This is where all the running, all the lying, was leading. It was all worth it because now I'm here with this beautiful man in this beautiful house.

Just one last thing to do.

Turning away from him, I twist the wine-glass in my hands. I can't see out the giant glass doors, only my own reflection, and Eddie's, as he leans against the marble-topped island separating the living room from the kitchen.

"This has been the loveliest night," I say, making sure to put the right note of wistfulness in my voice. "I'm really going to miss this place."

It's not hard to sound sad as I say it — even the idea of leaving makes my chest tighten. It's another strange feeling, another one I'm not used to. Wanting to stay somewhere. Is it just because I'm tired of running, or is it something else? Why here? Why now?

I don't know, but I know that this place, this house, this neighborhood, feels safe to me in a way all those other stopgaps never have.

In the glass, I see Eddie frown. "What do you mean?"

Turning to face him, I shrug. "I'm just not sure how much longer I'm going to be able to stay in Birmingham," I tell him. "I don't want to walk dogs forever, and my roommate is a nightmare. I've been looking at grad school programs out West, and . . ." I trail off, thinking about another shrug, but settling on a melancholy sigh instead.

"What about us?" he asks, and it's everything I can do to hide my smile.

I give him a look, tilting my head. "Eddie," I say. "This has been really fun, but . . . I mean, it's not like there's a future for us, right? You'll eventually want somebody more . . . polished." I wave my free hand. "Sophisticated. Prettier."

And then I take a deep breath. "I haven't even been totally honest with you about my past . . . about my life before this."

He stands still, watching me, waiting. "Okay," he says, and his voice is soft, patient. "Want to start now?"

I nod, and then I take one of the bigger gambles of my life. I tell him the truth.

"I was in foster care from the time I was three until I aged out of the system. That dad I mentioned the other day . . . he wasn't my real dad, he was my foster dad, and not a very nice one at that. I don't even know who my parents were. I mean, I know their names, but just on paper. I have no memories of them. I don't even know who I really am. Is that actually someone you want to be with? Someone who comes from nothing?"

He sets his glass down on the counter and crosses over to me in a few strides.

"Yes," he says. His voice is low, and his hands are resting on my bare arms. I feel that touch all the way down to my toes, and when I tug my lower lip between my teeth, I see the way his eyes follow the motion.

"Thank you for sharing that with me, Jane. Knowing that about you, imagining all that you must have gone through . . ." He trails off, his eyes searching mine, and there's so much empathy and kindness there, my legs buckle a little. "It doesn't make me want you less. It makes me want you more," he finishes, and it is the nicest thing anyone has ever said to me.

"Eddie," I start, and his grip tightens.

"No," he replies. "If I wanted an Emily Clark or a Campbell Reed, I'd be with them. I'm with you because I want *you,* Jane."

Eddie lowers his head, and his lips brush mine, just barely. A sharp sting, his teeth biting lightly, desire flooding through me so hard I nearly shake with it.

"My Jane," he says, his voice low and rough, and I swallow hard, nothing feigned now, no illusion.

"I'm not yours," I manage to say. "I'm free as a fucking bird."

That makes him smile, and when he kisses me again, I use my teeth this time, nipping at the same place on his mouth where he bit mine.

I'm not leaving tonight, and we both know it.

I'm not leaving ever again.

■ ■ ■ ■

PART II
BEA

■ ■ ■ ■

July, One Day after Blanche
I don't know who I'm writing this for.

Me, I think. A way to get this all down while it's still fresh in my mind. I can't let myself hope that someone will find it. It hurts too much to hope for anything right now.

But maybe if I write everything down in black and white, some of it will start to make sense to me, and I can keep from going crazy.

Last night was the first time I understood how easily sanity can slip right through your fingers.

Eddie included a book in the supplies he brought me, a cheap paperback I'd had since college, and I found a pen wedged in the back of a drawer in the bedside table we carried up here just a few months ago.

There's something especially bizarre about this, about writing my own story over the words I read and reread when I was younger.

But it's even harder to write the truth.

Last night, my husband, Edward Rochester, murdered my best friend, Blanche Ingraham.

Blanche is dead. Eddie killed her. I'm locked away in our house. No matter how many times I repeat these facts to myself, they still feel so wrong, so crazy, that I can't help but wonder if this is all some kind of awful hallucination. Or that maybe I drowned along with Blanche and this is hell.

That almost makes more sense than this.

But no. Blanche and I went to the lake house for the weekend, a girls' trip that was supposed to give us a chance to spend some time together. We'd both been so busy — me with running Southern Manors, Blanche dealing with Tripp — and to just sit and talk with my best friend, to drink wine and laugh like we'd been doing since we were teenagers had been . . . perfect. That weekend was perfect.

I'm replaying it all in my head to convince myself that there wasn't any sign of what would happen next.

It's hard to untangle, you see.

I remember Eddie showing up unexpectedly, and the three of us deciding to take the boat out for a midnight cruise. Eddie was driving, Blanche and I were dancing to the music piping out of the speakers. Then my head was heavy, my thoughts fuzzy, and it was dark. Blanche was screaming, I was in the water, and it was warm, warm like a bath, and I knew I had to keep swimming and swimming, but when I got to the shore, Eddie was already there, and there was a blinding pain in my head, and then blackness. When I opened my eyes, I was . . . here.

In this room.

It was Eddie's idea to add a panic room to the third floor, after watching some *60 Minutes* episode about how they were all the rage in new construction. I'd gone along with it when he'd renovated the house because I wanted our new home to have the best of everything, and if it made him happy, why not?

I would've done anything to make Eddie happy.

And it had been his idea to make it more than just an empty space, too. He'd been the one to suggest the bed.

"In case we get stuck in here for a while," he'd teased, grabbing me around the waist, pulling me close, and even though we'd been married for almost a year by that point, I felt the same thrill that had shot through me the first night he'd kissed me.

I'd never stopped feeling that for Eddie. Maybe that's why I'd never seen this coming. I'd been too in love, too trusting, too —

Eddie came in as I was writing that last entry. I was able to shove the book under the bed before the door was open, so he didn't see that I was writing, thank god. I'm going to have to be more careful in the future.

It's not much consolation, but he looks awful. Eddie has always been so polished, but today his eyes were red and his skin looked a little slack, almost gray. And as insane and fucked up as it is, for a second, I felt sorry for him. I wanted to help him. That's how our marriage had always gone, after all. I was the planner, Eddie was the doer.

I waited for him to say something, for him to at least try to explain what the fuck is going on. I probably should have screamed at him, rushed toward him, hit him. Anything.

But I just sat there, frozen.

I'd like to blame it on the lingering effects of whatever drug he slipped me and Blanche, but from the second he'd walked in, I'd felt paralyzed with some combination of fear and shock.

All I could do was watch as he put bottles of water and packets of peanut butter crackers, plus a couple of apples and a banana, on the table near the door, his back to me.

Eddie killed Blanche.

He killed her, and he could kill me.

Eddie, my husband, my partner. The man I thought I knew so well. Who smiled at me the day we met with such sweetness in his eyes. Who always listened so carefully when I talked about my day, my business, my dreams. Who remembered little, silly things — like my favorite hot sauce or how I always liked my coffee with one regular sugar, one Splenda.

That man, my Eddie, was a murderer.

If I think too much, I feel like screaming, and I'm afraid if I start screaming, I'll never stop, so instead, I'm taking deep breaths, even though the pattern — *in for four, hold for four, out for six* — reminds me of the yoga class Blanche and I took together just last month.

God, one month ago. It already feels like another lifetime.

Eddie didn't speak to me, just set the food and water down, then went back out the door, and when he was gone, I laid down on the floor and cried, shaking so hard that my teeth chattered together.

How had I married a monster and never seen it until it was too late?

Four Days after Blanche

Today, Eddie came in again, more water, more food, and this time, I tried to talk to him, but as soon as I said his name, he held up a hand, his face closed to me.

It was like looking at a stranger who shared Eddie's familiar features. This cold, dangerous man was no one I knew, and when he left, all I felt was relief. This time, there were no tears, no shaking. Maybe writing all this down is helping after all.

Six Days after Blanche

It's been two days since Eddie was last here, and in that time, I've felt myself growing calmer, saner.

I still don't understand what his plan is, or why he's keeping me here, why I'm not at the bottom of the lake with Blanche. But there has to be a reason, and I'm going to figure it out.

I have to be smart.

Smarter than Eddie.

It's the only way I'm getting out of this alive.

Bea didn't mean to be late, but traffic was bad and the rain hadn't helped.

By the time she slides into the booth opposite Blanche at their favorite restaurant, La Paz, Blanche is already on her second margarita and the chip basket is nearly empty.

As soon as she sits down, Blanche signals the waiter, pointing to her glass, then to Bea, who tries not to be annoyed. She does usually get a margarita, it's just that tonight, she hadn't planned on drinking.

And she clearly doesn't do a great job of hiding that annoyance because her voice is sharper than she'd intended when she says, "A three margarita Tuesday, huh?"

Blanche just shrugs and drags another chip through the little blue dish of salsa. "Smoke 'em if you got 'em!" she says, bright and, to Bea's ears, fake.

Something has been off with Blanche lately, but Bea can't figure out what it is. It might be

Tripp; he and Blanche have only been married a year, but there's already a brittleness there, a tension. Just last week, Bea went over to their house for drinks, and had to sit through two hours of the two of them steadily chipping away at each other, flinging little barbs, little insults wrapped in affection.

And sitting across from Blanche now, Bea sees that Blanche's eyes look a little puffy, her skin a little dull. She wishes she hadn't made that crack about the third margarita.

When their drinks are set in front of them, Bea picks up the heavy glass with its salted rim and touches it to Blanche's. "To us," she says. "And not drinking those sugar-bomb monstrosities from El Calor anymore."

That makes Blanche smile a little, as Bea had hoped it would. El Calor had been the cheap Mexican place near Ivy Ridge, the school she and Blanche had both attended as teenagers. They'd gone in nearly every Friday night, long before they'd turned twenty-one, and ordered the most obnoxious margaritas on the menu, frozen concoctions that came in giant bowls and were bright red or blue or neon green, colors that stained their lips and teeth.

Bea still has a picture of her and Blanche their senior year, sticking out their tongues for the camera, Blanche's purple, Bea's scarlet, their eyes shining with alcohol and youth.

She loves that picture.

She misses those girls.

Maybe tonight is the chance to recapture a little of that?

But then, Blanche lifts her menu and Bea sees the bangle around her wrist.

Without thinking, she reaches for Blanche's hand, and examines the bracelet. It's pretty, a thin silver circlet with a dainty charm — Blanche's zodiac sign, Scorpio, picked out in diamonds.

"We have something similar to this coming out next year," Bea says, turning Blanche's wrist so she can better see the bracelet. "But we did an enamel backing on the charm, and we're offering colored stone options. I'll get you one."

Blanche jerks her hand back, her elbow nearly upsetting her drink, the movement so sudden, so aggressive, that for a beat or two, Bea doesn't pull her own hand back and it just hovers there over the chips and salsa.

"I like this bracelet," Blanche says, looking at the menu and not meeting Bea's eyes. "I don't need another one."

"I just thought —" Bea starts, but then she drops it, picking up her own menu instead, even though she always orders the same thing.

So does Blanche, but you'd think the secrets of the universe were encoded among the various descriptions of burritos and enchiladas, that's how intently Blanche is staring at her menu now.

The silence between them is heavy and awkward, and Bea tries to remember the last time she felt this way around Blanche. Blanche, who's been her best friend since she was a nervous fourteen-year-old, away from home for the first time, trying to fit in at a new, fancy school.

Once the waiter has taken their orders — the usual for both of them, Bea's enchiladas verdes, Blanche's tortilla soup — that same silence returns, and Bea wonders if she's going to be forced to scroll through her phone when Blanche says, "So, how's the guy?"

Another spike of annoyance surges through Bea.

"Eddie is fine," she says, putting extra emphasis on his first name, which, for some reason, Blanche never wants to use. He's always "the guy," occasionally "that guy," and once, at a lunch with some of their friends from Ivy Ridge, "Bea's little boyfriend-person."

It was something Bea had heard Blanche say a lot over the years, her go-to dismissive phrase, but Bea had never had it directed at her before, and she'd ended up leaving lunch early.

Now Blanche drains the rest of her margarita and repeats, "Eddie." Folding her arms on the table, she leans forward, the sleeve of her tunic coming dangerously close to a splotch of salsa by her wrist. "I never trust men who go by nicknames like that," she says. "Like. Grown men. Your name is Robert, don't be Bobby, for Christ's sake, you know? Or Johnny for John."

"Right," Bea can't help but reply. "Like when a guy is 'the third' but goes by 'Tripp.' "

Blanche blinks at that, but then, to Bea's surprise, laughs and sits back. "Okay, touché, you bitch," she says, but there's no real heat in it. Bea feels some of the tension drain away, and wonders if this night will be salvageable after all.

But then Blanche leans forward again to take Bea's hand. She's drunk now, Bea can tell, that third margarita finishing the job the first two started, and her grip is surprisingly tight.

"But seriously, Bea. What do you know about this guy? You met him at the beach. Who comes back from vacation with a boyfriend?"

"A fiancé, actually," Bea says, looking Blanche in the eyes. "He asked me to marry him last week. That's why I wanted to have dinner with you. So I could tell you. Surprise!"

Bea holds her hands out awkwardly to either side of her face, wiggling her fingers, and smiling, but she knows she's not going to get it, the moment she's seen other women have, the moment she gave Blanche. That pause and then the squeal and the tear-filled eyes, the inelegant hugging, the immediate plans for showers and parties, questions about rings and dresses and honeymoons.

No.

Blanche, her best friend in the entire world, doesn't give her that.

Instead, she sits back against the booth, her lips parted in shock. Blanche is blond right now, and the color is well done, but it's too harsh on her, and for a second, she could almost be a stranger sitting across from Bea.

Then after a moment, she gives another shrug, rattles the ice in her glass. "Well, at least let Tripp set you up with a prenup."

Their food arrives then, and as the waiter sets their plates down, Bea can only stare at Blanche, waiting until they're alone again to lean closer and hiss, "Thanks for that. Really supportive."

Blanche throws up her hands, that silver bangle sliding up her skinny arm. "What do you want me to say, Bea? That I'm happy for you? That I think marrying a really hot guy who just strolled up to you on a beach is a great idea?"

"It wasn't exactly like that," Bea says, putting her napkin in her lap and glancing around. They're keeping their voices low, but she still feels like they are just a few seconds away from creating a *Real Housewives of Birmingham* scene, and that's the last thing she wants.

It's the last thing that the old Blanche would've wanted, too, but with this new Blanche — too thin, too drunk, too blond — who knows?

"You don't get it," Blanche insists, and now, okay, yes, a woman at another table is glancing over, her eyebrows slightly raised. "You're rich now, Bea. And not, like, normal person rich. You aren't a successful lawyer or doctor. You are on your way to having Fuck You Money, and this guy knows it."

"And that's why he's interested in me, right?" Bea says, feeling her face go hot even as every other part of her seems cold. "Because I'm rich. Which, coincidentally, is also what bugs you. Obviously, being my friend was a lot easier when I was some . . . some fucking charity case for you."

Blanche scoffs at that, sitting back in the booth hard enough to rattle it. "Okay, fine. I'm just trying to look out for you and remind you that you can't just attach yourself to anyone who's nice to you, but seeing as how that's your entire deal, I guess I'm wasting my breath."

Bea is almost shaking now, can't even conceive of eating her dinner, and she pushes the plate away and picks up her drink. The ice has melted, the margarita has turned salty and sour and too strong, but she downs it anyway.

"I just want you to be careful," Blanche says, her expression softened. "You hardly know him. You've been together, what? A month?"

"Three months," Bea replies. "And I know everything I need to know. I know he loves me, and I know I love him."

Blanche's face twists. "Right. Because love is definitely all that matters."

"I know things are rough with Tripp right now —"

"They're not 'rough,' " Blanche argues, making air quotes with her fingers. "It's just that marriage is a lot more work than you're thinking." Then she shakes her head, puts her fork down. "But then again, he's hot and you're rich, so hey, maybe it'll be easier for you two. Maybe that's the secret."

Anger drains out of Bea so quickly it's like someone pulled a plug.

Blanche is jealous of her.

That's what all this is about.

Blanche is jealous. Jealous of her money, jealous of her success, and now, jealous of her man.

Bea never imagined that Blanche would ever want anything of hers. And now, she wants everything.

Which makes it easier for Bea to gently take Blanche's hand. "Can we declare a truce?" she asks softly. "Because it's going to be super awkward to have you as my maid of honor if we're not speaking to each other."

Blanche snorts, but after a minute, she squeezes Bea's hand back.

■ ■ ■ ■

PART III
JANE

■ ■ ■ ■

10

I didn't know sheets could actually *smell* soft, but Eddie's do.

Every morning when I wake up in that big upholstered bed, I hold the sheets up to my nose and inhale, wondering how I got this fucking lucky.

It's been two weeks since I more or less moved in with Eddie, two weeks of soft linens and sinking into the plush sofa in the living room in the afternoon, watching bad reality shows on the massive television.

I'm never leaving this place.

I get out of the bed slowly, my toes curling against the plush rug awaiting my feet. The bedroom is luxurious in all the right ways — dark wood, deep blues, the occasional splash of gray. Neutral. Masculine.

This is one space where Eddie scrubbed out Bea's style, I can tell. Before, I bet it was decked out in the same swirling, bright shades as the rest of the house. Peacock blue, saffron yellow, brilliant fuchsia. But here, there's just Eddie.

And now, me.

Eddie is in the kitchen when I wander in, already dressed for work.

He smiles at me, a cup of coffee already steaming in his hand.

"Morning," he says, handing it to me. The first morning I'd woken up here, Eddie had made me a plain black cup of coffee, like I'd had the day we met. Sheepishly, I'd confessed that I actually didn't *like* black coffee that much, and now I have an expensive milk frother at my disposal, and all kinds of pricey flavored syrups.

Today's cup smells like cinnamon, and I inhale deeply over the mug before taking a sip. "I don't know how to tell you this, but I'm only sleeping with you for the coffee," I say, and he winks at me.

"My ability to make a great cup of coffee really *is* my only redeeming value."

"I think you have a few others," I say, and he glances at me, eyebrows raised.

"Just a few?"

I hold my thumb and forefinger up, putting them close together, and he laughs, which warms me almost as much as the coffee.

I like him. There's no getting around that.

This isn't just about the house or the money, although I'm fully into those things, trust me. But being with Eddie is . . . nice.

And he likes *me*. Not just the me I've invented, but the flashes of the real me I've let him see.

I want to show him more of the real me, I think. And it's been a long time since I've felt that way.

Turning back to the sink, Eddie rinses out his own coffee cup and says, "So, what's on your agenda today?"

I've been waiting for this moment for the past two weeks, hoping he'd ask what I was doing all day. Because I am still walking those damn dogs. I may stay in Eddie's house, I may eat the food Eddie buys, but I'm still on my own for everything else. Gas for my car, clothes, odds and ends. I still technically have rent to pay.

"Dogs," I reply shortly, and he looks up, frowning slightly.

"You're still doing that?"

Some of the warmth I was feeling toward him fades a little. What did he think I was doing all day? Just sitting around, waiting for him to come back?

I hide that irritation, though, standing up from the stool with a shrug. "I mean, yeah. I have to make money."

He pulls a face, wiping his hands on one of those Southern Manors towels that are all over the kitchen. This one has a slice of watermelon printed on it, a perfect bite taken out of one side. "You're welcome to use my card to get whatever you need. And I can add you to my checking account today. My personal one, not the Southern Manors account. Lot more fucking paperwork to that one, but we can get that worked out eventually, too."

I stand there as he turns away again, balling up the towel and tossing it into the laundry room just off the kitchen.

Is it that easy for men like him? He's handing me access to thousands and thousands of dollars like it's nothing, and I could just . . . take it. Take everything, if I wanted to.

Maybe that's what it is — it would never occur to him that I would do something like that. That anyone, especially any woman, could do that.

But since this is exactly what I wanted, I smile at him, shaking my head slightly. "That would . . . that would be amazing, Eddie. Thank you."

"What's the point of having it if my girl can't spend it, hmm?" He comes around the bar, putting an arm around my waist

116

and nuzzling my hair.

"Also," he says before pulling away, "why don't you go ahead a pick up your things from your old place, bring them back here? Make it official."

Pressing a hand against my chest, I give him my best faux-flirty look. "Edward Rochester, are you asking me to move in with you?"

Another grin as he walks backward toward the door. "I think I am. You saying yes?"

"Maybe," I tell him, and that grin widens as he turns back around.

"I'll leave the card by the door!" he calls out, and I hear the soft slap of plastic on marble before the door opens and closes, leaving me alone in the house.

My house.

I make myself another cup of coffee, and carry it back upstairs to the massive en suite, my favorite part of the house so far.

Like nearly everything else here, the bathroom is oversized, but not overwhelming. Bea's stamp is here, too, of course. Had Eddie designed this room, I think it would probably be sleeker, more modern. Glass and steel and subway tile. Instead, it's marble and copper with a tile floor with a mosaic of — shocker — a magnolia in the center.

I scuff my bare toe against one of the dark green leaves before making my way to the tub.

We had a bathtub in the apartment, but I'd have to be high to actually take a bath in it. Not only is it cramped and stained with black mold in the corners, but the thought of my naked body sitting where John takes a shower? Too horrible to contemplate. No, I've always taken the world's fastest showers, cringing every time the shower curtain touches me.

I fucking deserve this bathtub.

Sitting on the edge, I lean forward and turn on the hot tap, coffee cup still in one hand as I test the water with the fingers of the other.

I'll get to take a bath in here every day now, forever. This is how I'll spend my mornings. No more drive from Center Point.

No more dog-walking.

And once I'm done with today's soak, I'll get dressed and drive over to that dingy little apartment before putting it behind me and never looking back.

I take what Eddie calls "the sensible car," a Mercedes SUV, and make my way from the shady enclaves of Mountain Brook to the strip malls and ugly apartment complexes of my old home.

It feels strange, parking such a nice car in the space where I used to park my beat-up Hyundai, and stranger still to walk up the concrete steps in my new leather sandals, the clack of my heels loud enough to make me flinch.

Number 234 looks even dingier somehow, and I dig my keys out of my purse.

But when I put the key in, I realize the door is unlocked, and I frown as I step inside. John's a moron, but he's not the type to be this careless.

And then I realize it's me who's the careless one because I should've called the church before I came here this morning, should've made sure John had actually gone into work and wouldn't be doing what he is currently doing — namely, sitting on the couch with my afghan draped over him, watching boring morning television.

"She returns," he says around a mouthful of cereal. He could eat cereal for every meal, I think, always the cheap, sugary shit they make for kids. Never brand names, no things like "Fruity Ohs" and "Sugar Flakes." Whatever he's shoveling into his mouth now has turned the milk a muddy gray, and I don't even bother to hide my disgust as I ask, "Shouldn't you be at the church?"

John shrugs, his eyes still on the TV. "Day off."

Great.

He turns to say more then, and his eyes go a little wide when he sees me. "What are you wearing?"

I want to make some kind of joke about saving those lines for his internet girlfriends, but that would prolong this interaction and that's the last thing I need, so I just wave him off and make for my room.

The door is open even though I distinctly remember closing it, and I press my lips together, irritated. But my bed is still made up, and when I open a drawer, all my underwear appears to be accounted for, so that's a relief, at least.

Reaching under the bed, I pull out my battered duffel bag, and have already un-zipped it before I stop and look around.

It's not like I didn't know my room was deeply sad. No matter what I did, it always looked grubby and just a little institutional, almost like a cell.

But now, after two weeks living in Eddie's house?

There is not a single thing I want to take with me.

I want to leave all of this — the dullness,

the cheap fabrics, the frayed edges — behind.

More than that, really.

I want to set it all on fucking fire.

When I walk out of the bedroom, I'm not carrying anything. Not the duffel, which I'd shoved back under the bed. Not my underwear, which John was now welcome to be as pervy as he liked with. Not even the little trinkets and treasures I'd taken from all the houses in Thornfield Estates.

John turned off the TV, and he now faces me on the couch, my afghan still on his upraised knees. He's smirking at me, probably because he's expecting me to ask for the blanket, and he's ready to say something that just skirts the line, something that's supposed to make me wonder if he's being gross or not (he is).

He can keep that blanket, too.

"I'm moving out," I say without preamble, shoving my hands in my back pockets. "I should be all paid up on rent, so —"

"You can't just leave."

Anger sparks inside my chest, but, right on the heels of it, there's something else.

Joy.

I am never going to look at this asshole's face again. I'm never going to sleep in this depressing apartment or take a sad shower under trickling, lukewarm water. I'm never going to dig money out of my pocket to hand over to John Rivers ever again.

"And yet I *am* leaving. Wild."

John's eyes narrow. "You owe me two weeks' notice," he says, and now I laugh, tipping my head back.

"You're not my landlord, John," I say. "You're just some sad little boy who thought I'd sleep with you if you let me stay here. And you overcharged me for rent."

There's a dull flush creeping up his neck, his lower lip sticking out just the tiniest bit, and once again, I am so relieved that this is it, the last time I'll ever have to talk to him.

But soon, people like John Rivers won't even exist to me. He barely exists right now.

"I never wanted to sleep with you," he mutters, his tone still sulky. "You're not even hot."

That would've stung once upon a time. Even coming from someone like John. I've always been aware of how completely plain I am, small, nondescript. And I've definitely felt it when I look at pictures of Bea, her dark, glossy hair swinging around that pretty face with its high cheekbones and wide eyes. That body that was somehow lush and trim at the same time, in contrast with my own straight-up-and-down, almost boyish body.

But Eddie wanted me. Small, plain, boring me.

It made me feel beautiful, for once. And powerful.

So I look at John and smirk. "Keep telling yourself that," I say, then I turn and walk out.

I'm not sure hearing a door close behind me has ever been this satisfying, and as I walk back to the car, I actually welcome the slap of my heels, love how loud they are.

Fuck. You, I think with every step. *Fuck. You. Fuck. You.*

I'm grinning when I reach the Mercedes, and I grab my keys, pressing the little button to unlock the doors. It takes me a moment to realize that there's a familiar red car parked just across the parking lot, and my first thought is that it's weird anyone here has that nice of a car.

It's not until Eddie is stepping out of the driver's side and walking toward me that my brain fully absorbs that it's his car, that he's . . . here. In Center Point. In my shitty apartment complex.

Seeing him is so jarring that my instinct is to run away, to jump in my car (his *car,* my asshole brain reminds me), and get the hell out of here.

"Hey, beautiful," he says as he approaches,

keys dangling from his fingers.

"You followed me?" I blurt out, glad I'm wearing sunglasses so that he can't see my full expression. I'm rattled, not just because it seems weirdly out of character for Eddie to *follow me,* but because he's *here.* He's seen this place now, this ugly little hole I tried to hide from him. Doesn't matter that I'm leaving it all behind. The fact that he knows it existed at all makes me feel close to tears.

Sighing, Eddie shoves his hands in his back pockets. The wind ruffles his hair, and he looks so out of place standing in this parking lot, in this life.

That sense of vertigo gets stronger.

"I know," Eddie says. "It's crazy and I shouldn't have done it."

Then he gives me a sheepish grin. He's not wearing his sunglasses, and he squints slightly in the bright light.

"But you make me crazy, what can I say?"

Even though the sun is beating down on us, I feel a chill wash over me.

Eddie is romantic, for sure. Passionate, definitely. But this . . . doesn't feel like him.

You've known him for about five minutes, so maybe you don't actually *know him,* I remind myself.

There's only one way to play this. I smile

in return, rolling my eyes as I do. "That is so cheesy," I say, but I make sure to look pleased, tugging my lower lip between my teeth to really sell it.

It must work, because his shoulders droop slightly with relief, and then he steps forward, sliding his arms around my waist.

Pressing my forehead against his chest, I breathe him in. *You're being stupid,* I tell myself. I'm so used to men lying to me, manipulating me, that now I see it where it doesn't exist. Maybe Eddie is the type to go a little over the top when he's into someone. There could be all sorts of stuff about him that I haven't worked out yet.

"Are you the boyfriend?"

We both turn to see John standing there on the stairs in his T-shirt and loose sweats. He's barefoot, his hair greasy and sticking up in spikes, and observing them near each other, it's hard to believe he and Eddie are from the same species.

"So it seems," Eddie replies, his voice easy, but I can feel him stiffen slightly, his muscles tense.

"Cool," John mutters, his eyes darting between the two of us, clearly trying to make sense of what's happening here.

Eddie is still smiling at him, still friendly and relaxed, but there's something radiating off him, something dark and intense, and when I glance down, I see that his hand is curled into a fist at his side.

John doesn't notice, though, walking down the steps to stand right in front of us. This close, I can smell his sweat, smell the sugary scent of whatever cereal he was eating.

"Jane owes me two weeks' notice before she moves out," he says, and Eddie's eyebrows go up.

"I don't," I say. "That's not even a thing."

"It is," John insists, and I see this as the desperate grab for control that it is. Doesn't mean it sucks any less, though, and my face has grown hot in that dull throbbing way, a blush creeping up from my chest.

"Send the paperwork over to my lawyer," Eddie says, fishing around for his wallet before pulling out a business card. He keeps grinning at John as he hands it to him, and I see John's eyes flick between the card and Eddie's face before he takes it.

"Will do," he says, but I know this is the last we're ever hearing from John Rivers. His kind of bullshit only barely works against women with no options. Against someone like Eddie? With his nice car and casual use of "my lawyer"? John has nothing.

But he can't keep from delivering one last

parting shot.

"Good luck, man," he says, his gaze skating over to me. "She's a fucking handful."

The shame that rises up in my throat threatens to choke me. I hate this, that Eddie now knows this asshole was a part of my life, that he fully understands just how shabby everything was before he found me.

Slipping an arm around my waist, Eddie gives me a brief squeeze. "Janie, would you go grab my phone out of my car? I want to be sure I get John's phone number in case there are any other issues."

It's not the reaction I expected at all, which is maybe why I just nod and start to cross the parking lot to Eddie's car.

I've just reached the back bumper when I glance over my shoulder at Eddie and John.

They're standing closer now, Eddie's head lowered as he speaks to John.

He never lays a hand on John, never uses his superior height to loom over him or threaten, but there's something there, etched in every line of his body, that speaks of violence. That makes me think he wants nothing more than to send John through the windshield of the nearest car.

And John, stupid though he may be, sees it, too. His face goes even paler, and whatever Eddie is saying, smiling all the while, has John backing up the steps, his hands deep in the pockets of his sweatpants. In his haste, he actually stumbles, arms pinwheeling, and Eddie makes no move to steady him, letting him flail before John rights himself. With one final dirty look at me, he turns and heads back up to his apartment.

His now. His alone. Never mine again.

Eddie walks over to the car, then, his gait loose and rolling again, all that tension vanished like it was never even there.

And when he reaches me, he holds out his hands, takes mine, and squeezes.

"Please tell me that douchebag wasn't your ex," he says with a grin, and I'd be lying if I said a little shiver of lust didn't go through me. Is it because of his proximity or because protecting me from John is a turn-on?

In any case, it's not totally feigned when I press closer and say, "Please have a better opinion of my taste in men."

Still grinning, Eddie leans forward and kisses the tip of my nose. "How can I when you're in love with me?"

11

It takes forever to plan my first "accidental" meeting with the ladies of Thornfield Estates. The moment had to be perfect, after all — I was only getting one shot at this, and I wanted to be sure I nailed it. I'd thought about trying to engineer something in the village, bumping into them at Roasted, maybe just strolling down the sidewalk, bags from one of the pricier boutiques hanging off my arms.

I'd spent hours imagining that scenario, and while it was satisfying, it didn't have quite the impact I wanted.

Then I'd thought about being really bold and just texting them, inviting them over for lunch at Eddie's, but the house still held too much of Bea, and I was worried that I'd look like a pale imitation standing in her space.

Then I remembered that Emily Clark and Campbell Reed both loved to walk the neighborhood in the mornings, and suddenly I knew exactly how I wanted that first meeting to go down.

So here I am, walking the sidewalks of Thornfield Estates, Adele on her leash pulling me along.

Walking a dog when you're not being paid to do it is actually kind of fun. The weather is nice, Adele is well-behaved, and I like how she looks back over her shoulder at me whenever she spots something new, wagging her tail, giving me her little doggy smile.

Or maybe I just like her more now because she's mine. Mine and Eddie's together, bought after Bea was long gone.

I'm so busy thinking about that, this idea of Eddie and me having something that's only ours, that I almost miss the moment when Emily and Campbell see me.

But when I glance up, there they are, both wearing white and brightly colored neon sneakers, both with sunglasses so huge half their faces are covered.

That's a shame because it means I don't catch as much of their expressions as I'd like, but the subtle parting of Emily's lips, the way Campbell's stride stutters just a little, is enough.

"Jane?"

Emily moves forward, a little faster than Campbell who ambles up behind her, hands pressed to her lower back.

"Oh, hey!" I say, raising my hand, then tucking my hair behind my ear, ducking my head a little, in full Sheepish Mode.

"I thought you'd quit dog-walking?" Emily asks, glancing down at Adele, and I laugh a little, winding a part of the leash around my palm.

"I did," I say. "I'm just out walking Adele for a little exercise."

I wait for it to click. They have to put the pieces together themselves because if I push it, the gossip will be about how smug I was.

Look, don't get me wrong — I am super fucking smug right now. But I also want Emily and Campbell and Caroline McLaren to eventually see me as a friend, not an enemy, and that means I have to nail this delivery, the moment they first see me as Eddie's girlfriend, not the dog-walker.

"Did Eddie give her to you or something?" Emily asks, and I stifle a sigh. Of all the ladies in the neighborhood, Emily is the nicest, but definitely not the brightest. I suddenly wish Caroline were there. I'd have to do a lot less work for her.

Luckily, Campbell comes to my rescue. Shoving her sunglasses up on her head, she looks at me, eyes wide. "You're the mystery girl," she says, then nudges Emily. "Remember, we said that we thought Eddie was seeing someone?"

Emily's jaw drops comically round, a little "oh" escaping her mouth.

I wave my free hand, shifting my weight slightly. "It was really sudden," I say, "and it's still really new, and I felt awkward saying anything, and . . ." I trail off, then give a sort of groan, rolling my eyes. "Well, now I feel *really* awkward."

This is another trick I've learned over the years — make people think they have the upper hand, and they trust you so much faster. I can already see Campbell's expression softening, and Emily's smile seems genuine.

I'm not a threat, not an interloper. I'm just Sweet Jane Who Got Absurdly Lucky and Knows It.

They can work with that.

Emily reaches out and slaps affectionately at my arm. "You minx," she teases. I'm not sure I've ever heard anyone use that word, but it sounds right coming out of Emily's mouth.

And then, just like I'd hoped, she gestures back toward her house. "This is too good a story to hear while we're standing in the middle of the street. Let's go back to mine."

It feels different, being in Emily's house as a guest.

I let Adele out into the backyard with Major and Colonel, smiling as the dogs wag their tails at me, then go back inside to the kitchen, where Campbell and Emily are standing at the counter. They've totally been talking about me — they look up too quickly when I come in, and move a little farther apart — but they don't seem suspicious or pissed off. Just surprised, probably.

And if I'm honest, I like being the subject of conversation.

Emily is shoving pieces of fruit into a juicer, the motor whirring, and the resulting juice is a dark, viscous green, but I take it anyway, smiling as I sip.

It tastes like someone dumped half a pound of ginger into grass cuttings, but this is what women like Emily and Campbell drink, so fuck me, I guess I'll develop a taste for it.

"Sooooo," Emily drawls, leaning on the counter, propping her chin on her fist like she's a teenager at a slumber party. "Tell us everything."

I laugh and shrug. "I mean, it's really not that interesting. We got to talking one afternoon, he asked me for coffee, and then . . ." I trail off, grinning and looking demurely down at the counter.

Always better to let people use their imaginations, rather than giving them every detail.

Except that Campbell wants details, because of course she does.

"So, like, what are you two now?" she asks, tapping her nails against her glass. She's got a new ring on her index finger, a thin gold band studded with diamonds, and I try not to stare at it, try not to want it. "Like, is it serious?"

She's smiling when I meet her gaze, her head titled down in that conspiratorial "girl talk" pose I've seen her, Emily, and Caroline do a thousand times, but there's something hard in her eyes, and a muscle ticks in her jaw.

Careful, careful.

For a second, I think about going the helpless ingenue route again, all, "Oh, I don't know, we're taking it day by day," that whole song and dance. But there's another part of me that doesn't want to do that. That wants them to know I'm here to stay, so they better get used to it, and fast.

No shrugging, then. No blushing. I look

Campbell directly in the eyes as I say, "It is, yeah."

Emily gives a little squeal and reaches out to squeeze my arm. "This is so *exciting!*"

Campbell glances over at her, and I can see her waver. If Emily throws her support behind me, then what choice does Campbell really have but to do the same?

She must figure that out, too, because she finally smiles at me, and says, "It really is. Congratulations, Jane."

Now I can go back to the "aw shucks" thing. "I mean, we're just dating," I say. "It's not like we're getting married."

"But you're living together, right?" Emily asks, and when I don't immediately answer, she says, "I mean, I just assumed. If you're walking Adele for funsies."

"We are," I reply, glancing down, feigning a little embarrassment. "My apartment was on the whole other side of town, so it just made sense to move in."

I catch a little look between Emily and Campbell, but don't know what it means exactly. Do they think I'm slutty for moving in with a man so fast? Do they think Eddie's stupid for letting me?

I don't know, and before I can say anything else, Emily shrugs. "So you might get married one day. Seems likely."

I see her gaze slide over to that massive stainless-steel fridge of hers. There's a picture there, of Emily and Campbell at some backyard barbecue thing, Bea Rochester and Blanche Ingraham standing between them.

They're all smiling, Emily's arm around Bea's waist.

I let them see me noticing the picture, then look back at both Emily and Campbell. "You both must really miss her. And Blanche, too."

Emily frowns slightly, her fingers coming up to play with the little gold-and-pearl-inlay cross around her neck, and Campbell finishes the rest of her juice.

"It's definitely different without the two of them around," Emily finally says, the words a little slow and halting, her frown deepening.

"Less drama, that's for damn sure," Campbell adds, then looks back over at me, waving a hand. "I shouldn't have said that."

I actually want her to say a whole lot more of *that*. What drama?

A little of the smugness leaks out of me, deflating me as I sit at Emily's counter. It's a reminder that there's a whole world here full of undercurrents and stories and connections and voids. Just when I feel like I've got a handle on it, some new thing pops up, some indication that I'm a newcomer here. An outsider.

"That was actually the last time we were all together," Emily says, walking over to the fridge. "Fourth of July. It's so weird, but I keep thinking I'll get a text from Blanche, or Bea will email me about the Neighborhood Beautification Committee or something." She shakes her head. "I don't know when I'll get used to them not being here."

Fuck, this is not going the way I'd hoped at all. I can practically feel myself scrambling for some ledge to hold on to, some way to turn this all around.

Unfortunately, what I latch on to is, "The Neighborhood Beautification Committee?"

Kill me now for letting those words come out of my mouth.

Emily's eyebrows go up a little, her eyes widening. "Oh, yeah," she says. "We haven't had a meeting since . . . well, since Bea and Blanche, because it just felt too weird without them there. But with summer coming up, we should probably plan something. Don't you think, Cam?"

Campbell nods, getting off the stool and carrying her glass to the sink. "Definitely. Those flower beds by the sign at the front of the neighborhood look like complete dog shit."

I'd just passed those flower beds yesterday, and thought to myself that they looked lovely, all colorful and a little wild. But now I agree with Campbell, giving a way too enthusiastic, "Totally!"

There's a beat of silence, just a little too long, and I find myself rushing into it. "I know I'm pretty new to actually living in the neighborhood, but if you need someone on that committee, I'd love to help."

The idea of spending time talking about flowers with the women in this neighborhood makes me want to die, but if Bea did this, then I want to do it, too. Let them get used to me. To the idea that I'm not going anywhere anytime soon.

I can see that Campbell wants to object, probably on the basis of me just living with Eddie rather than being a homeowner myself or whatever, making up some rule that didn't exist until right this second. I know her type, after all.

But Emily beams at me. "That would be so fun!"

Campbell smiles, too, but it takes longer, and when she looks at me, it feels more like she's baring her teeth. "Super fun."

12

May

I had no idea you could spend over a thousand dollars on fucking solar lamps that look like gaslights.

But here I am, loading up packages of those lights into the back of Eddie's SUV, his credit card practically smoking in my wallet. He won't care, I know — he told me to get "whatever it is Emily has decided she can't live without" — but I was eating ramen and cereal for just about every meal only a few months ago, so hearing the cashier at Home Depot say, "That'll be $1023.78," as I checked out with nothing more than *lights* made my chest hurt.

My first week on the Neighborhood Beautification Committee is obviously going really well.

So far, we've had one meeting over at Emily's house, and there were only five of us there — Emily, Campbell, Caroline, another woman named Anna-Grace who I'd never met, and me. Mostly everyone just drank white wine for an hour and made vague noises about what kinds of things might look good around the neighborhood, and it wasn't until the last ten minutes or so that Emily suggested the fancy solar lights. "They'd brighten up that front flower bed so much, and if we got enough, we could even use them around the sidewalks!"

Like an idiot, I'd volunteered to go get them, somehow not grasping that that also meant paying for them and lugging them back to Thornfield Estates.

Now, as the guy in the orange apron helps me put the last bag in the car, I wish I'd waited for the weekend. This could've been a fun trip with Eddie, but it's a Wednesday afternoon, so he's at work. He's at work a lot lately, as he's had to manage both his contracting business and the Southern Manors office, and he sometimes doesn't get home until late at night.

I'm surprised that I kind of miss him being around. I'd thought that having access to the house, the cars, and the money would assuage any loneliness I might feel, but the house is . . . big. And still full of Bea's stuff because god knows I don't have any stuff of my own to contribute. Maybe that will be the next project I tackle.

I press the button on the key chain to lower the tailgate of the SUV, and am just turning toward the driver's side when I hear, "Jane."

John is standing there in the parking lot, a plastic bag in his hand, squinting at me in the bright sunlight.

For a second, I feel like maybe I hallucinated him, because why in the fuck would John be here, but then I remember that I purposely didn't go to the fancier hardware stores in Mountain Brook, that I drove to this Home Depot in Vestavia because I thought it might be cheaper.

Old habits, I guess.

And John's church is in Vestavia, something I should've remembered, but in the weeks since I've moved out, it's been so easy to forget about John altogether.

Now I ignore him, but I'm flustered, and when I press the button to unlock the car, I hit the alarm instead, the shrill beeping seeming louder than it actually is.

"Fuck," I mutter, trying to hit whatever button will make it stop, but then as soon as I find it, John is right there, so close to me that I can smell his cheap deodorant, probably something called "Mountain Lynx," or "Fresh Iceberg."

"I'm actually glad I bumped into you," he says, and I move back, my shoulder blade hitting the side mirror of the SUV.

"Well, I'm having the opposite reaction to bumping into *you,*" I reply, "so I'm —"

"Someone called the apartment looking for you."

I freeze, a numbness starting in my fingertips, spreading up my arms. Which is stupid because it could be anyone. Maybe Roasted wanted to offer me my old job back. I had written down the apartment's landline as a contact, hadn't I? And I'd applied for tons of jobs when I first moved here. That had been a long time ago, but still, people could be looking through old applications. There were a million people it could be. It didn't have to be *them.*

But some primal part of me knows.

"Okay?" I say, but there's no real bite to it and definitely none of the casual "I-don't-give-a-fuck," I was trying to convey. I feel trapped and scared.

I *am* trapped and scared.

"Apparently they were calling from Phoenix."

My heart is heavy in my chest now, thudding too fast, too hard. The numbness has spread up to my face, and I'm suddenly afraid my mouth won't work.

"They were trying to track down anyone who might know a woman named Helen Burns."

John's tongue flicks out as he licks his lips, and I hate that I can't control my reaction to this, hate that he's seeing how freaked out I am. I hate giving him this moment.

But that name.

Turning away, I fumble for the door, not bothering with the key fob now, just wanting to unlock my car *(Eddie's car, it's Eddie's, none of this is yours)* and get away from John.

"I don't know anybody by that name," he goes on, stepping so close that he catches the back of my shoe with the tip of his sneaker, the rubber scraping my ankle.

"But the way the guy was talking, it sure did sound like you. Said Helen would be in her early twenties now. Short, brown hair, brown eyes. A scar on her right arm."

I turn around then, trapped between him and the car, the metal and glass hot against my back. "What did you tell him?"

John smiles then. He doesn't look as weaselly and pathetic as he did that day with Eddie. There are no stains on his clothes, and his hair has been combed, and I suddenly have this awful feeling that he didn't just run into me by chance — that he's been following me, tracking me all the way to Vestavia, because he wanted to have this confrontation, wanted to be sure it would go the way he wanted.

The thought of it is somehow worse than any of the creepy shit he did when I lived with him.

He's not supposed to exist in this new life. He, and everything that happened in Phoenix, is supposed to be behind me, forever.

John makes me wait for his answer a few beats too long, seconds in which I feel my stomach sink and my heart race, and I hate him, I hate him, I hate him.

Then he shrugs. "Told him he had the wrong guy. I don't know anyone by that name or fitting that description."

The relief that floods through me is so sweet it almost hurts, but right on the heels of that is the knowledge that I now owe John Rivers something, and the sweetness curdles in my mouth.

"Of course, he didn't really believe me," John goes on, shoving his hands in his pockets and rocking back on his heels. The fucker is *loving* this.

"He gave me his number, told me to call him if anything jogged my memory."

Looking down at me, he grins. "And you

know, running into you today *has* jogged
—"

"What do you want?"

A little of the light dims from his eyes. He wanted to draw this out longer, probably. Wanted to watch me wiggle on the hook. Eddie humiliated him in front of me, and now it's my turn to suffer, fine. I just want to get out of this giving him the least amount of satisfaction possible.

"Is it the rent?" I go on, reaching into my purse. There's a wad of cash stuck in there — my money, not Eddie's. Left over from dog-walking and pawning stolen shit, money I kept in the bottom of my bag and had planned on keeping forever because I wanted it to remind me of what I'd left behind, because I'd wanted to be the kind of woman who could just have two hundred dollars in a purse and never think about it, never even need to spend it.

I take it out now, and shove it into John's hand. "There. It's actually more than I would've owed for my *two weeks' notice,* so we're good."

John stares at the wrinkled bills, blinking, and then looks back at me. I don't know what he'd wanted or expected out of all this.

Maybe he didn't even know.

But the money wasn't quite it, and I can

feel him struggling to gain control of the situation again even as he stuffs the cash in his pocket. "Thanks," he finally says, and then another smile.

"And what do you know, just like that, my memory has gone blank again." He taps the side of his head with one finger. "Funny thing, memory. Comes and goes, I guess."

He probably practiced that fucking line in front of a mirror, and normally, I'd call him out, but now I just get in the car, my hands shaking as I slide the key into the ignition.

When I look in the rearview mirror, I see John walking away toward his own car, and I wait until he's out of sight to lower my head to the steering wheel, taking deep breaths through my nose.

John never knew about Phoenix. Or Helen. All that shit was years before I met him at the group home, so when things had gotten bad, when I'd had nowhere else to go, John had seemed safe.

Or safe enough.

But I should've remembered that no place was ever safe, no *person* was ever safe.

Except Eddie, I remind myself. *Eddie is safe. Thornfield Estates is safe.* You're *safe now.*

But I check my rearview mirror the whole drive home.

13

"Girl, if I eat another cheese straw, I am going to *die.*"

Emily takes another cheese straw as she passes me the plate, so I'm not sure her death is all that imminent, but I give her a sympathetic smile. "Same," I say before tacking on a "girl," about a beat too late.

Luckily, Emily doesn't seem to notice. We're sitting on the floor in her living room: me, her, Campbell, Anna-Grace, and Landry. I still don't know their last names or even what streets they live on, but both Anna-Grace and Landry look a lot like the women I already know here in Thornfield Estates. Pretty, thin, good teeth, good jewelry, and a casual way of wearing clothes that I will never be able to mimic. The only thing that sets them apart is that they are both pregnant, Landry slightly further along, her belly rounded underneath her light blue top, Anna-Grace looking like she maybe just ate an extra piece of pizza at lunch. Earlier, I'd heard her tell Emily that they'd already decided to call the baby "Hilliard," whether it was a girl or a boy, so I shoot her bump a sympathetic glance as I sit on the floor.

At the last meeting, my first one, I'd worn a Lilly Pulitzer dress and ended up having to perch awkwardly on the couch while the rest of them sprawled gracefully on the hardwood in leggings and drapey tops, their feet bare. I'd expected something a little more formal and fancy, hence the dress, but once again, I'd somehow gotten it wrong.

Today, however, I am dressed nearly identically to Emily. Both of us are in neutral shades, Emily a sort of sand color, me in an eggshell cream that I know makes me look sallow, but Anna-Grace and Landry aren't looking at me like I'm a gate-crasher this time, so I guess that's an improvement.

Or maybe I somehow proved my worth by buying all those solar lights and not being so gauche as to turn in a receipt.

In any case, I'm on the floor, too, now, sitting next to Emily on one side of the giant upholstered ottoman she uses as a coffee table. There's a big wooden tray on it today holding a bucket of ice where our white wine currently sweats, and I think all of it

— the ottoman, the tray, the wine bucket, the painted glasses we're all drinking out of — came from Southern Manors.

I almost ask, but the last thing I want to do is raise the specter of Bea here and now. No one had said anything at that first meeting, thank god, and I wasn't about to give them an opportunity to do a little compare and contrast where the two of us were involved.

"So," Campbell says, pulling out the monogrammed binder she'd brought last week. "Sweet Jane here got us the new solar lights like a rock star, thank you, *Jaaaaaane.*"

I raise my wineglass, smiling at all of them. "No problem!" No problem at all except my ex-roommate threatening me in a Home Depot parking lot, and over a thousand dollars racked up on Eddie's credit card for something as stupid as *lights.*

"And," Campbell goes on, sliding her finger down the page, "Anna-Grace said her father-in-law's landscaping company can donate sod for the front entrance."

She presses a hand over her heart, tilting her head down with an exaggerated sad face. "You are an actual angel."

Anna-Grace made a fucking phone call and got some free shit, which doesn't really

149

seem to qualify her for angel status, but what do I know?

I take another cheese straw off the plate. I'm just jumpy because of everything with John, which is making me bitchier than usual. I'm supposed to be proving to these women that I'm one of them, not thinking of them as the competition, and I need to remember that.

Campbell turns back to her binder, sitting back on her heels. "Okay, so that ticks off most of our summer goals. We should probably go ahead and start looking at fall."

"Girl, if you say the word *mums,* I am leaving," Landry says, rolling her eyes, and they all laugh.

I laugh, too, but once again, I'm about a beat too late again. As far as I can tell, they're speaking some foreign language.

"No, no mums, don't be *basic,* Landry," Campbell assures her with a smile. Then she clasps her hands underneath her chin, her rings sparkling. "I was thinking we could do something fun with football," she says. "You know, half the front flower bed in red and white, half in orange and blue."

The other ladies all *ooh* at that, and I look around, smiling, but once again, having no clue what's actually going on here.

Landry must notice my face because she

grins a little, leaning forward. "The Iron Bowl," she says, like that explains anything, and I raise my eyebrows, still smiling, still lost as fuck.

"Are you a Bammer or a Barner?" Anna-Grace says as she pulls the bottle of wine out of the bucket. It's nearly empty, though, so with a tutting sound, Emily gets up and heads to the kitchen.

"Jane isn't from the South," Campbell says as she ticks something off of her list. Then she glances up at me. "Auburn and Alabama," she explains. "Big colleges here, big football rivalry. Most everybody declares for one or the other since birth."

"Landry and I both graduated from Alabama," Anna-Grace says. "So, 'Roll Tide' and all that."

"And I'm an Auburn girl," Emily adds, coming in from the kitchen, open bottle of wine in hand. "So, War Eagle!"

I accept her offer of more wine, my head spinning, wondering how *college football* is now a thing I need to care about.

"Where did you go to school, Jane?" Anna-Grace asks.

She's not quite as pretty as Campbell and Emily, her features a little too sharp, her hair a little too blond for her fair skin. As she crosses her arms, bangles jingle on her wrist, and I have to fight down the urge to want one. Not just one I can buy, but one of *hers.*

I think about lying to them. Making up some obscure college they've never heard of. But I've already got too many lies going at this point, and there's something about the way Anna-Grace is looking at me that makes me think she'd go home and Google, or invent a friend who went there, too. Something to throw me off.

So I tell . . . okay, not the *truth,* but something that at least feels closer to it. "I did community college, then online courses. I was working a lot, so that fit my schedule the best."

"Yeah, Campbell and Emily were telling me you were their dog-walker?"

She says it like a question, but it's not.

I smile. "Yup, sure was."

"And that's how you met Eddie?"

"Mmm-hmm." I take another cheese straw even though I don't want it. The crumbs leave greasy little dark spots on my new beige leggings, and whoever made them used too much cayenne. It stings my nose, making my eyes almost water.

"God, if I'd known you could meet hot, rich widowers walking dogs, I wouldn't have bothered with those stupid dating apps,"

Landry offers, and now I remember that her name was familiar because Emily and Campbell were gossiping about her doctor husband having an affair with a drug rep a few months ago.

"Guess I'm just lucky," I say, making myself smile. I can't quite manage the faux-humble thing I did with the others, though. Maybe because of how she's looking at me, maybe just because I'm tired of doing that shit. I'm here, aren't I? Isn't that enough?

"So where were you before Birmingham?" Landry asks as she sits up a little, fluffing the couch cushion she's propped up against.

I'd been expecting this, and had already decided that vague was the way to go here. "Oh, gosh, lots of places," I say, shrugging. "My family moved around a lot."

It was actually me who did the moving, sliding into different families. A cousin here. Another cousin there. Eventually foster homes. Then the last home, in Phoenix.

The memory makes the wine go sour in my mouth, my stomach suddenly roiling, and I sit my glass back on the tray, almost catching the lip and dumping pinot grigio everywhere.

"Obviously, I never lived in the South before now," I say, grinning again and trying to cover the awkwardness of the moment. "Or I'd know my Roll Tide from my War Eagle."

That makes them laugh, like I'd hoped, and I'm hoping we can move back into talking about flowers or flags or whatever other dumb shit they want. I'll spend another grand on fucking light-up lawn ornaments if we can stop talking about me.

"But I sure hope you're planning on staying in the South," Landry says, all saccharine now. "Now that you and Eddie are . . ."

She trails off, waving one hand.

There's nothing pointed about it, and her gaze is nowhere near as searching as Anna-Grace's was, but I feel a question hanging in the air.

Campbell finishes her train of thought. "I do not know why he doesn't just go ahead and wife you up, girl."

"Seriously," Emily says, nodding and pouring herself more wine. "If he's going to have you living with him, the least he can do is put a ring on it."

"Caleb wanted us to live together before we got married," Anna-Grace says, shaking her head so that her ponytail brushes her back. "And I was like, 'I don't think so!' If a man wants a woman to basically *be* a wife, he needs to *make* her a wife."

The others all hum in agreement, and I look around, at these ladies drinking in the middle of the afternoon on a random Thursday, all of whom seem to have decided that "getting married" is a woman's chief accomplishment.

And I finally get it.

I can join all the committees, wear all the right clothes, learn about fucking football, say all the right things, and none of it will matter.

I'm never going to be one of them until Eddie proposes.

14

For the next week, I try so hard not to think about Emily or Campbell or any of that, try not to want more than I have. What I have is, after all, like winning the fucking lottery, and I've learned the hard way that wanting more is what fucks you in the end.

But it sits there under my skin, itching — the way they'd looked at me, the questions, the insults disguised as jokes.

And it's not just the Thornfield ladies. It's John, it's whoever was calling him and asking questions. I feel like he got what he wanted that day in the Home Depot parking lot — to lord something over me, to watch my fear and anxiety creep in, *plus* two hundred bucks out of the deal. Surely that was enough for him. And as weird as it sounds, I trust John.

Okay, *trust* is not the right word.

I *know* him, I guess. People like him. All of us who stayed permanent foster kids, who met at group homes or shelters. John might follow me and maybe even call one of these days, making insinuations, but he's not going to turn me over to the cops.

Or at least, I don't think he will.

Being Mrs. Rochester feels like another brick in the wall between me and threats like that, like maybe John wouldn't even attempt it if he thought it would involve Eddie.

So that's the plan. The new plan.

It's not enough to live with Eddie. Being the girlfriend is not the way in. I have to be the *wife.*

Which means I have to be the fiancée first.

So, for the next few days, I study Eddie. I don't know what the signs are that a man is thinking of proposing to you — I've actually never known anyone who got engaged. People I've met are either firmly single or already married, and not for the first time in my life, I wish I had an actual friend. Someone to talk to, just one person who knew the whole truth about everything.

But I've only got me.

About a week after the committee meeting, Eddie comes home from work a little early and asks if I want to take Adele to the Cahaba River Walk.

It's a park not too far from us, and one of the places he brought me when we first started dating. I like the quiet of it, the meandering trail along the water, the shade of the trees, and as soon as he suggests it, my spirits lift.

It's a place he knows I like. It's special to us because we've been there before.

And he never comes home early.

The idea that maybe I won't have to do anything at all to get him to propose is dizzying, and when we get out of the car, I'm practically bouncing on the balls of my feet.

Laughing, Eddie takes my hand as Adele runs ahead of us, barking at squirrels. "You seem happy," he says, and I lean over to kiss his cheek.

"I am," I reply.

And I really am. Right until Eddie settles us both on a bench by the river and pulls out his phone.

"Sorry," he says as Adele flops at our feet, panting. "I just have a few emails to send, and I need to get them out before the end of the day."

So much for our nice afternoon in the park. I sit there, sweating and fuming, while he types and a couple of guys kayak on the river.

There are also people walking, and as two

women move past us in their workout shorts and fitted tops, I see their eyes slide to Eddie, see one of them, a brunette with the same shiny hair and tiny waist as Bea, look over to me like she's thinking, *Huh. Wonder what that's about.*

My face is warm from more than the heat now, and I sit there, wondering, too. What the fuck *is* this about?

Eddie is still on his phone, and I decide to go for subtle.

"I need a manicure," I say on a sigh, wiggling my fingers in front of my face. "When I was at Emily's the other day, all I could see were everybody's perfect nails. Well, perfect nails and a metric fuckton of jewelry. I'd be nervous wearing more than one ring."

Okay, so that last little bit was maybe not as subtle as I *could* have been, but desperate times and all.

Eddie snorts at that, but doesn't look up. "Bea always thought it was tacky how much jewelry they all wore. Especially when they're mostly just staying home all day."

"Okay, well, I don't have to be dripping in diamonds, but I should probably take better care of my nails."

Still looking at his phone, Eddie catches my hand, absently bringing my fingers to his lips.

I want him to say something about not minding my nails like that or not noticing, but instead he says, "The place in the village is supposed to be good."

Nodding, I take my hand back, twisting my fingers in the hem of my shirt. "Is that where Bea went?" I ask, and finally, I have his attention.

He looks up from the screen, blinking, before saying, "As far as I know, yeah. All the girls in the neighborhood go there."

"Women," I say, and when he screws up his face, I sit up a little taller. "Just . . . they're all in their thirties at least. They're not girls."

His face clears, and he gives me a smile I haven't seen before.

It's not the sexy grin, or that delighted quirk of lips I get when I've said something that charms him. It's . . . indulgent.

Slightly paternalistic.

It irritates me.

"Right, sorry," he says, turning back to his phone. *Women.*

"Look, I get that you're older than me, and have, like, seen more of the world or whatever, but you don't have to patronize me." The words are out before I can stop them, before I can remember to be the Jane he wants, not the Jane I actually am.

160

Then again, I'm remembering, he sometimes likes the Jane I actually am.

He lowers his phone and gives his full attention to me. "I'm being a dick, aren't I?"

"Little bit, yeah."

There's his real smile now, and he takes my hand again, squeezing it. "I'm sorry," he says. "I'm just swamped. But I wanted to spend time with you today, and to get you out of the house for a little bit. You've seemed out of sorts the past week or so."

Ever since John.

I sit there, my mind working, wondering what I can say, how much I can share. There's an opening here, an opportunity, one of those chances to mix a little lie in with some actual truth, and it occurs to me that it might get me what I want a lot faster than dropping hints about fingers and rings.

"I guess I'm just wondering where all this is going," I say, and he frowns, that crease deepening between his eyebrows. On the river, one of the kayakers calls to the other, and another pair of women jog by, glancing down at me and Eddie.

"It's not that I don't love living with you," I go on. "I do. I really do. But when you've been a charity case for most of your life, you start to really resent that feeling."

Eddie puts his phone down now and sits

up straighter, his hands clasped between his knees. "What does that mean?"

I keep my own eyes trained on the river in front of me, on the families pushing strollers around the trail. The one couple with their arms around each other's waists.

"You saw where I used to live. You know what my life was like before I met you. I don't . . . I don't belong here."

He snorts at that. "Okay, again, I don't know what that's supposed to mean."

Now I turn toward him, pushing my sunglasses up on my head. "It means that I'm not Emily or Campbell or —"

"I don't want you to be any of them," he says, taking my hand. "I love you because you're not them. Because you're not . . ." He trails off, and I see his throat move as he swallows.

He wants to say *because you're not Bea.* I know it, and he knows I know if the way he suddenly looks away is any indication. But for the first time, I'm left wondering what *that* means. He had obviously adored her, so why is being different from her such a bonus to him?

"I'm sorry." Eddie squeezes my fingers. "I'm sorry if I haven't made it clear how much I want you here. How much I need you and how, yes, you do belong here."

Turning to look at me, he ducks his head so that our foreheads nearly touch, his lips almost brushing mine. "I am fucking in love with you, Jane," he murmurs, the words sending an electric spark down my spine, his breath warm on my face. "That's all that matters. None of this shit with the neighborhood, with Emily, any of that. That's all just noise. This." He lifts our joined hands between us, squeezing again. "This is real. This is what matters."

Eddie kisses my knuckles, and I wait, practically holding my breath because if ever there were a moment to propose, it's now, here in the park at sunset, him looking at me like that, me not even having to fake the wide-eyed swoony thing. How did I not realize sooner that I wanted this?

But then he drops our hands and turns away, sighing. "I'll try not to be gone so much, though, okay? I'll let Caitlyn handle more things at Southern Manors. Running two businesses is too much, but I can't really give up either of them right now. You understand that, right?"

I'm still sitting there feeling the imprint of his lips on my fingers, wondering how this moment got away from me, wondering why we're back to talking about his work and not getting engaged, so all I can do is nod and manage a feeble, "Yeah."

Clearing my throat, I shake my head a little. Jesus, Jane, get it together.

I scoot closer, threading my arm through his elbow and resting my head on his shoulder. Disappointment sits like a rock in my stomach, heavy and hard. And not just because I feel even further away from cementing my place as Mrs. Rochester.

Because I genuinely want him to want me.

Because I want Eddie.

15

We have the next meeting for the Neighborhood Beautification Committee at Eddie's house.

My house. Sometimes I think of it like that. But thinking it and actually feeling it are two different things, and as I carry our empty wineglasses to the sink once the meeting is over, I can't shake the feeling that I'm right back where I started: a servant, rather than the lady of the house.

The meeting was mostly pointless, and I think the ladies only agreed to it for the chance to get back inside this place. The whole time we'd been sitting in the living room, talking about Pinterest boards and "Festive Fall Fun Décor," I'd felt their eyes cataloguing what was gone, what was new.

Campbell and Emily linger after the other women have gone home, saying it's to help me pick up, but I know it's to do some more digging.

"This place looks great," Campbell says, putting our wine bottle in the recycling. "I mean, it always did, but it just feels brighter now, doesn't it, Em?"

Emily hums, nodding as she sips the last of the wine from her glass. "Totally."

The house can't look any different from how it did the last time they were in here. There might be a few pictures missing, but it's not like I've gone on a redecorating spree.

I can't tell if they're being nice or fishing, so I decide to do a little fishing myself.

"Everything was so gorgeous that I didn't really want to change anything. Bea really had excellent taste." A self-conscious little laugh for effect. "I mean, I guess that was her whole career, having excellent taste."

Emily and Campbell share a glance I pretend not to see.

"She did know how to put things together," Campbell agrees at last, coming to stand next to me at the kitchen counter, propping her elbows on the granite. "But you know what? I always thought Blanche's place was even cuter. No offense, Jane," she hurries to say, and I wave it off even as I think back to the Ingrahams'. There was some cute stuff there, for sure, but maybe Tripp had made everything so grubby I

166

hadn't been able to see it.

"God, remember how *pissed* Blanche was when Bea's living room got the big *Birmingham Magazine* spread at Christmas?" Campbell says, and I see Emily look over at me for just a second.

"Blanche was funny about Christmas," she replies delicately, and Campbell pulls a face.

"Blanche was funny about Bea."

Turning to me, Campbell tucks her hair behind one ear. "Sorry. We're just here in your kitchen rehashing old gossip, aren't we?"

"I don't mind," I say, and I really don't. I feel like I keep getting these glimpses of Bea and Blanche that don't line up with what I thought I knew, and I want more of them. Maybe if I can paint a full picture of Bea for myself, I won't feel like she's still here.

Like she could just appear around any corner.

Sometimes it feels like she has. Just last week a delivery truck showed up with fresh flowers for the house. A standing order from Bea, one that Eddie had never canceled.

She's been gone for nearly a year, but the arrangement of lilies and magnolias on the front table of my house were hers, and every time I walk past them, it's like I've just missed seeing her, that she's just stepped out for a second.

But now both Emily and Campbell shake their heads. "No, we've imposed enough on you today." Emily comes around the counter, kissing my cheek. "Thank you so much for hosting!"

"Happy to do it anytime," I reply, and Campbell smiles, patting my arm.

"You are so sweet. Be sure to tell Eddie how much we appreciate him letting us meet here today!"

Aaaand there it is. They don't see this as my house, either.

My smile is tight when I walk them to the door. I didn't want to have to be this unsubtle about it, but I'm not sure I have a choice anymore. I can feel all this starting to slip away, slowly, sure, but still. If we're not engaged soon, any of the ground I've won with the neighborhood women will be lost.

So when Eddie comes in, nearly an hour later, I'm on the couch, iPad in hand.

As I'd known he would, he leans over the side of the couch to kiss my temple. "There's my girl," he murmurs, and I can actually feel when he looks at the screen.

Behind me, his body goes tense.

"UCLA?"

I shrug, making no effort to hide the iPad or look sheepish. If I want this to work, he has to think I'm very serious about it.

"I told you I was thinking about grad school."

He stands up straight, his hands still on the armrest of the couch, knuckles white. "In California?"

I turn, putting my feet down on the floor, and look up at him. "Eddie, I love you, and I love staying here. Love being with you. But I have to look out for myself. You understand that."

He steps back, his arms folded over his chest. "I get that, but I thought . . . I thought I made it clear that I want you here. That you belong here. With me."

Standing up, I face him, tilting my chin up. "I've been depending on myself for almost my entire life. I have had people say they love me and make promises they couldn't keep in the end."

Another step closer. I lay my hand on his wrist. "*I'm* the only person I can trust, Eddie. I learned that the hard way. You can't blame me for making plans. It's what I do."

A muscle works in his jaw, and I wait, almost holding my breath.

He turns away, stalking toward the bedroom, and everything in me sinks.

I've fucked it up. I pushed too hard too fast, and now he's going to throw me out. For fuck's sake, I can't even *go* to grad school, I never finished college, what am I —

Eddie comes back into the room, and I see the little velvet box in his hand.

I'm almost dizzy from the emotional whiplash of it all, but suddenly he's in front of me, he's dropping down on one knee, the box is opening . . .

"Marry me," he says, his voice gruff.

My eyes are fixed on the emerald ring sparkling in front of me, a huge green stone surrounded by a halo of diamonds.

"I should've asked you weeks ago," he goes on. "I've been wanting to."

"Obviously," I say, my voice shaky, and that makes him laugh a little, too, his features relaxing as he reaches out and takes my hand.

"Please, Jane. Be my wife."

He slips the ring on my left hand, the metal silky and smooth, burnished with age, and even though it's a little snug, it's perfect.

I stare at it there on my hand. This gorgeous piece of jewelry on my plain, small fingers, my nails still a little ragged, pale pink polish chipped, and it's like there's no breath in my lungs, like my heart is trying to leap out of my chest. I want to tell myself it's satisfaction, victory, *fuck yeah, I won,* but it's more.

It's so much more. And that scares me, but for the first time, I feel like I'm allowed to want this much.

That I get to have this.

"Oh, shit," I whisper, and Eddie grins at me, still there on one knee.

"Is that a yes?"

I look at him, at his handsome face, and his blue eyes, kneeling on that gorgeous hardwood floor, and I nod.

"Yes," I say, and he surges up from the floor, gathers me up in his arms, and kisses me hard. It sparks something inside me, that kiss, and soon I'm tugging him down onto the couch, pulling at his clothes, arching up against him.

Afterward, we lay there in a slightly sweaty heap, our clothes half-off, half-on, and I play with his hair, damp at the nape of his neck.

"I should've asked you somewhere nicer," he mumbles against my collarbone. "Taken you out to dinner."

"But then we couldn't have done this," I remind him, nudging him with my thigh. "Or we could have, but I feel like the restaurant would've asked us to please leave and never come back."

He laughs lightly, then lifts his head to stare down at me.

"You're sure about this?" he asks. "About marrying me, even though I'm a disaster?"

I lift myself up to brush a kiss over his lips. "I'm marrying you *because* you're a disaster," I reply, which makes him laugh again, and as he settles back against me, I catch a glimpse of my ring over his shoulder.

Mrs. Rochester.

16

I'm engaged.

Motherfucking *engaged.*

I can't stop looking at the ring, the way it sparkles in the sunlight, the heavy, cool weight of it on my finger.

But weirdly, it's more than just the ring, gorgeous as it is.

It's knowing that Eddie bought it before I even knew I wanted him to propose.

He wanted this. He *chose* me.

No one has ever chosen me before. I've spent my life being passed around and looked over, and now this.

I've passed it dozens of times before, the village bridal shop that's a world away from the big dress emporiums in strip malls and shopping centers. I've looked in its plate glass window at the delicate bits of lace and silk on display, and even though I've never been a girly-girl, I'd always felt a little . . . wistful, maybe.

And even now, as I open the door, the little bell overhead jingling, something flutters in my chest.

There's no overhead lighting, only strategically placed lamps, huge windows, and a skylight. And the dresses aren't just hanging up on crowded racks, row after row of heavy skirts and beaded bodices, all so jumbled up you can barely tell what's what.

Instead, some dresses are displayed on old-fashioned wire dress dummies, and others are draped over bits of antique furniture, like the bride just slipped out of her dress and tossed it casually over the nearest armoire.

It's the kind of place where they're not scared of anyone getting something on the dresses or messing them up somehow — no one who shops here would be that gauche. So there's no need for the miles of plastic that protect dresses from all the grubby hands at those cheaper bridal places.

The woman who approaches me has soft blond hair arranged in an elegant chignon, and she's wearing an outfit that reminds me of the things I've seen Bea wear in pictures. It's elegant but feminine at the same time, a sleek black sheath dress and pearls paired with houndstooth pumps that have a tiny hot pink bow on the back.

Her name is Huntley, because of course it is.

I see the way she clocks my ring, and while I'm sure Huntley here would never be so crass as to actually start adding up numbers in her head, her smile definitely warms a little.

I know plenty of girls dream about their wedding day, but I never had, not really. Maybe it had just seemed like something so far out of the realm of possibility for me, or maybe I just had bigger things to worry about.

Turns out, I fucking *love* this shit.

We move around the store, talking about shades of white and ivory, the difference between eggshell and cream, whether I'd like my hair up or down, what kind of veil options that might entail.

When Huntley brings out a book full of fabric samples for me to look at, I almost swoon.

By the time I leave the shop, my head is swimming, but I'm pleasantly high, and not just on the two glasses of champagne I sipped while Huntley and I talked.

I'm marrying Eddie Rochester.

I'm going to be his wife, and live in that gorgeous house, and afternoons like this, afternoons not spent walking dogs or waiting tables or driving for Uber or making someone else coffee, aren't just a temporary reprieve — they're my future.

"Jane?"

Emily is standing there, paper cup of coffee in hand, her face hidden behind those huge sunglasses.

She glances up toward the striped awning of Irene's, and her mouth drops open. "*Girl.* Tell me you were in there for a reason."

My smile is not even a little bit faked. "Turns out he *did* put a ring on it."

She squeals at that, rushing forward to throw her arms around me, pulling me into a hug that smells like Santal 33.

I smell like it, too, since I stole a bottle from her bathroom just two months ago.

"Let me see, let me see," she says when we pull apart, flapping her hands toward mine.

Another rush of what feels suspiciously like joy, but is probably just the adrenaline rush of winning.

I haven't perfected this move yet, the ring display, and I fight the urge to mimic girls I've seen on TV, all arched wrist like I'm waiting for her not just to ogle the ring, but to kiss it.

As a result, I feel like I just sort of hold my hand out for inspection, awkward and suddenly very aware of how ridiculous that sparkly emerald looks on my stumpy fingers with their raggedy manicure.

But Emily just sighs. "It's gorgeous. And *so* you!"

I raise my hand again, studying the ring myself. "I still can't get used to it," I say. "I mean, all of it has been kind of a whirlwind, but the ring makes it feel real, you know?"

I give her a smile.

"I remember feeling like that," she offers. "The ring definitely cements it."

Raising her eyebrows, she asks, "Did you pick that one out?"

I shake my head, looking back at the emerald surrounded by its halo of diamonds. "No, Eddie did. It's bigger than anything I would've chosen, but I love emeralds, so I can't complain."

She nods. "He has the best taste in jewelry. I always thought —"

Her words break off, and she presses her lips together, and I know there's a comment about Bea there, caught in her throat. I don't want Bea's memory to ruin this moment, so I rush in.

"I was just in there peeking around, we're not sure when the wedding is going to be yet," I say lightly, and her shoulders loosen a little.

"Are y'all doing something big?" she asks. "Lots of family?"

Until that moment, it hadn't really hit me what a wedding with Eddie would look like. I'd been so caught up in the idea of marrying him, of being Mrs. Rochester, that I'd basically skipped the wedding part of things.

But now it's all I can see, a giant church, Eddie's side of the church full, his family from Maine all turning up, mine completely empty except for John Rivers sitting there, eating a bowl of cereal.

The image is so grotesque and awful that I literally shake my head to will it away, which apparently looks like an answer to Emily.

"Small, then!" she says, smiling. "I love it. Classy, elegant. Appropriate."

Eyes on my hand again, and this time, I do rearrange my bags so that they're covering the ring, and I give her my best bland smile, the one I actually learned from her and Campbell and Caroline McLaren. "Exactly," I say, all sugar, then I gesture back up the road. "Anyway, I have more errands to run, so —"

"Oh, sure," Emily says, waving a hand. Her own engagement ring is a princess-cut diamond, at least three carats, and it sparkles in the sunlight. "And my lips are sealed!"

"They don't have to be," I reply with a little shrug. "It's not a secret."

The truth is, I want her to spread this news like wildfire, I want everyone in Thornfield Estates to be talking about it by dinner.

We make vague plans to get coffee one of these days, and then go our separate ways, Emily already texting on her phone. By the next Neighborhood Beautification Committee meeting, everyone will know, and I'll be the center of attention.

On the way home, I decide to stop at the Whole Foods and pick up some groceries. I haven't cooked a single meal for Eddie since we've met, and that might be nice. It's a pretty late spring day, and we could go full suburban basics and grill out.

The idea makes me smile as I turn into the parking lot.

The store is soothing, all wide aisles and calming Muzak, a world away from the Piggly Wiggly where I used to shop.

I push the cart down the aisle, wondering if Eddie would notice if I picked up some junk food. I love the fancy shit as much as the next girl, but truth be told, I'm getting a little sick of it. The other day, I found myself longing for macaroni and cheese — not the Annie's Organics kind, not even the frozen kind that's halfway decent, but the blue cardboard box kind that costs a dollar.

Snorting, I turn down another aisle. Who am I kidding? This is a nice grocery store, not the Pig. So instead, I stare at the fifty varieties of hummus and olive tapenades, wondering if I should also make a gas station run on my way home. Maybe they'd have macaroni and cheese there?

"Fancy meeting you here."

I recognize the voice without turning around.

Tripp Ingraham stands behind me in a polo shirt and khaki shorts, a basket slung over his forearm.

A quick peek inside reveals cans of craft beer and a bunch of frozen but ostensibly healthy meals.

Tripp looks a little better than he did the last time I saw him. He's still bloated, the pink polo stretching over a disturbingly round and smooth belly, but his face isn't as puffy, and his eyes aren't red. He's even brushed his hair.

Maybe he's managed to make it all the way to noon without a drink.

Smiling tightly, I give a little wave. "Hi, Mr. Ing— Tripp."

One corner of his mouth lifts, half attempted smile, half smirk. "That's right, you don't work for me anymore," he says, then adds, "and I hear congratulations are in order."

Jesus, Emily worked even faster than I thought.

"Thank you," I say. "We're very happy. Anyway, it was nice to see you —"

I move to scoot past him, but he's still standing there in the middle of the aisle, and even though it would be deeply satisfying to clip Tripp Ingraham with my cart, I stop, raising my eyebrows at him.

"So, when exactly did all this happen?" he asks, waving his free hand. "You and Eddie? Because I gotta say, I never saw that one coming."

"Neither did we," I say, still smiling, remembering that I need to be the girl Tripp thinks I am, the innocent barely-out-of-college dog-walker who made good. I wonder when I'll feel like I can drop that act, when it will feel normal to just . . . be me.

"You know, I never got the whole Eddie 'thing.' "

He actually raises his hands to make air quotes, the basket dangling heavily from the crook of his elbow.

I don't bother asking him what he means

because for one, he clearly wants me to ask him that, and for another, I just want to leave, but a little thing like lack of interest has clearly never stopped Tripp Ingraham where a woman is concerned.

"I mean, he's good-looking, I guess, and he's charming in that used-car-salesman way, but Jesus, from the way the women in this neighborhood acted, you would've thought the dude had a twelve-inch cock."

Okay, maybe I misjudged how not-drunk Tripp actually is.

But this is good — now he's given me every reason to push my cart past him, head held high, like I'm mortally offended and embarrassed instead of just kind of irritated.

He steps aside right before my cart actually hits him, and as I reach the end of the aisle, he calls after me, "Just hope you don't like boats."

When I glance back at him, his expression is curdled and nasty. "Women have bad luck around Eddie Rochester and boats," he adds, before turning and trudging away.

I get all the way back to the produce before I abandon my semi-full cart and head for the doors.

The drive home isn't long enough for me to shake the unease, the sudden fear that Tripp Ingraham — fucking *Tripp Ingraham,* of all people — has instilled in me, and again, I see Bea pale and greenish under the water. My stomach lurches as I pull into the driveway.

"Stop it, stop it, stop it," I mutter, my hands over my face. Eddie's wife drowned in an accident with her best friend. Eddie wasn't even there, and the women were drunk and possibly had some unresolved drama. Shit happens.

I try to think about the bridal store again, the way Huntley smiled at me and treated me like I had just joined an exclusive club, how good that had felt. Emily's hug and bright smile as she'd looked at the ring.

That's what matters now.

When I walk in the house, Eddie is already home, changed into shorts and another one of his button-down shirts. Now that I've seen inside his closet, I know he has dozens of them in a variety of colors. Men can do that — find one thing that looks good, then wear it for the rest of their lives, pretty much.

"There's my girl," he says brightly as I walk in. I smile as I greet him, but it's clear I'm upset because he immediately frowns.

"Everything okay?"

I step easily into his arms, sighing as they come around me, my head fitting just there underneath his chin.

"Long day of wedding dress shopping," I say, and he chuckles at that, his hands making soothing strokes up and down my back.

"Sounds exhausting," he says. "Beer?"

I nod even though I already have a slight headache from those two glasses of champagne earlier, plus it's barely even three in the afternoon.

Pressing a kiss to my forehead, Eddie lets me go and walks to the fridge while I set my purse down and go into the kitchen, grabbing a couple of limes from the silver bowl on the counter.

"You're sure you're alright?" Eddie rubs a hand down my back, and I make myself smile at him as I chop limes into wedges for our beers.

"Yeah, fine," I say, then shake my head, using the back of my hand to push back a lock of hair from my forehead. "I just ran into Tripp Ingraham today, and he was weird."

Eddie stills, looking down at me. "Weird how?"

I'm not actually sure how much of this I want to get into with him. My nerves are still jangled, and I'm afraid Eddie will get the wrong idea if I tell him the truth. That he might think what Tripp said about Eddie and boats got to me, scared me.

I tell myself that it didn't.

So, I smile up at Eddie, letting the knife fall to the counter. "Oh, you know. The kind of thing you'd expect from a guy like him."

I twine my arms around Eddie's neck, pressing my body close to his. "He thinks I'm marrying you for your money."

Some of the wariness leaves Eddie's face, and he puts both arms around my waist, hands resting on my hips. "Hope you told him that you were actually in it for the sex."

"Obviously," I say, and when he lowers his head to kiss me, I nip at his lower lip, Tripp Ingraham and his bullshit forgotten.

17

Later, we sit outside in the big wooden Adirondack chairs in the yard, a fire crackling away in the big stone ring in front of us. Nearby, the grill smokes, and the scent of cooking meat reminds me of those summer nights in Phoenix, when the air was so still and so dry it felt like a loose spark could send everything up in flames.

The grill turned over, the burning coals spread over the gravel yard, Jane, the real Jane, crying, Mr. Brock's red face, a sweating beer can in one hand, a pair of tongs in the other.

HIS KISS THE COOK apron with a giant frog on it, its lips red and obscene in a pucker, me sprawled in the rocks, my hand burning, my face stinging, thinking how stupid that apron was, how stupid it was that a man like him had this much power over all of us.

I haven't thought about that for such a long time. I've pushed it all away, but now here it is, this ugly memory, in this perfect place.

Looking down, I study my engagement ring again, turning my hand this way and that, catching the light of the flames.

That's over. That can't touch you. No matter what John says.

Next to me, Eddie sighs, his long legs stretched out in front of him.

He really does look good tonight. I think of how slightly ragged he was when I first met him, how those edges have smoothed a little in the past few months, and I feel a little surge of satisfaction. *I did that,* I think. *I've made him happy. He's like this because of me.*

And soon, I'm going to be his wife.

I think about the wedding dresses I saw today, the veil there in the window I'd itched to put on my head.

"I think we should elope."

I don't know I'm going to say the words until they're out, but then they are, and I realize I don't want to take them back.

Eddie pauses, his beer lifted to his mouth. Then he takes a sip, swallows, and lowers his arm before looking over at me and saying, "We don't have to do anything you don't want to do."

"It's just . . . I don't have a big family," I say. "And I hardly know anyone in Birmingham, or at least no one I'd want at my wedding."

Eddie smirks slightly at that, raising his eyebrows.

"I don't want that John asshole at my wedding, either."

Reaching over, he takes my hand, his thumb making circles on the heel of my hand.

"Janie, say the word, and we'll get married at the courthouse tomorrow. Or we'll go to the lake. Hell, we can go up to Tennessee if you want, rent one of those cheesy mountain chalets. I think they even have drive-through wedding chapels in Gatlinburg."

I smile, but don't say anything, ignoring the weird sinking in my stomach at the idea of marrying a man like Eddie, but still having the kind of wedding girls like me always get. Cheap, fast, tacky. When I suggested eloping, I was imagining saying our vows on a white-sand beach, an intimate wedding night in a big bed with gauzy mosquito netting. I wasn't imagining pulling up to a window like we were grabbing french fries and heading to a motel advertising free parking on a neon sign.

Still, what I know for certain is that I can't get married here. I can't walk down an aisle at a big church in a big dress and see the Campbells and the Carolines, Bea's friends, comparing me to her.

I head inside, picking up our empty beers as I go. When I slide the patio door open, there's a sound from somewhere above me.

I freeze there in the doorway, one ear cocked toward the ceiling, waiting.

There's another thump, followed by a second, a third.

Sliding the patio door closed behind me, I glance back out at Eddie.

He's still sitting in his Adirondack chair, hands behind his head now, his chin lifted to the evening sky, and I creep a little deeper into the house.

The sounds are rhythmic now, a steady *thump thump thump* like a heartbeat.

I think about that story they made us read in middle school, the one with the man buried under the floorboards, his murderer thinking he could still hear the old man's heart, and for a horrified moment, my brain conjures up Bea.

Then the sounds stop.

I stand there, practically holding my breath, the empty beer bottle dangling from my fingers as I wait.

Three sharp raps at the front door make me nearly jolt out of my skin, one of the bottles crashing to the floor as I make a sound somewhere between a shriek and a gasp.

It's coming from the front of the house, though, not upstairs. Someone knocking at the door.

"Jane?"

I see Eddie through the glass door, still sitting outside, the words tossed casually over his shoulder, his head barely turned toward me.

I scowl at the back of that head, that perfectly tousled hair. "I'm fine," I call back. "Just someone at the door."

There's another knock just as I reach the foyer, and when I open the door, a woman is standing there.

She's wearing khakis and a blue button-down, and there's a badge snapped to her waist.

She's a cop.

My heart is beating so fast in my chest that I feel like she must be able to see it, and I lay a hand there against my collarbone, suddenly grateful I have the diamonds and emerald on my finger, to let her know I am somebody.

I have no reason to be afraid anymore, I remind myself. The woman standing on the porch doesn't see the girl I used to be, doesn't know the things I've done. There's no suspicion in her gaze, no narrowed eyes and thinned lips. She sees a woman who belongs in this house, a woman wearing Ann Taylor and real jewels, a woman whose dishwater-blond hair isn't pulled back into a scraggly ponytail, a woman wearing the kind of expensive makeup that's meant to make her look like she's not wearing any makeup at all.

That's who she sees — the future Mrs. Jane Rochester.

But my body doesn't seem to want to acknowledge that. Heart still pounds, stomach churns, knees go watery.

"Hi there." She smiles, offers her hand to shake.

"I'm Detective Laurent, and I sure am sorry for interrupting your dinner."

Her hand is warm and callused, and I shake it even as my left hand stays where it is, pressed to my chest.

"We weren't eating," I say, and then I think about Campbell and Emily, how they would handle a detective on their doorstep on a spring evening.

"Has something happened?" I ask, furrowing my brow with concern and also confusion. A police officer showing up at their houses would only be confusing, after all, hardly a cause for personal concern, because of course they hadn't done anything wrong. In Thornfield Estates, police weren't to be feared, they were to be trusted. They were always on your side, after all.

Detective Laurent frowns, deep parentheses forming on either side of her mouth. She's older than I'd first realized, and now I can see the slight sprinkling of gray in her black hair.

"Is Mr. Rochester at home?" she asks, and my mouth is dry now. It's happened. John has called someone, they know, that's why I was remembering Phoenix earlier, because I somehow sensed that it was coming for me, that this was all over, that —

"Detective Laurent."

Eddie is just behind me, and he slips an arm around my waist, his hand laying heavily on my hip. Just his touch makes me feel better, and I hate that a little bit. I've never been the type to cower behind a man, but I have to admit it's nice to have him there, as the detective's eyes drop to Eddie's Rolex, to his bare feet on the marble floor.

"Nice to see you again," he says, flashing a smile, and I blink, looking up at him.

Eddie's nervous.

His body may be loose and relaxed against mine, but I know that Eddie doesn't do this, doesn't turn on this kind of charm for no reason.

And when I lower my eyes to his throat, tan, framed by the vivid green of his shirt, I can see his pulse thumping steadily there.

Detective Laurent smiles at him, but it's tight, a perfunctory response rather than a genuine expression.

"We just had a few more questions to ask you, if you don't mind," she says. "About your wife."

■ ■ ■ ■

Part IV
Bea

■ ■ ■ ■

Bea hadn't wanted to do dinner with Blanche and Tripp tonight, but tradition is tradition, and this is theirs — every other Thursday night, the four of them meet up somewhere. Tonight, it's a new place in Homewood, fancy barbecue, overpriced drinks. They sit outside in a courtyard at a wrought-iron table, fairy lights in the trees, and Bea fights the urge to check her phone every ten minutes.

She's started to realize how little she actually has in common with Blanche these days, and lord knows, Eddie and Tripp don't have much to talk about. They exhaust football as a topic of conversation before the first drinks arrive, and then Tripp launches into some diatribe about a new family moving into the neighborhood, how they've put up a basketball hoop, how he's going to complain to the HOA.

Eddie smiles at him, but his voice has an edge to it as he says, "Or you could just let the kids play in their own driveway? Maybe the better option?"

"That's what I told him," Blanche says, rolling her eyes and reaching over to shove at Tripp's arm. She hadn't shown up half-drunk tonight, and her wineglass is still mostly full, which Bea takes as a good sign.

She also notices that Blanche looks nicer tonight than she has in a while, her makeup subtle, but pretty, her simple pink sheath dress making her complexion glow.

Another good sign.

Bea knows Blanche is unhappy, knows she's bored with Tripp and Thornfield Estates and her life, that all the committees and boards she's signed up for aren't filling the void, but it's nothing they've been able to talk about. Every time she tries to bring it up, Blanche changes the subject or, if she's had too much wine, makes some catty comment about Bea working all the time.

But tonight, she's relaxed, happy, and Bea is relieved to see it. Maybe the old Blanche is still in there after all.

They've just gotten their main courses when Blanche says, "You know, we were so inspired by the work y'all did on your house that Tripp and I were thinking about doing some renovations of our own."

That's a surprise. Bea knows that money has not exactly been abundant for the Ingrahams lately, but it's not like she can say that out loud.

Apparently, she's not the only one surprised. "We were?" Tripp asks. He's on his third bourbon now, leaning back in his chair, his food mostly untouched on his plate, his cheeks red. He's still handsome in his way, but every time they do one of these dinners, Bea can't help but think how much better Eddie looks in comparison.

Blanche waves her husband away. "I talked to you about it," she says. "You probably just forgot. Or weren't listening. Or were drunk."

There's the bite Bea has gotten used to hearing in Blanche's voice whenever she talks to Tripp.

Tripp is used to it, too, though, and he just snorts, taking another sip of his drink. "Do what you want, my love," he tells Blanche. "You always do."

Ignoring him, Blanche leans forward, focusing on Eddie. "Of course, we'd want you for the job," she says, and Eddie grins as he slices his brisket.

"I was going to say, I hope you're bringing this up because you're planning on hiring me, otherwise this is going to get very awkward."

They all laugh at that, and Bea reaches over to lay a hand on Eddie's thigh, squeezing slightly. "Your schedule is kind of full right now, honey," she reminds him, and she sees the way Blanche glances at them, at Bea's hand there on his leg.

She can't explain why she doesn't want Eddie working on Blanche's house. She wants to tell herself that it's because she knows Blanche and Tripp don't have the money, that this is going to be a waste of everyone's time, and besides, since she gave Eddie the capital to start his contracting business, she has a say in what projects he takes on.

But it's more than that. There's something going on here, something she can't quite put her finger on.

Something about the hard look in Blanche's eyes even as she smiles at Bea.

Eddie pats her hand, and goes back to his food. "I can always make time for friends," he says easily.

Blanche's smile widens. "Great!" she says. "I already have, oh god, about a hundred and five different ideas."

The rest of the dinner passes in something of a blur for Bea. She drinks a little more than she's used to, and she keeps watching Blanche, wondering what this is all about, fighting the urge to blurt out what she knows about Blanche and Tripp's money problems.

And when Blanche says, "I've always loved how open y'all's kitchen is. Maybe that's something we could do?" Bea comes so close to making a snide comment, she actually feels the words sitting heavily on the tip of her tongue.

Of course, Blanche wants what they have. Of course, their house is nicer. Of course, Blanche can't stand it that Bea has come out on top after all these years.

The evening wraps up as it so often does, with Tripp drinking too much. This time, it's bad enough that Eddie has to help him to the car.

Bea and Eddie are parked on the street while Tripp and Blanche are in the small parking lot in the back of the restaurant, so Bea goes to the car alone, the keys in her hand.

It's only when she's opening the passenger door that some urge overtakes her, and suddenly she's hurrying across the pavement, ducking around the side of the restaurant to the little lot where Blanche and Tripp's car is parked.

She sees Eddie and Blanche clearly in the streetlights, standing next to Tripp's massive SUV. Eddie must've already gotten him in the backseat because it's just the two of them, just her husband and her best friend, standing there.

Blanche is standing close to Eddie, too close, in Bea's opinion, her face awash in the orange light. She's smiling up at him, and Eddie is smiling back.

It's the same smile he turned on her in Hawaii, the deep one that gives him a trio of wrinkles at the corner of his eyes, the smile that had made something in her chest feel warm, because she'd somehow known he didn't smile like that at everyone.

That smile she'd thought was just for her, and now it's Blanche's, too.

Bea feels numb as she turns away from them, her heels clicking on the asphalt.

So, this is what Blanche wants. This is what the "renovations" are about.

She doesn't want Bea's house.

She wants Bea's husband.

September, Two Months after Blanche

This is going to sound bizarre (but then again, what about this doesn't?), but I'm settling into a routine in here.

We're settling into a routine.

Eddie doesn't come every day, but every three days. Every time is the same. He brings food and water, enough to get me through until the next time he sees me. Actually, more than enough. I've got extra bottles of water lined up against the wall.

For the first few weeks, I hoarded all of it, rationing out food and water to myself in case he didn't come back, but — another bizarre thing — I've started to trust that he's not going to just leave me up here to starve to death.

He still doesn't talk to me, though, and there are a million questions I want to ask him. Not just the obvious things like, "Why the fuck are you doing this?" but little things. I want to know what he's told the world about me, I want to know what's happened to Southern Manors.

Do people here miss me? Do they miss Blanche?

There has to be some way to get him to talk to me.

I think if I don't talk to someone soon, I'm going to lose my mind.

Today, finally, a breakthrough.

Thanks to a shirt, of all things.

When Eddie came to bring me supplies, I noticed he was wearing the blue dress shirt I got him for our last anniversary. It was the exact same shade of blue as his eyes, which is why I'd bought it, and he still looked great in it. He's been looking better in general lately, more like himself.

And so I said, "You look good."

That surprised him. Instead of turning away from me, he glanced down at himself, like he'd just realized what he was wearing. Saw the significance of it.

"Thanks," he said at last. "I forgot you got this for me."

"I got most of your clothes for you," I replied, "except for that godawful houndstooth tie you like. That was all you."

He smiled a little at that, his eyes crinkling

at the corners. "I love that tie."

Well, now you can wear it all the time, I guess.

The words were right there, a pithy comeback, the kind of thing he used to like from me. But I held my tongue because I knew it would just make him leave. And I needed him to stay.

"It did look good on you," I said. "Which was very irritating."

A snort, then he turned for the door, and was gone. I'd wanted him to linger, to keep talking, and it was hard not to feel disappointed. But there was a looseness to him as he left that hadn't been there when he came in.

It's a start.

October, Three Months after Blanche
Eddie came back today, which surprised me. He'd just been here yesterday, and I was used to waiting three days between visits, counting the time as best as I can up here.

He brought more food and water with him, but I still had plenty, and after he dropped them off, he just stood there by the door for a long while, his hands in his back pockets.

"Do you want some more books?" he

finally asked, and it took me a minute to respond.

"That would be great," I said, and meant it. He doesn't know I've been using this one as a journal, and I could really use some more reading material.

He nodded and, as he left, said, "Bye, Bea."

He hasn't done that before. It's the first time I've heard my own name in weeks.

Another day, another visit from Eddie. He's coming every day now. Not staying long, and twice now, he's been here while I've been asleep, and I wonder if that means he's coming at night. I don't have the best sense of night and day right now, but I still sleep, and I assume that I must be keeping a semi-regular schedule. I don't know why he'd suddenly be coming up at night, though.

But no, I told myself that I can't do that, can't try to guess at his reasons or his motives. If I do that, I'll go crazy.

Well, crazier.

Eddie stayed for an hour today. Maybe longer.

He didn't even bother bringing food and water, and for the first time since I woke up in here, I felt something in my chest loosen, like I could breathe again.

He'd brought me books like he promised, and as soon as he came in, I held up one of them, a political thriller I remembered him reading. "This was maybe the stupidest book I've ever read," I told him, and he crossed the room, taking it from my hand, studying the cover.

"Is this the one where they replace the president with a clone?"

"It was the vice president," I reminded him, "but yes."

Reading the back, Eddie smiled faintly. "I bought it in an airport. No one can be judged for the books they buy in airports."

"I remember that," I said, and suddenly I did. We'd been going to a conference in Atlanta. Well, I'd been going to the conference. Eddie had come with me so he could go to some football game there the same weekend.

"Women and Leadership, Leaders and Womanhood," I said. "Some workshop like that. Three days of lectures with titles like, 'A Gentle Hand: Commanding Respect without Fear,' and 'Women on Top.'"

He smiled. "You hated that shit."

"I did," I replied, nodding. "That one was especially bad, though."

I sat on the edge of the bed, remembering

that weekend, how miserable and bored I'd felt, overdressed in my pencil skirts, wasting my time.

I could still see the woman who led one of the group workshops, standing in front of us, her hair short and prematurely gray, a cream-colored cashmere cardigan nearly swallowing her birdlike frame.

"We keep so many things in our brains," she'd said. "More than men do. They're allowed to only worry about business, while we have to worry about business *and* our families. Our children. I bet if I were to ask a male CEO, 'How much milk do you have in your fridge *right this second*?' he'd have no idea. But all of you know."

The woman had smiled, beatific, then lowered her voice to a conspiratorial whisper. "You all know, don't you?"

A wave of chuckles and knowing nods, and I'd looked around thinking, *Are all of you for fucking real?*

I told Eddie that story now, and he laughed, folding his arms across his chest. "Right, but every day, when I got back to the room and asked how your day had gone, you'd said, 'Fine.' "

I shrugged. "What was I supposed to say? I was the one who'd chosen to go. I didn't want to admit that you were right, and it was a waste of time."

I didn't add that things had been strained between us then. That we'd been arguing more, even before Blanche and her renovations.

I didn't want him to remember that.

"That weekend wasn't exactly a barrel of laughs for me, either. I ended up giving my ticket to the Falcons game to one of my clients, so I think I mostly watched ESPN in the hotel room and ate bad room service."

He glanced around then, and I realized he was looking for a place to sit.

But of course, there wasn't one, because this wasn't my parlor, it was a cell.

A cell he'd made.

Thinking fast, I patted the bed next to me. "It's surprisingly comfy," I said, smiling a little. This was the most we'd talked, and I wanted him like this, relaxed and a little more open.

He hesitated, and for a moment, I thought he'd leave instead.

Then he sat.

The mattress dipped under his weight, making me lean toward him more, and I caught the scent of his soap, and underneath that, the clean, warm smell that was just Eddie.

That weekend in Atlanta hadn't been all

bad. Even with the tension between us, we'd taken advantage of that big hotel bed every night.

Things had always been good between us in bed.

Eddie looked over at me, his eyes very blue, and my mouth went dry.

He wasn't looking at me like he hated me, like he wanted me gone. And there had to be a reason I was still here, after all.

Blanche was dead, while I was alive.

That had to mean something.

"We should've gone on more vacations," I said, letting my gaze drift to his lips. "Maybe back to Hawaii."

I glanced up at him then, and his face was open to me, finally. His eyes warm, his lips parted, the Eddie I knew.

The Eddie I understood.

And suddenly the best way to get out of here was very, very clear.

She hadn't come to Hawaii to meet a guy. She'd come to sit in the sunshine and drink overpriced frozen cocktails. To look out at the Pacific Ocean, which she'd never seen before that trip. In fact, the only ocean she'd ever been to was the Gulf of Mexico, that one summer Blanche's family took her to their place in Orange Beach.

Blanche hadn't approved of the trip to Hawaii. "It's tacky," she'd told Bea, wrinkling her nose as she'd tucked her hair behind her ear. "And you can afford better. Do Bali or something. Fiji, even."

But Bea had wanted Hawaii, so that's where she'd gone, and Blanche could get fucked with her judgey face and pointless opinions. She was just jealous, anyway. Tripp hadn't taken her anywhere since their honeymoon in Italy, and Bea knew for a fact he was still paying off the credit card bills.

But she sat there in her beach chair day

after day, looking out at the ocean — as blue as she'd hoped it would be — and Blanche's words had spun around her mind. Should she have gone somewhere a little more exotic? Somewhere harder to get to? Somewhere where she wasn't spending her days avoiding families and honeymooners?

It was always a balancing act, separating the wants of the girl she used to be from the needs of the woman she was now.

Another mai tai, too sweet, but she drank it anyway. No, Hawaii was good. Hawaii was *accessible,* and that's part of what Southern Manors was selling, right? Class, but in a comfortable way. She might do an entire Hawaiian line for next summer. Hibiscus blooms painted on glass tumblers. Napkin rings in the shape of pineapples. A cheeky hula girl print.

Thinking about work calmed her as it always did, made her brain cease that constant circling, like she was forever looking for the places where she'd stepped wrong, or *could* step wrong. She never had that uncertainty and self-doubt when it came to her business.

Bea pulled her iPad out of her beach bag where it sat next to the three magazines and two books she'd picked up at the airport, but knew she wouldn't read.

Within a few minutes, she had a page of

ideas for the summer line, and was trying to think of a name for the collection that would be fun and catchy, but not overly cutesy. Another fine line she walked all the time, but easier.

She was on her third attempt ("Something with Blue Hawaii? Too dated?") when a shadow fell across her chair, and she heard someone say, "Working at the beach? I'm not sure if that's inspiring or depressing."

It was the smile that did her in, almost from that first moment. Looking up at the man standing there in striped trunks and a white T-shirt, one hand casually in his pocket, his sunglasses spotted with dried seawater, his hair falling over his brow like he was the hero of some rom-com she'd just stepped into.

Bea smiled back, almost without thinking. Later, she'd realize that he was good at that, at breaching walls before you'd even had a chance to put them up, but on that sunny afternoon, there hadn't been anything sinister about his charm.

"Beats working in an office," she heard herself reply, and his grin had deepened, revealing a dimple in his left cheek.

"I'll drink to that," he replied, and then he was offering her his hand, that smile as bright as the sun overhead.

"I'm Eddie."

Eddie. It was a boy's name, Bea thought, but it suited him because there was something boyish in his smile.

And she liked that. Liked it enough that she let him sit in the empty chair next to her and that she accepted his invitation for dinner that night.

Why not? she'd thought. Wasn't this the kind of thing that was supposed to go along with this new life of hers? Expensive vacations, fancy cocktails, dinner with a handsome stranger?

They ate in the hotel restaurant, near the big plate glass window overlooking the sea, the sky a violent mix of pink, purple, and orange, a candle flickering between them, expensive wine sweating in a bucket of ice by the table.

Looking back, Bea could see how it was almost too perfect, too much of a romantic cliché, but at the time, it had just felt exciting and . . . right, somehow. Like she was finally getting everything she deserved.

They talked, and she was surprised at how easy it all was. How easy *he* was. He was from Maine, originally, and loved boats. He was in Hawaii because he had a friend looking to get into the yacht charter business, and they were scouting out other companies, seeing how it was done.

And she'd told him about growing up in Alabama, leaving out the more Southern gothic aspects of her childhood, focusing on the fancy boarding school, the debutante scene, the all-girls college she'd attended in South Carolina. As she spun out her tales, she realized that she was doing it again, papering parts of Blanche's life over the less savory parts of hers, but she'd been in the habit for so long that it hardly registered anymore.

Over dessert, laughing sheepishly, a little chagrined, rubbing his hand over the back of his neck: "You are really fucking beautiful."

Shake of his head. "And I am clearly really fucking drunk," he added.

But he hadn't been. He'd had one old-fashioned earlier, and his wine was mostly untouched.

Maybe it should have alarmed her, that he was faking being drunk as an excuse to say something like that to her, a woman he'd just met.

But it didn't alarm her. It interested her. It felt like it might be a hint at a weakness in a man who, from what she could see, had no reason to be weak. Good-looking, smart, successful . . .

Bea would eventually find out that he wasn't in Hawaii "on business" like he'd said, that the charter yacht idea was closer to a pipe dream than an actual pursuit, but by then it was too late and she didn't care anyway.

"I'm sure you get that a lot," he went on, and Bea had looked at him, really looked at him.

His eyes were blue, and there was just a hint of red high on his cheekbones, from the sun she thought, not booze or embarrassment.

"I do," she replied, both because it was true and because she wanted to see how he'd respond. If the script he'd come up with in his head had counted on her playing that mythical creature boys sang about, the pretty girl who didn't know it.

But he didn't seem flustered at all. He narrowed his eyes slightly, tilting his glass at her. "So, beautiful *and* smart enough to know it."

"And rich," she added. Also true, and again, she wanted to see the look on his face when she said it.

To his credit, he didn't give anything away. He just smiled again. "A triple threat, then. Lucky me."

Bea laughed, tucking her hair behind her ear, sincerely charmed for maybe the first time that evening. She liked that he didn't bluster about it, didn't pretend it was no big deal. He probably already knew, of course — later, she'd wonder a lot about that first encounter — but something about the way he handled it appealed to her. He accepted her, right from the start. She'd built an image of the person she wanted to be, and Eddie was perhaps the first person who truly understood it.

Probably because he was little more than an image himself.

■ ■ ■ ■

PART V
JANE

■ ■ ■ ■

18

Eddie takes the detective out to the back-yard. There's no ride to the police station, no Eddie in the back of a car, and I tell myself that this isn't serious. This is nothing, really.

If it *were* something, he wouldn't be offering the detective bottled water with a smile.

I stand in the kitchen, absentmindedly cleaning the counters, putting glasses in the dishwasher, anything to keep my hands busy and make me look just as relaxed as Eddie does right now.

But I'm not Eddie, and when Detective Laurent comes back inside, I have to fight the urge to go hide in the bedroom and lock the door.

It sounds stupid, but I'd thought this kind of money and lifestyle insulated you from things like this, the police showing up at your door with questions and hard eyes.

The detective is friendly enough, though, holding up her empty bottle. "Recycling?" she asks, and I take it from her, smiling like I'm totally unbothered.

She leans on the counter, casual, and asks, "How long have the two of you been seeing each other?"

I have no idea if this is an actual question she's asking as a police officer, or if she's just making small talk, and my palms sweat as I reach up to tuck my hair behind my ear.

"A few months?" I say. "Eddie and I met back in February, started dating in March?"

Great, I'm doing the questioning thing that makes me sound like an unsure little girl, not the kind of woman who belongs in a house like this.

But the detective just smiles at me, her dark eyes warm, the skin around them crinkling.

"Your fiancé says you used to be his dog-walker." Wrinkling her nose, she gestures around us. "I said, 'What the hell do people in this neighborhood need a dog-walker for?' but that's the bougie set for you, isn't it?"

I laugh along with her, nodding even as my heart keeps pounding and my hands keep shaking. "I said the same thing. But it was a good job, and I like dogs."

I could not sound more insipid if I tried, but that's the point, right? Make her think I'm no one worth even talking to. And whatever *this* is, it has nothing to do with me. Plain Jane, blending into the background again.

Drumming her nails on the counter — sensible, short, square, only one thin gold band on her left hand — Detective Laurent nods. "We all have to do what we can to get by," she says, not unkindly, and then gives me a nod before checking the phone she has clipped to her belt.

"I better get going. Sorry again for interrupting y'all's evening."

"It was no problem at all," I tell her, dying to ask why she's here, what she said to Eddie, but also wanting her to go, to pretend that this night never even happened.

"Let me walk you out," I offer, but she waves me off.

"No need." Then, reaching into her jacket, she pulls out a business card and hands it to me. Unlike the card Eddie handed to John that day, this one is thin, the paper cheap. It's stamped with the Mountain Brook PD's crest, and has her name — Detective Tori Laurent — and number. "I told Mr. Rochester to call if he has any questions. You do the same, okay?"

And then she's off, her sensible shoes squeaking on the floor, the front door opening and closing.

As though he'd been waiting for her to leave, Eddie comes in through the back sliding glass door and lets out a long breath, shoving his hands through his hair.

"Are you okay?" he asks, and I make myself smile up at him as I wrap my arms around his waist.

"Yeah, fine," I say, even though I definitely am not. "What did she want?"

He leans in close, resting his chin on the top of my head. "To talk about Blanche. And Bea."

"Did they find her?" My voice is quiet. It's such a gruesome question, a gruesome image, them finding Bea after she's been in the water this long . . .

"Not Bea," Eddie replies, his voice rough. "Blanche, though. They found Blanche."

"Jesus," I mutter, trying hard not to think about what exactly they found as I pull out of his embrace.

His skin has gone a sort of grayish-green, and a muscle keeps ticking in his jaw. He looks more like the Eddie I first met than he has in ages, and my stomach lurches.

"Is there more?"

"She was . . . there was a fracture on her skull. Like she'd been hit by something. Or someone."

He turns away from me, then, rubbing the back of his neck, and I stand there, absorbing the news, peeling through the shock and fear to see what this means.

Now I'm not just nauseous, I'm cold. Numb, almost as I reach up and press my fingers to my lips. "She was murdered?" I ask, my voice barely above a whisper.

Eddie still has his back to me, his shoulders tense, and I can't help but add, "And Bea?"

"Considered a homicide, now, too," he says. "That's what they wanted to talk to me about. To tell me they're now investigating her disappearance as a murder."

I feel like my vision is graying out, and my knees are suddenly weak, watery. "Oh, god. Eddie."

I don't know what else to say.

We were finally starting to make peace with Bea's ghost. We're *engaged,* for fuck's sake. Talking about a wedding. And it's one thing to have lost your wife in a tragic accident. But to find out someone did it on purpose? That's a nightmare.

And then another thought occurs to me. "They don't . . ." I don't even want to finish the sentence. Don't want it hanging there in the air between us.

"Think I did it?" he asks, turning around. He's still pale, but his expression isn't quite so intense now. "No, they just wanted to let me know that things had changed. They'll have questions, of course, but I got the impression they were looking at me as the grieving widower, not a suspect."

The more he talks, the more that the normal Eddie, the Eddie I'm used to, starts bleeding back into his face and voice. I can practically see his other persona sliding on like a shell. Or a mask.

He looks at me then, frowning. "Christ, Jane, I'm so sorry."

"Sorry?" I step toward him, taking his hands. "Why would you say that?"

Sighing, he pulls me into his arms. "Because this is such a fucking mess, and I don't want you to have to deal with this. I don't want you . . . I don't know, sitting in some little room, answering questions about something that happened before you even fucking knew me."

I thought I'd felt as scared as I could, but now a new horror rushes over me, making my mouth dry as I look up at him. "You think they'll want to question me?"

"They mentioned it," he says, distracted.

"Just that you should come along when I go in."

I've spent the past five years avoiding attention, avoiding questions, definitely avoiding cops. Fuck, if they look into Eddie over this, they'll look into me. His fiancée. The girl he got engaged to less than a year after his wife disappeared.

John, the call from Phoenix, now this. I can practically feel the teeth of a trap starting to snap closed, and I close my eyes, pressing my forehead against Eddie's chest and taking deep breaths.

Eddie's hand goes to the back of my neck, rubbing. "Don't let it worry you, though."

"It doesn't," I automatically reply, but he gives a rueful smile, reaching out to cup my cheek.

"Janie, you're pale as a ghost."

I capture his hand before he can pull it back, pressing it closer to my face. His skin feels so warm. Mine is still freezing. "This is a lot, I know," he says. "I'm still trying to wrap my mind around it. But I want you to know you have nothing to worry about, okay? I'm not going anywhere, and we're going to get through this."

He's speaking in this calm, measured tone, but it doesn't help. In fact, I think it might actually make it worse, and I step back from him, running a hand through my hair.

"Eddie, your wife was murdered," I say. "It's not going to be okay. It *can't* be."

Things like this weren't supposed to happen here. I was supposed to be safe here, this place was supposed to be safe.

And even though Blanche and Bea had disappeared before I even arrived in Thornfield Estates, there was a part of me that felt like maybe this was my fault. Had I brought this here? This sordidness, this violence? Did it cling to me like some kind of virus, infecting anyone who got close to me?

It was a silly, self-absorbed thought that didn't make any sense. But what made even less sense was the thought that Bea and Blanche could've stumbled into something that got them killed. Who would've wanted to hurt either of them? And why?

And why was Eddie so calm?

"I know, it's fucking awful," he says on a sigh. "Believe me, I know." Closing his eyes, he pinches the bridge of his nose. "But there's nothing we can do about it now. Worrying about it isn't going to change it."

Worrying about it isn't going to change it. I want to tell him that it's pretty fucking normal to worry about who might have wanted your wife and her best friend dead, but something stops me.

Eddie takes my hands. "Focus on the wedding," he says. "On the rest of our lives. Not this."

"It's just that . . . I don't really like the police," I say, and he frowns in confusion.

"Why not?"

Spoken like a rich white guy, I think to myself.

Instead, I consider my response very carefully. This is another moment where I feel like a bit of truth in the lie might be useful.

"There was a foster family I lived with," I say. "In Arizona. They weren't exactly in it to do good work for kids, you know?"

When I glance back over at him, he's got his arms folded across his chest, watching me with his chin slightly tucked down. His listening face.

"Anyway, when I was sixteen, they thought I was stealing from them, and they called the cops on me."

I *had* been stealing from them, but given that they were using most of the money the state gave them on themselves, rather than to take care of me and two other kids in their care, I hadn't really seen what the big deal was.

"The officer they sent was a friend of my foster dad's, so they took me down to the station, and it was . . ."

Even as I talked about it, I remembered sitting there, smelling burnt coffee and Pine-Sol and shaking with so much rage that I could barely talk. But I can't tell Eddie about the anger. He won't get that.

"It was scary," I finally say. "And I guess I never really got over it."

Not the full story at all, of course. No mention of the real Jane. Of that last night in Phoenix.

But Eddie doesn't need to know those things.

Making a clucking noise, Eddie uncrosses his arms, pulls me back into them.

"This isn't supposed to be about me," I say, tilting my head up to look at him. "Sorry."

"Don't be," he says before kissing my forehead. "And don't worry about any of this. Bea and Blanche are gone. This doesn't change anything."

But when he lets me go and turns away, I see his hand at his side, fingers flexing and unflexing.

19

The casseroles start showing up the next day.

First, it's Caroline McLaren with chicken Divan and a big hug. "Oh god, this is all just so *awful,*" she says, before tapping the foil covering her glass dish and saying, "And this can't go through a dishwasher."

Emily and Campbell are just a couple of hours behind her. They bring three big paper bags full of things from the gourmet store in the village, the place that makes the fancy dinners you can pass off as your own.

As I stack the foil containers in the freezer, Emily and Campbell sit at the island, sipping the iced coffees they'd brought with them, which is kind of a shame because I already feel like drinking today. I know they're just dying to ask a thousand questions, and I could use the fortification.

"How's Eddie holding up?" Emily asks when I close the freezer and turn back to them. Outside, it's started to rain, and I think back to that first day I met Eddie, the gray skies, the slick roads.

"Not great," I reply. "I think he's still in shock, really."

"We all are," Campbell says, stabbing her straw into her drink. "I mean . . . it just never occurred to any of us that they'd been *murdered*. I've never known anyone who was murdered."

For the first time, I notice that her eyes are red, and that Emily isn't wearing any makeup, and shit.

Shit.

I was so sure they were coming over here to get the dirt, but Bea and Blanche were their friends. Two women they'd loved whose deaths had seemed tragic, but at least accidental. Finding out that someone had killed them had to be awful, and here I am, thinking they just want gossip.

"How are the two of you?" I ask, leaning against the counter, and they glance at each other.

"Oh, honey, this isn't about us," Emily says, waving her hand, but Campbell says, "Not great, either."

Another shared glance, and then Emily sighs, nodding. "It's just a lot to absorb. That someone wanted them dead, that we've suddenly got the police around, ask-ing questions . . ."

I'm starting to get too familiar with that feeling of my stomach dropping, the icy wave that breaks over me every time some new, ugly bit of information is revealed.

"They're asking you questions?"

Campbell sighs as she rises. "Not yet, but I've got an interview scheduled with them later this week. Em?"

Emily nods again. "Yeah, Friday for me."

I think of the two of them, sitting in a police station, answering questions about Bea and Blanche.

About me.

Because the detectives are going to ask, aren't they? Where did I come from, how soon did Eddie and I start dating?

They're going to look into whether I was around last summer or not, and suddenly I want both of them to leave, want to huddle in a ball on the sofa until this somehow magically all goes away.

But then Emily reaches across the counter and squeezes my hand. "I just hate that you have to deal with all this."

My gut reaction is to snarl at her, to search her face for some sign that she's actually loving this, but when I look at her, there isn't any. Her gaze is genuinely warm and sympathetic, and I think back on all those times, sitting at lunch tables by myself, self-consciously tugging at the hem of a Salvation Army T-shirt, knowing it never mattered what shoes people were talking about, or what CD everyone wanted, I was never going to be able to have those things.

I'd always thought it was just the money that I wanted, but looking at Emily now, I know I've wanted this, too. People to care about me. People to accept me.

And while it is weird as shit that, of all people, it would be this crew of Stepford Wives who let me in, they had.

And I was grateful for it.

"Thanks," I reply, squeezing back.

My phone starts ringing on the counter, and as I glance at it, both Emily and Campbell stand up. "Get that, honey," Emily says. "We can show ourselves out."

I hear them make their way to the front door as I look at the screen.

A 205 number, which means Birmingham.

Which could mean the police.

If they'd found something bad, they'd be over here, I tell myself as I slide my finger across the screen to answer the call. *Sound normal. Sound calm.*

"Hello?"

My voice only cracks a little on that last syllable.

"Jane." Not the police, not Detective Laurent. John fucking Rivers.

"What do you want?"

I can practically see him smirking on the other end. "Good to talk to you, too."

"John, I don't —" I start, but he cuts me off.

"I know you're busy doing whatever it is Mountain Brook housewives do, so I'll make it quick. The church is raising money for a new sound system, and I thought you'd like to contribute."

I'm still so shaken up by everything else going on that at first, I don't see the threat beneath his words. It takes a second for my brain to turn them over and see what's really being said.

"I thought we were good after the other day," I reply, the fingers of my other hand curled around the edge of the counter.

He pauses, and I hear him swallow something. I imagine him standing in the kitchen of his apartment, drinking Mountain Dew, and fight back a shudder of revulsion because he's not supposed to be here. I was supposed to be able to leave him behind forever, but he keeps rising back up, the world's most pathetic ghost.

"Well, we were. But that detective from Phoenix called again, which was just a real hassle for me, Jane. And I was going to ignore it, but then I saw in the paper where you and your boyfriend got engaged."

Fuck. I hadn't ever heard of people announcing their engagements, but Emily had submitted it for us, saying, "It's what everyone does!"

And I'd let her because I wanted to be like everyone here.

"So I thought to myself, 'You know, now that Jane is marrying money, she'd probably really like to help me out. Pay me back a little for taking her in.' " Another pause. "And for keeping secrets."

"You don't know shit about my 'secrets,' John," I say, my voice low.

"I know you have them," is his too-quick reply. "And I think that's enough."

Just like that day in the parking lot, I feel my throat constrict, the sense of a tightening noose around me. I wish I'd never met John Rivers, wish I'd never been desperate enough to message him on Facebook from that library in Houston two years ago, wish I'd never taken him up on his offer of a place to stay.

But if I hadn't, I wouldn't be here now.

Wouldn't have met Eddie.

Eddie, with his murdered wife.

Gritting my teeth, I lower my head, pushing the heel of one hand against one eye. "How much."

"Twenty-five hundred," he says, and I flinch even though I know that's a small amount of money to Eddie. He'd probably never even notice it was gone.

"Cash is preferable," John continues, "and you remember the address."

I nod even though he can't see me.

"I'll put it in the mail this week," I say, and I can hear the grin in his voice.

"You're a saint, Jane. The church will really appreciate it."

"Don't call me again. We're done now."

"I can't even call to check in with you? As a friend?"

"We're not friends," I reply, then end the call, my fingers trembling.

The police asking questions. John asking for money.

And in the middle of it, me. And my secrets.

20

June

"We should go to the lake this weekend."

I'm sitting at the kitchen counter, paging through another bridal magazine when Eddie speaks, his tone casual as he pours himself a cup of coffee.

It's been a week since Detective Laurent showed up and while neither of us have mentioned her visit, it's still been there between us, a third presence in the room all the time.

And now Eddie wants to go to the lake? The same place where Blanche and his wife died? Oh wait, were *murdered*?

"Like, the house there?" I ask inanely, and he smirks slightly.

"That was the idea, yeah. Might be nice to get out of town for a little bit, you know? And you've never seen the house."

I'm temporarily stunned into silence.

Finally, I say, "Are you sure that's a smart idea?"

Eddie fixes me with his eyes. He's still smiling, his posture loose and relaxed, and it's somehow worse than if he were angry. "Why wouldn't it be?"

It feels like a dare. It *is* a dare. He wants me to say it out loud, to ask about the police investigation. Does he wonder if I read into Detective Laurent's visit, if I suspect him at all? Because, if I'm being honest with myself, I don't know what to think anymore. But I also think that in a twisted way, going to the lake could give me some clarity.

"Okay," I say. "We'll go to the lake."

We leave on Friday afternoon, Eddie wrapping up work early. The drive to Smith Lake is about an hour from the house in Mountain Brook, and it's pretty, taking us away from the suburbs and into the more rural parts of Alabama, hills rolling gently, the sky a blazing blue.

We stop in a town called Jasper to eat lunch, Eddie as at ease in a little barbecue joint with plastic tables and a roll of paper towels for napkins as he is at the fancy French place back in the village.

Watching him with his sloppy sandwich, managing to get not one drop of sauce on his pristine white shirt, I laugh, shaking my head.

"You fit in anywhere," I tell him, and he looks up, eyebrows raised.

"Is that a compliment?" he asks, and I'd meant it as one, definitely. But not for the first time, I wonder about Eddie's past. He rarely talks about it, like he just sprang into the world, fully formed when he met Bea.

"No, if I wanted to compliment you, I'd tell you how hot you look with barbecue sauce on the corner of your mouth."

He smiles and winks. "You think I'm hot, huh?"

Shrugging, I poke at the lemon in my sweet tea with my straw. "Most days you're just passable, but right now, yes."

That makes him laugh, and he tosses a balled-up napkin at me. "This is why I love you, Jane," he says. "You won't let my head get too big." Even though it's dumb as hell, I almost want to tell him my real name then. Just to hear him say it.

Instead, I finish up my lunch, and we head back to the car, the drive short now.

We make our way down winding roads, dim under the canopy of leaves, the lake sparkling in the distance. There are lots of houses, but the farther we drive, the more spread out they become until finally, there's just the woods, the lake, and as Eddie rounds a corner, the house.

It's not as grand as the one in Thornfield Estates, and it was clearly built to *look* like a rustic lake house, the kind of place where you bring kids fishing, but it's still sprawling, and I feel the coziness of lunch start to ebb away.

It's so quiet here. So isolated.

And it's the last place Bea was ever alive.

As Eddie gets our bags from the trunk, I think he might be feeling something similar because he's quiet except to call out, "The code for the door is the same one at the house."

6-12-85. Bea's birthday.

I enter it into the keypad on the front door, and step inside.

More similarities to Eddie's house — *our* house. It's clearly been expensively decorated, but it's designed to look lived-in, too. There's darker wood here, darker furniture, the whole place a lot more masculine, a lot less . . . Bea.

As I stand beside the heavy front door, my surprise must register on my face because as Eddie steps past me with our stuff, he asks, "What?"

"It's just . . ."

This house looks so much more like him.

241

Even though Bea died here, her ghost doesn't feel nearly as present.

"This is a very man-cavey place," I finally say, and one corner of his mouth kicks up as he tosses his leather bag onto a couch done in green-and-blue tartan.

"This place was Bea's wedding present to me," he says. "So, she let me decorate." Another smile, wry this time. "Which means I said yes to everything she picked out."

So, Bea's stamp is still here — it's just her version of what she thought Eddie would like. Should like.

I move into the living room, seeing it through Bea's eyes, imagining how she saw Eddie. Even though this is on a lake, not the ocean, there's a whole coastal theme happening. Paintings of schooners, decorations made with heavy rope, even an old Chelsea Clock on the wall.

"I worked on sailboats when I was younger, up north. Charter boats in Bar Harbor, that kind of thing," he says, nodding at the seascape over the fireplace. "I guess Bea wanted to remind me of it."

"Because you liked it or because you hated it?"

The question is out before I realize what a stupid thing it is to ask, how much it reveals.

His head jerks back slightly, like the ques-

242

tion was an actual physical blow, and he narrows his eyes. "What does that mean?" he asks, and I feel my face go hot as I shrug, nudging the edge of an area rug with my toe.

"You've just never mentioned that to me before, so I thought . . . maybe you were trying to forget it? Your past. Maybe this reminder of it might not have actually been a nice thing to do."

"You think Bea was that kind of bitch?" he asks, and god, I have royally fucked this up.

"Of course not," I say, but to my surprise, he just laughs, shaking his head.

"I can't blame you for it. I imagine you saw some real cunty stuff when you worked in the neighborhood."

It's a relief, both that he doesn't think my question was that weird, and also that he gets me. I may not always be honest with Eddie, but he still sees these parts of me sometimes, and I like it.

It makes me think that even though I've been playing a certain role, he might have picked me — the real me — anyway.

"It was still a dumb thing to say," I tell him now, sliding closer to him. Over his shoulder is a glass door leading out to a screened-in porch; beyond that is a sloping green lawn, a narrow pier, and the dark water of the lake. This time of the afternoon, the sun sends little sparks of gold dancing across its surface.

It's hard to believe that this pretty, sparkly water took Bea's life. And Blanche's. And it's even harder to believe Eddie would want to be anywhere near it again. How can we sit out there tonight and drink wine and *not* think about it?

But Eddie just gives my ass a pat, propelling me slightly in the direction of the hallway off the living room. "Go ahead and get settled, and I'll unpack the groceries."

The master bedroom is nowhere near as big as the one back at Thornfield, but it's pretty and, like the rest of the house, cozy and comfortable. There's a quilt on the bed in swirling shades of blue, and a big armchair near the window with a good view of the lake.

I settle into the chair now, watching the water.

After twenty minutes, I still haven't seen a single person out there.

No boats, no Jet Skis, no swimmers. The only sound is the lapping of the water against the dock and the wind in the trees.

When I come out of the bedroom, Eddie is pouring us both a glass of wine.

"It's really quiet out here," I say, and he nods, looking out the back door toward the water.

"That's why we picked it."

And then he releases a long deep breath and says, "It made me crazy. After Bea."

I look up, startled. I hadn't expected him to voluntarily mention her after my fuckup earlier.

"The quiet," he goes on. "Thinking about that night and how quiet it would've been, how dark."

He keeps his eyes trained on the water. "It's deep out there, you know. The deepest lake in Alabama."

I hadn't known that, and I don't say anything. I'm not even sure if he's talking to me, to be honest. It's almost like he's talking to himself, staring out at the lake.

"They flooded a forest to make it," he goes on. "So there are trees under the water. Tall ones, sixty feet high in some places. A whole fucking forest under the water. That's why they thought they never found her. They thought she was somewhere in the trees."

The image seeps into my mind. Bea, her skin white, her body tangled in the branches of an underwater forest, and it's so awful I actually shake my head a little. I'd wondered why it had been so hard to find the bodies, and now that I knew, I wish I didn't.

I wish we'd never come here.

A muscle works in his jaw. "Anyway."

"I'm sorry," I say, rubbing his lower back. "If this is too much —"

"No," he says, then takes a sip of his wine. "No." It's firmer this time. "I loved this place, and she loved this place, and one bad memory can't taint it forever."

I want to point out that it's more than a bad memory — it's the death of his wife, the death of a close friend, but then what he's actually said crystallizes in my mind, sucking the breath out of my lungs.

One bad memory.

Eddie wasn't here that night. He can't *remember* it.

Okay, no, I'm being stupid. It was a simple turn of phrase, he doesn't mean it like a literal memory, just that *thinking* about what happened here is like a bad memory. Right?

But my voice is still brittle when I ask, "Have you been here since it happened?"

He takes a moment before answering me. "Once."

It's all he says, that one word, and then he turns away. "Let's go out to eat tonight," he says. "There's a great restaurant on the other side of the lake."

And then he's moving past me into the bedroom, leaving me there in the silence, watching the sun over the water.

21

Dinner is nice. Some fish place with slightly tacky décor and Christmas lights strung up everywhere, but the food is good, and Eddie seems a little looser, back to how he'd been earlier in the day, before we arrived at the house.

There's no talk of Bea this time, only us, and when we drive back to the house after the sun has set, Eddie reaches over to hold my hand, his fingers stroking my knuckles.

But the closer we get to the house, the more I can feel him tense up, and when we come in, we end up just watching TV and drinking more wine. Maybe too much in my case because when I get into bed close to midnight, my head is spinning and I feel too warm, my skin sweaty, so that when Eddie tries to slide an arm around me, I scoot away from him.

I fall into a fitful sleep only to wake up to find myself alone.

For a moment, I lie there, one hand splayed over the spot where Eddie should be, the sheets still warm.

Then there's a sound from the living room.

It sounds like something scraping against the floor, and my mouth is suddenly dry from more than the wine.

When I hear it again, I get out of bed.

I come out of the bedroom, my eyes burning, my head still fuzzy, and Eddie is there in the living room, crouched down, looking at the floor.

"Eddie?"

His head jerks up. "Hey," he says and rises to his feet. He's wearing the boxers he wore to bed, his feet bare on the hardwood, and even though the house is cool now, he seems to be covered in a thin sheen of sweat.

"What are you doing?" I ask, and there's a beat. A small one, barely noticeable, but I feel it. The moment when he has to shift himself into a sheepish grin, a hand on the back of his neck.

But before he managed it, I saw a flash of irritation. He was pissed.

At me.

For seeing him. For interrupting him.

"Sorry," he says. "I didn't want to wake you, but I just remembered I pulled the key to the boat shed off my key ring earlier, and then I couldn't remember where I put it, and then I started wondering if I'd dropped it. You know how it is when you're trying to sleep and one little thing is bothering you?"

I did. Funny how having your future husband disappear in the middle of the night will do that to you.

"Did you find it?" I ask now, feigning more sleepiness than I feel. But I know he's lying. And that flash of anger in his eyes, that moment when he clearly wished I hadn't gotten out of bed to find him.

It scared me.

Eddie scared me.

"No," he says. "It's probably in the drive-way. I'll check tomorrow."

I see his eyes drift over me. I'm wearing an oversized T-shirt that hangs to my knees, but we hadn't had sex when we'd gone to bed, and I catch the interest in his gaze now.

I could lean into that, smile back, give him some cheesy line about having something that might help him sleep.

Instead, I turn away, going back into the bedroom.

And later, when I lie in bed next to him, I keep seeing that look on his face, and wonder if there is even a boathouse key at all.

■ ■ ■ ■

"Did you take money out of the account?"

I'm standing on the dock the next afternoon, looking out at the water. It's basically all I've done today. I slept late, and have been reading since I woke up, trying to ignore the way Eddie keeps prowling around the house when he thinks I'm not paying attention.

The sun is hot on my shoulders, but I feel cold as I turn to see him behind me. He's wearing swim trunks, his gaze hidden behind those mirrored sunglasses, and he's frowning down at his phone.

Fuck. I'd thought I'd been so careful with John's money, taking three hundred out of an ATM in the village, getting a hundred dollars back at the grocery store, spreading it out over a few days so he wouldn't see a big chunk of money coming out. How did he notice it?

He's still watching me, still waiting.

"Wedding stuff," I say, waving a hand, even though the truth is I haven't done shit for this wedding yet besides look at dresses. "You have no idea how many little things you have to put deposits down on."

Eddie nods, but says, "I actually do have

an idea. Had a wedding before, remember?"

That Eddie grin, the one that makes his dimples deepen, but there's an edge to it now, and I suddenly remember that this is the same grin he gave John that afternoon in the parking lot when I went to get my stuff.

I've never had this directed at me before. "Of course," I reply, giving a flustered little laugh. "You know all about this kind of thing. Anyway, it just seemed easier to use cash. I meant to tell you, but I guess the lake trip distracted me."

I try to give him a sultry sideways look at that, but he's already looking back at his phone.

"Gotcha. It's just that the bank thought it looked suspicious and froze the account."

My face flushes hot. Here I was, thinking I was being smart and subtle, and instead his bank saw a petty fucking thief.

"Shit," I say. "Sorry."

"It's fine," he says, waving his free hand. "I'll just let them know the charges were legit, and they'll unfreeze it. Just."

He looks up at me then. "Use the credit card I gave you, okay?"

"Sure, of course," I say, and he nods at me, heading back inside while I stand there, blushing and sick to my stomach and nearly shaking.

We go out to dinner again that night, and this time I make sure not to drink so much, but it doesn't matter. Neither of us can relax, and I get the sense Eddie is watching me just as carefully as I'm watching him. And when he suggests we leave early on Sunday, I agree too quickly. This place gives me the creeps.

We leave before nine, and when I get into the passenger seat, I tell myself I'll never come back here, that we'll sell this place and buy something new.

"I should get another boat," Eddie says as we drive away, the house and the lake slipping from view. He sets a hand on my knee, squeezes. "Would you like that?"

Tripp Ingraham stands there in my mind, his basket on his arm, his face twisted in a smirk, and I push the image away, making myself smile at Eddie. "I'd love it."

22

For the next two weeks, all I can think about is the way Eddie kept creeping around the lake house, and I find myself doing the same thing back in Thornfield Estates. Going down hallways, opening closets, pacing.

Standing in front of closed doors.

For the first time since I started seeing Eddie, I feel lonely.

I imagine bringing it up to Emily or Campbell, power-walking around the neighborhood, all, "Hey, girls, Eddie took me to the lake house where his wife died; weird, right?"

Fuck that.

But people are still talking, I know.

When I do manage to leave the house, even just to go to Roasted for a fancy coffee, I hear two women I don't even know talking about Bea.

Two older ladies, sitting at a table near a window, one of them with her phone in her hand. "I ordered things from her website every Christmas," she says to her friend. "She was such a sweetheart."

I edge closer just as the other one says, "It was the husband, you know it was."

"Mmmhmmm," her friend agrees, lowering her voice to whisper, "It always is."

But *which* husband? There are two involved here, and one of them is about to be *my* husband.

Then the lady holding her phone says, "It's just such a shame she got caught up in it. You know that's what happened. He probably didn't want to kill both of them, but they were both there, and . . ."

"And what else could he do?" her friend says. "It was the only option."

Like "murdering someone" is the same as saying, "Sure, Pepsi is fine," when you order Coke.

These fucking people.

I keep listening, trying to discern whether they mean Tripp or Eddie, Bea or Blanche, so that the barista has to call, "Hazelnut soy latte for Jane?" three times before I remember *I'm* Jane.

I can't keep doing this.

I need to talk to someone. I need to know what happened out there on that lake.

■ ■ ■ ■

Detective Laurent's card is still in my purse, and I think about calling her, just casually checking in, seeing if there's anything I can do to help, but even I can't fake that level of confidence.

No, the less I talk to the police, the better.

So, I decide to talk to someone I dislike nearly as much.

When Tripp accepted my text invitation to lunch, I'd been a little surprised, but now here we sit at the pub in the village, the one I've never been to because it always seemed like the kind of place guys like Tripp would frequent.

"I'm sure you're wondering why I asked you to lunch," I tell him, going for the whole "hesitant college girl" thing. My hair is loose today so I can nervously tuck it behind my ears as I talk, and while I'm not in the jeans and T-shirts I always wore to work at his house, I'm in one of the more casual outfits I picked up after the engagement, a plain beige shirtdress that I know doesn't particularly flatter me.

Snorting, Tripp picks up his Rueben and dips it in the extra Thousand Island he ordered. "Let me guess," he says. "Someone told you the rumors about Blanche and Eddie, and now you want to know if it's true."

My shock is not feigned. I really am that blinking, stammering girl I've pretended to be so often. "What?" I finally say, and he looks up.

Tripp's gaze sharp. "Wait, it's not about that?" He frowns a little, licking dressing off his thumb. "Well, shit. Okay, then. So what, you just wanted to hang out?"

I sip my beer to buy some time, and I hate this, feeling like I'm out of control, that this thing *I set up* is already fucked.

"I wanted to talk to you because I know you're going through the same thing Eddie is, and I just wanted to see how you were doing, to be honest."

A little wounded sharpness in my tone, eyes meeting his then sliding back to the table. I can still keep this on track, even if I do want to lunge across the table and shake him until he tells me everything about Eddie and Blanche.

Some of Tripp's smugness drains away, and he puts his sandwich down, picking up his beer. "Yeah. It was . . . different when I thought she drowned. Now this, it's . . . well, it's a hell of a thing."

He drains nearly half his beer, setting it back on the table with a not-so-discreet burp into his napkin. "How is Eddie?"

Tripp's stare is pointed, and I see now that he has his own reasons for accepting this invitation, and they have nothing to do with being neighborly.

"I can't really speak for him," I reply, careful now, pushing my fries around my plate. "But I know he offered to cooperate with the police. Anything he can do to be helpful."

Which is true. Eddie's gone down to the station twice now to answer questions, questions he'd never told me the specifics of, and I wonder if that's what Tripp is fishing for. Wondering how much Eddie is saying, what is he saying, and not for the first time, I wonder if this was more dangerous than I'd thought, arranging to meet him. And not just because someone might see us.

Drumming his fingers on the table, he nods, but his gaze is far off now, and we sit there in an excruciating silence for too long before he says, "There wasn't anything. Between Blanche and Eddie. It was just your usual neighborhood bullshit. Eddie's company was doing some work on our house, I was busy, so I let Blanche handle it. They hung out a lot, but Blanche and I were good. And honestly, even if I thought she'd cheat on me, she never would've fucked over Bea."

He grimaces before adding, "Although Bea never deserved that loyalty if you ask me, but . . ."

His words just hang there, and I push, the littlest bit.

"You said that Bea took a lot of . . . inspiration from Blanche."

"Basically took her whole life, yeah, but they both ended up in the same place, didn't they? Bottom of Smith fucking Lake."

Tipping his head back, he sighs. "Anyways, if Emily Clark or Campbell or any of those other bitches try to tell you Eddie and Blanche were sleeping together, it was just gossip. Maybe even wishful thinking, since it's not like I was ever all that popular with that crowd."

Whatever I was going to get out of Tripp is gone now, I can tell. He's slipping back into his bitterness, and when he orders another beer, I make a big show of checking my watch. "Oh, shit, I have a hair appointment," I say.

"Sure you do." His tone is sarcastic but he doesn't press further, and when I try to leave a twenty to cover my lunch, he waves it off.

Back at the house, I go back to my computer, pulling up Emily's Facebook page, looking for any pictures of Blanche with Eddie, but there's nothing. Not on Campbell's, either, and while Blanche is clearly tagged in a few pictures, it's a dead link to her page, which I assume someone in her family took down.

I've been so fixated on Bea, it never occurred to me to look that closely at Blanche.

Now it seems that was a mistake.

Eddie doesn't get home until late. I'm in the bathtub, bubbles up to my chin, but I hear him long before I see him — the front door unlocking, his footsteps down the hall, the door to the bedroom opening.

And then he's there, leaning against the door, watching me.

"Good day?" I ask, but instead of answering, he asks a question of his own.

"Why did you have lunch with Tripp Ingraham today?"

Surprised, I sit up a little, water sloshing. I fucking love this tub, so deep and long I could lie down flat if I wanted to, but right now, I wish I weren't in it, wish I weren't naked and vulnerable. Usually, the size difference between us is kind of a turn-on. Eddie is sleek, but brawny — he's got real muscle, the kind you get from actually working, not just going to the gym. He makes me feel even smaller and more delicate than I am.

But for the first time, it occurs to me how easy it would be for him to hurt me. To overpower me.

"How did you know about that?" I ask, and I know immediately it's the wrong response. Eddie isn't scowling, but he's doing that thing again, that forced casualness, like this conversation doesn't really mean that much to him even though he is practically vibrating with tension.

"I mean, it's a small town, and trust me, people were dying to tell me they saw you out with him. Thanks for that, by the way. Really fun texts to get."

Pissed off, I stand up, reaching for the towel hanging next to the bath. "Do you honestly think I have any interest in Tripp Ingraham?"

Sighing, Eddie turns away. "No," he acknowledges, "but you have to think about how things look. Especially now."

He moves back into the bedroom and I stand there, still naked, still holding the towel, dripping onto the marble floor and looking after him.

I have worked so hard to present a certain version of myself to Eddie, to everyone, really, but in that moment, it snaps.

"How it *looks*?" I repeat, following him into the bedroom, wrapping the towel around myself. "No, Eddie, I didn't think about how it *looks*."

"Of course, you didn't. Let me guess, you also didn't think about how it might *look* for my fiancée to be handing over wads of money to the guy she used to live with."

I am frozen standing there in my towel, my stomach clenching. I'm too rattled to even try to lie. "What?"

Eddie is looking at me now with an expression I've never seen before. "Did you think I didn't know, Jane? Did it never occur to you to come to me?"

How? How the fuck could he have known? That first time, the money I gave him was mine. The second, yes, that was Eddie's, but I was careful. I was so careful.

"He called me, too," Eddie says, his hands on his hips, his head tilted down. "Some bullshit story about people in Phoenix looking for you."

This can't be happening; he can't know. I can't breathe.

"Did he tell you why?" I ask, my voice barely above a whisper, and Eddie looks up at me again, his eyes hard.

"I didn't ask. I told him to go fuck himself, which is what you should've done the

262

second he called."

He steps closer, so close I can practically feel the heat radiating off of him. I'm still standing there, not even wrapped in my towel, just holding it in front of me, shivering with more than just cold.

"That's what you do when people threaten you, Jane. When they try to fuck you over. You don't give in to them, you don't give them what they want, you remind them that you're the one in charge, you're making the rules."

Eddie reaches out then, taking me by the shoulders, and for the first time since I met him, I stiffen at his touch.

He feels it, and the corners of his mouth twist down, but he doesn't let me go. "I don't give a fuck why someone in Phoenix is trying to find you. What I care about is that when he came to you with this shit, you didn't trust me enough to tell me about it."

I don't know what to say, so I just stand there, looking down, wanting him to let me go, wanting him to leave, and finally, he sighs and drops his hands.

"You know what?" he says, stepping back and reaching into his jacket pocket. "Here."

He pulls out a slip of paper and forces it into my hand.

My damp skin nearly smudges the ink, but I see it's a phone number, one with a Phoenix area code. "This is the number of whoever was calling John."

I startle, blinking down at the paper. "He gave this to you?"

Eddie doesn't answer that, saying, "The point is, Jane, I've had this number in my wallet for the past month. *Before* I asked you to marry me. And I never called it. Not once. You know why?"

I shake my head even though I know what he's about to say.

"Because I trust you, Janie."

He turns, heading for the bedroom door, and then stops, looking at me. "It would be nice to get the same in return."

With that, he's gone, and I sink to the edge of the tub, my knees shaking.

But it's not because of the number I hold in my hand. It's not knowing that Eddie's had it all this time, that at any point over the past month, he could've called it and learned . . . everything.

It's because of what he said. How he looked.

That's what you do when people threaten you, Jane.

His eyes had been so cold. His tone so flat.

I'd looked him in the eyes and hadn't recognized him at all.

I can hear those women at the coffee shop again. *It's always the husband.*

And for the first time, I honestly believe that it could've been.

Not Tripp, sitting across from me at lunch. He was a little bit drunk, a little bit belligerent. He's also clumsy, and unfocused.

He's nothing like Eddie.

23

"Girl, I swear you've gotten even skinnier!"

Emily is smiling as she says it to me, and I think it's a compliment, but I can barely make myself smile back at her. We're standing in the open courtyard of the First Methodist Church, people milling all around us, and I'm too aware of both how hot the evening is — even though the sun is going down — and also how wrong my outfit is.

In my defense, I had no idea what the fuck one was supposed to wear to a silent auction at a church on a Wednesday night, and black had seemed a safe choice — sophisticated, respectable. But all the other women are in bright colors, flower prints, that kind of thing, and I feel like a crow standing around a bunch of flamingos.

Eddie must've known it was wrong, but he hadn't said anything, and I fight the urge to glare at his back as he stands there, talking to the reverend.

Now I smooth my dress over my thighs and say, "Pre-wedding jitters," to Emily, who nods and pats my arm sympathetically.

"You're lucky. When I got married to Saul, my stress response was to eat everything in sight."

Her husband is over near a giant azalea bush, chatting with Campbell's husband, Mark, and Caroline's husband, Matt.

I realize that I hardly ever see Eddie with those guys, and that he never mentions them. Did the neighborhood pull back from him after everything with Bea and Blanche, or does he find these people as insufferable as I do?

Okay, they're not all bad. Emily is actually nice, steering me around groups of people, introducing me as Eddie's fiancée and never once mentioning the dog-walker thing.

It almost makes me feel sorry for all the shit I stole from her.

The auction items are inside the church's Family Life Center, but despite the heat, everyone is congregating out here in the courtyard, probably because it's so pretty and lush.

Maybe we should get married here instead of eloping after all.

But then thinking about the wedding is

too hard when Eddie is barely speaking to me.

It's been two nights since our fight in the bathroom, two nights of Eddie sleeping god knows where in the house, of him leaving for work early and coming home late.

The worst part is that I've been relieved he's been gone so much. It's easier with him not there, without looking at him every second, wondering if that flash of hardness, coldness will come back.

The number he gave me is still in my purse. I'll never call it, but I want it there as a reminder of how badly I almost fucked up, how little I even really know about Eddie.

But here we are at the church's little party, mingling in a garden, drinking lemonade because even though the Methodists aren't the Baptists, no one wants an open bar in front of Jesus, I guess, and I'm just about to get another glass of the lemonade when Caroline approaches us, her blond hair swinging over her shoulders.

"Holy shit," she breathes, surprising me because I've never heard her curse before and also, Jesus. I'm going to hell for all kinds of things, but even *I* manage to keep it PG at church.

She clutches my arm, her nails digging in.

"Tripp Ingraham has been arrested."

That last word is hissed in a whisper, but it doesn't matter. I see other people looking over at us, and Emily already has her phone out, frowning at the screen.

Eddie is still talking to the reverend, and my insides feel frozen, my feet locked to the soft grass beneath my too-tight heels.

"What?" I finally say, and she glances behind her at her husband.

"Matt just got a text from his friend in the DA's office. Apparently, they found something when they did the autopsy? Or something in the house? I don't know, but I texted Alison who lives on his street, and she said a cop car full-on showed up and took him away in handcuffs."

Now Emily is glancing over at me, and I can see little groups start to form, practically watch as the gossip moves through the gathering, all thoughts of fundraising replaced with this, the biggest story to hit this neighborhood since Bea and Blanche died, I'd guess.

When I turn toward Eddie, he's staring at me. And even across the courtyard I can see it in his eyes.

He's relieved.

The house is dark and quiet as we walk in,

both of us absorbed in our own thoughts.

When I tell Eddie I'm going to take a shower, I wait for some of this old spark to come back, for a sly grin and an offer to join me.

Instead, I get a distracted nod as he keeps scrolling through his phone. He'd barely spoken on the car ride home, just confirming that yes, he'd heard the same thing, that they'd arrested Tripp; yes, it had something to do with the night Bea and Blanche died; no, he didn't know what the actual charges were.

In the master bathroom, I step out of my dress, letting it pool there on the marble floor, not bothering to hang it up. I probably won't wear it again anyway.

The water is scalding hot, which feels good after the weird chill I experienced on the way home, and when I step back out of the shower, the room is filled with steam.

Wrapping myself in a towel, I walk to the mirror, wiping the steam off with one hand.

My face stares back, plain and starkly pale, my hair wet and shoved back from my face.

You're fine, I tell myself. *You're safe. It was Tripp the whole time because of course it was.*

But that doesn't really make me feel better, and I'm frowning at my reflection when

Eddie steps into the bathroom.

He shucks his clothes easily, and I can't help but watch him in the mirror. He's so beautiful, so perfectly male, but I feel no surge of desire when I look at him, and he's not meeting my eyes.

I take my robe from the hook near the door, wrapping it around me as he showers, and then I sit on the little tufted bench in front of the vanity, combing out my hair for much longer than I need to.

I'm waiting.

Finally, the water shuts off and Eddie steps out, wrapping a towel around his waist as I fumble in a drawer for the expensive moisturizer I bought the other day.

"The other night. When we argued. Were you scared of me?"

I sit very still there at the bathroom counter, watching him in the mirror. He's got a towel around his waist, water still drying on his skin, his hair slicked back from his face, and there's something about the way he's looking at me that I don't like.

"Did you think it was me? That I killed them?"

I blink, trying to recalibrate, trying to get this back on track. "The last few weeks have just been a lot," I finally say, adding a little tremor to my voice for effect. "Everything was finally so perfect, and we were so happy, and then . . ."

"And then you thought I murdered my wife and her best friend," he says, relentless, and my head snaps up.

This isn't how this is supposed to go. He's supposed to feel sorry for snapping at me, for even suggesting I thought such a thing.

But he's still watching me, arms folded over his chest, and since the lowered lashes and tremulous voice aren't working, I turn and meet his eyes.

"Yes," I say, and honestly, it feels kind of good to tell the truth. "I did. Or I thought you may have done it."

He blows out a long breath, tilting his head up to look at the ceiling before saying, "Well. At least you're honest."

I step forward, curling my hands around his wrists and pulling his arms down. "But I was wrong," I insist. "Obviously. And I'm sorry, Eddie. I'm so sorry."

And the thing is, I am sorry. I'm sorry I ever thought he might have been involved with Bea's and Blanche's death, and not just because I almost fucked up everything.

I'm the one lying to him, I'm the one who's stolen from him, from everyone I've grown close to. I'm the one who has pretended to be something she's not.

I'm the one who has actually done something terrible.

I press my forehead to his damp chest, breathing in the scent of his soap. "I'm sorry," I say again, and after a long beat, I feel his hand rest gently on the back of my head. "And you were right, the other night. I should've trusted you about John, I should've come to you —"

"It's alright," he murmurs, but I'm afraid that it's not. That I've let all my suspicions and distrust ruin this perfect thing I've found, this new life.

"Do you think it really was Tripp?" I ask him, still standing there in his arms, wanting him to tell me that yes, he does. That it's that awful, but that simple, and there's an easy person to blame.

"I don't want to think he could've done it," he says. "How many times did I have that guy in my house, or played golf with him, for fuck's sake." Another sigh, one I can feel as well as hear. "But he and Blanche were having issues. God knows he drinks like a goddamn fish. If he was drunk and they fought . . ."

He lets it trail off. I remember now how uneasy Tripp has made me feel. I'd never thought of it as anything truly threatening, but that didn't mean it wasn't. Who could ever really know what someone was capable of?

"The police are doing their job," Eddie says, his hand still stroking the back of my head. "If they think it was Tripp, I'm sure they've got good reasons."

"I'm sorry," I say again. "Eddie . . ."

But he dips his head then and kisses me. "Shh," he murmurs against my lips when we part. "It doesn't matter, Janie."

He kisses me again, harder this time, and I wrap my arms tightly around his waist, holding on not just to him but to this moment, to this chance I nearly threw away.

When we part, Eddie lowers his forehead to mine. "Tell me you trust me," he says, his voice husky.

And for the first time in my life, I say, "I trust you." And I think I actually mean it.

■ ■ ■ ■

PART VI
BEA

■ ■ ■ ■

November, Four Months after Blanche
Eddie didn't hesitate today.

He came right in and sat down next to me, his thigh touching mine. When he said, "Are you okay up here?" I could smell the mint on his breath.

For some reason, that made it easier. Knowing he'd brushed his teeth before coming to see me, that he was expecting — hoping? — for this.

But then I'd gotten ready, too. I don't have much in the way of makeup in here, but I'd taken a shower, pinched my cheeks to put some color in them, brushed my hair. It was a little longer now, closer to how it looked when we first met, and I figured that could only help with what I needed to do.

Ever since that last visit, when the look on his face changed as soon as I mentioned Hawaii, I'd known we would end up here, that the easiest and best way of keeping myself alive, reminding him that he needed me, was through the one thing that had never let us down.

Sex.

But it's one thing to consider seducing the man who murdered your best friend, the man who's keeping you locked up, the man you thought you knew, the man you married.

It's another thing to go through with it.

I took his hand in mine, feeling the calluses on his palms, remembering that I'd always liked that about him, how he worked with his hands, how he wasn't like the Tripp Ingrahams of the world with their soft, pale fingers.

He was beautiful.

He always had been.

I focused on that, taking a deep breath as I let my fingers run over his knuckles.

I couldn't think about those hands on Blanche, couldn't think about them pulling me into this room. Instead, I thought of all the times I'd wanted those hands on me, the times I'd thought I'd die if he didn't touch me.

It had been like that, right from the start.

"Bea, what are you doing?" he murmured as I leaned closer, letting my lips brush the shell of his ear.

"I miss you," I answered, and realized all at once that it was true.

I did miss him.

Not the Eddie who killed Blanche. I didn't know that Eddie. But the Eddie from before, the one who had swept me off my feet with his easy smiles, his charm, the way he'd known exactly what I wanted before *I* knew it myself.

I focused on those early days now. Before we moved here, before things went darker than I knew they could.

"Do you remember that first night in Hawaii?" I asked him, rising up from the bed to stand in front of him, my hands on his shoulders.

His own hands easily came to rest on my waist, almost like a reflex.

"I invited myself to your room," he said as I slid my hands from his shoulders, down his chest, moving even closer so that he had to open his legs to let me step between them. "You said you weren't that kind of girl."

The corner of his mouth kicked up a little at that, a dimple deepening, and I leaned down to kiss that spot, feeling him suck in his breath.

"I wasn't," I said. "Until you."

Then I kissed him.

This part was so much easier than I thought it would be, maybe because kissing Eddie had always been one of my favorite things.

Or maybe because as I re-created that first night for us, it was easy for *me* to slip into it, too. I wanted Eddie to forget where we were, what had happened, what he'd done, but I was doing it, too.

Forgetting.

Slipping.

His mouth under mine made that so easy, and I wrapped my arms around his neck, pulling him in, my fingers in his hai—

"No, no, Jesus, Bea, this is fucked up."

Eddie pushed me away, his breath coming fast.

I stepped back from the bed as he stood up, nearly stumbling in his haste to get to his feet.

His face was red, his eyes almost glassy as he raked a hand through his hair.

"We can't," Eddie said, and my heart sank.

"I shouldn't have come today," he continued, moving past me. "I don't know what the fuck I was thinking, I don't know —"

I reached for him before he could walk out, and he stopped, looking down at my fingers loosely cuffing his wrist. The energy in the room shifted, tightened, and sharpened.

Moving toward him, I cupped his face in my hand and he didn't turn away.

"It's okay," I told him, my voice soft. "It's okay."

"It's not," he protested, but he didn't move, and I leaned in.

"If you really don't want to, we don't have to," I said, keeping my voice steady. "But I want to. I want you to understand that. I want this, Eddie. I want *you.*"

And I did.

I honestly did.

Which was maybe the worst part of all of it.

There was no holding back when I kissed him this time, no tentative testing of lips and tongue. I kissed him like I had that very first night, and he gave in, like I'd known he would.

It was amazing, really, how easy it was. How quickly our bodies remembered each other.

You love me, I told him with every kiss, every touch, every gasp.

Remember that you love me, that what we have is good and right and worth something.

Remember you're mine.

But in trying to make him remember all

that, I'm remembering, too.

How good he feels. How much I loved him.

Reader, I fucked him.

And when it was over and we lay in the bed, sweat still sticking his skin to mine, something about the quiet made me reach out, tracing my finger over his heart. "You know that I still love you," I said, my voice barely above a whisper. "You know I'd never do anything to hurt you."

I wanted him to hear what I was trying to say. *If you let me out, I'll never tell what happened. We'll figure it out.*

But it was the wrong thing to say.

Eddie sighed heavily, pulling away from me and reaching for his clothes, still in a pile beside the bed.

I could see in the stiffness of his movements that I'd pushed too far. He'd heard what I was saying, and he didn't like it.

And when he walked out without another word, I wondered if I was going to have to start all over again.

Bea had put that moment with Eddie and Blanche out of her mind when she sees them at lunch in the village.

She was supposed to be at the Southern Manors offices in nearby Homewood, but she'd wanted to drop by one of the Mountain Brook boutiques and see what was in the front windows.

Instead, she sees her husband and her best friend sitting at one of the café tables, laughing over salads like they're in a fucking Cialis commercial, and the anger nearly chokes her, shocking in its force.

It isn't just the two of them together — it's that it's so public, that anyone can see them, that people *will* see them, and they'll talk.

People might even feel sorry for her.

She stands there on the sidewalk underneath an awning, shielded by her sunglasses, and in her mind, Bea can see other faces turned to her, other expressions of pity with just a touch of schadenfreude, and suddenly her hands are shaking, and her feet are moving and she's crossing the street to stand in front of their table, taking a small, savage delight in the way they both flinch at her bright greeting.

There are blueprints on the table between them. Eddie's contracting business (the business she paid for, the one she *gave* him) is doing an addition on Blanche's house. It's all innocent really. Just a friendly working lunch to go over some details.

But it's not just this lunch. It's that ever since Blanche came up with this idea for Eddie to renovate her house, Eddie has been there all the time.

Or Blanche has been at Bea's house, sitting on the back deck with Eddie, drinking Bea's wine and showing Eddie some Pinterest board of her "dream kitchen."

And Eddie just smiles at her, indulges her.

Takes her out to lunch, apparently.

"You embarrassed me," Eddie tells her later, the two of them making dinner in the kitchen together, Bea on her third glass of wine, the stereo up just a little too loud. "Actually," he goes on, "you embarrassed yourself."

Bea doesn't answer because she knows that will infuriate him, and it does.

With a huff, Eddie tosses the kitchen towel

he'd had on his shoulder to the counter and heads out to the back deck, taking her glass of wine with him.

They don't talk about it again, but the next time Blanche and Bea have coffee, Blanche is all apologies and brittle smiles and then —

"You always overreact, Bea."

Bea thinks about that for a long time, that tossed-off statement as Blanche scraped the whipped cream off her coffee with a wooden stirrer, the slight bite in the words, the implied judgement.

But two days later, Bea picks up Eddie's phone — he doesn't password lock it, wouldn't even think to, which is classic Eddie — and sees the text.

It's a selfie of Blanche. Nothing sultry or sexy, nothing tacky, but a shot of her face pulling an exaggerated frown.

Missed you today!

Bea stares at that text, then scrolls up.

Again, it's maddening how little actual evidence there is, how there's not one definitive thing that tells her they're having an affair, one thing she could point to and ruin them both, but collectively . . .

A series of moments, of conversations. Of a closeness they've both denied is there.

Blanche's bad day, Eddie's frustration with how often Bea is gone. Funny little phrases that make no sense, but read like in-jokes, snapshots of something they share that has nothing to do with her.

It has honestly never occurred to her that Eddie would cheat on her, but it's the betrayal from Blanche that stings the most.

That actually hurts.

So really, it's only fair what happens between Bea and Tripp.

They're all over at Caroline's for a neighborhood barbecue, and Tripp is, as usual, drunk as a fucking skunk before the sun has fully set.

"They sure are getting cozy, aren't they?" he says to Bea as they watch Eddie and Blanche chat by the grill, Eddie holding a beer, Blanche a margarita. They're laughing, and it's the most relaxed and happy Bea has seen Eddie look in a while.

Blanche glances over then, seeing Bea and Tripp, and she just grins, raising her glass in greeting. Bea and Tripp raise their glasses, too, and everything is fine, everything is like it should be, all of them just the best of friends.

Only Bea notices the way Blanche's smile turns up at the corners, curdling into a smirk.

Only Bea notices how Eddie reaches out to touch Blanche's elbow to make a point.

"So, if they're fucking, do you think Eddie should give her a ten percent discount?" Bea asks Tripp now, and that startles a laugh out of him.

Tripp is better looking when he laughs. More like the Tripp that Blanche married.

The Tripp that Blanche had been in love with.

"Blanche should actually probably give him a twenty percent bonus," he replies, and Bea looks over her shoulder at him, grinning slowly, letting him see her gaze drift over him.

"I think maybe you're selling yourself a little short there, Tripp."

He's not, it turns out.

The sex he and Bea have in Caroline's upstairs bathroom is decidedly mediocre, and Bea doesn't even bother pretending to come, focusing instead on the heinous print Caroline has hanging on the wall, a banal picnic scene.

As Tripp groans against her neck, Bea thinks about how she'll have to send Caroline one of those new block color prints they just got in for Southern Manors' summer line.

As soon as it's over, Tripp is surprisingly remorseful, rubbing his hand over his face and saying, "I don't know why I did that."

Bea knows exactly why she did it — to get back at Blanche and Eddie, to take from Blanche before Blanche can take from her —

but she feels empty all the same.
  Later, Tripp texts her.

I'm sorry, but I'm not sorry, either.

Bea knows exactly how he feels.

■ ■ ■ ■

PART VII
JANE

■ ■ ■ ■

24

July

Over the next few weeks, I resolve to trust Eddie, to be the fiancée he wants and deserves. I go ahead and buy the dress I wanted from Irene's in the village, complete with a veil, new shoes, the whole thing.

And we talk about the wedding more. We're still planning on something small and simple, but here in Birmingham now, no more talk of eloping. We're back on track, finally.

I take up jogging even though the summer weather is getting oppressive, and Eddie warns me that I'm going to die of heatstroke. But I actually like the heat early in the morning, before the humidity sets in, the grass still wet and jewel-green as the sun climbs over the horizon. It feels good, the sweat running down my back, stinging my eyes behind my sunglasses.

Sometimes I see Emily and Campbell.

They're always walking, not running, and while Emily always waves at me and grins, there's something tight in Campbell's smile.

This morning, though, the streets are empty, the July temps too much for most people, even at 8 A.M., and I find myself turning down Tripp's street.

A first-degree murder charge, and he's still at home.

That's rich white guys for you, though.

I try not to think of Phoenix, of Mr. Brock gasping on the floor, of the sick fear I've lived with ever since that moment. If they'd caught me, if they'd found out what I did, do you think I'd be able to just hang out at Eddie's until the trial?

No, I'd be in an orange jumpsuit before I'd even had time to say the words *not guilty.*

It's another reminder that this world, the world these people live in, might as well be a different planet.

Tripp's lawyer was able to prove his client wasn't a flight risk, so he's still here in Thornfield Estates, waiting for the trial, which is still months away.

I tell myself that by the time he goes to trial, it won't matter as much. Eddie and I will be married by then, and even though Eddie will certainly have to testify, I can stay out of it.

That hasn't stopped me from reading everything I can about the case, though. I know that when they found Blanche, there was a massive fracture in her skull, and that Tripp had bought a hammer just a few days before Blanche went to the lake.

Dumbass used his credit card at the hardware store in Overton Village.

The theory is that Tripp surprised the women, talked them into taking out the boat even though they were all completely fucked up, and that *something* happened. A fight, an argument. Tripp was drunk, they all were. And it ended with Blanche in the water.

They don't know about Bea. Maybe she was screaming and he hit her, too. Maybe she was passed out, or down below in the boat when it all started going down. Maybe she came up, confused, disoriented, and Tripp pushed her overboard.

The cops have admitted to Eddie that getting a murder charge to stick to Tripp for Bea might be harder since they still haven't found her body and since there's no evidence on the boat. No blood, no DNA. It's all conjecture at this point, which is another part of why Tripp's lawyer was able to get him bail.

Well, that and Rich White Dude Privilege.

I pause now outside his house, a stitch in my side that I pinch with one hand as I stare at the windows, wondering what Tripp is doing in there. What he's thinking.

Eddie says he won't do much jail time, even if he's found guilty, because guys like him never do. Since the case is still mostly circumstantial, the DA might lower the charge to manslaughter, for a better shot at conviction. Tripp's lawyers will argue that all the prosecution has is Blanche's body, and a crack running up the back of her head. The fact that Tripp bought a hammer doesn't mean he used it to kill his wife, and she could've hit her head when she fell off the boat.

Upstairs, there's a flicker of movement, a drape being pulled back slightly, and I know Tripp is watching me.

I wait on the sidewalk for a bit, wondering if he'll come out or try to talk to me, but there are no further signs of life, and after a moment, I jog on.

The house is empty when I get home, Eddie already off to work, and I stop in the kitchen, grabbing a bottle of water out of the fridge and resting one hip against the counter as I drink deep, the water so cold it makes my teeth and my temple ache.

I've just set the bottle down when I hear a noise.

It's a thump from somewhere upstairs, just like the one I heard that night the cops first came to tell us about Blanche, and I stand there, frozen, listening.

Thump. Thump. Thump.

Like someone picking up and dropping something heavy.

"Hello?" I call. "Is someone there?"

Excellent, I've gone the full horror movie. Soon I'll be running down to the basement in my underwear in the dark.

But then there's a thump again, and my heart beats faster.

I move across the living room slowly, quietly, my ear cocked toward the ceiling, but there isn't another sound. I can't hear anything except the purring of the air conditioner and my own rasping breath.

The silence feels loud, weighted, my sweat cooling so fast on my skin that now I'm cold, and when my phone trills, I shriek.

My hands are even shaking slightly as I pull it out of the little pocket in my yoga pants, and I see Eddie's name on the screen.

"Hey, gorgeous," he says when I pick up, and he sounds so relaxed, so casual, that my heartbeat slows a little, some of the fear draining from my veins. "Just calling to see how your day was going."

I can hear noise in the background, the *thwap* of hammers on boards, a distant buzzsaw, so I know he must be on a job site, and I try to picture him there, his shirt rumpled, his sunglasses on.

"You just saw me two hours ago," I remind him. "Miss me already?"

I try to sound flirty, sexy, but Eddie must pick up on something in my voice because he asks, "Hey, everything alright over there?"

"I'm fine," I tell him, even as I keep my ear cocked toward the ceiling, still listening. "I just heard something in the house."

"Like what?" Eddie asks, and suddenly I feel very young, getting spooked by a noise in the house, like a kid left on her own.

"Just a thump," I tell him, shaking my head even though he can't see me. "Or a few thumps. It's so stupid, I know. Now I'm creeping around upstairs like I'm in a gothic novel or a bad horror movie."

I expect him to laugh, or make a joke. Instead, he says, "It's a big house, Jane. It makes all kinds of noises, especially in the summer."

"Sure," I say. "Like I said, stupid."

"Why don't you go back to bed, Nancy Drew?" he says, cajoling, and a spike of irritation shoots through me, angry and hot.

But I shove it down. He's trying to be nice, and I can't keep doing this, I can't keep trying to destroy a good thing that's right in front of me.

"Well, right now, I'm all sweaty and gross, so maybe a shower instead," I say, and he makes a low sound that would usually send desire spiking through me.

"Wish I were there and not here," he says, and I make myself sound appropriately intrigued as I reply, "You could always come home for lunch."

He sighs, and I'm actually a little relieved when he says, "Would that I could. But it's a big day on the Connors' place, then I need to drop by Southern Manors. I'll be home before five though, promise."

"I will hold you to it," I say, and after Eddie hangs up, I stand there in the hall, hands braced on the now-empty table.

There's a mirror over the table, and I look into it now. I'm pale despite my run, my hair scraggly and slightly greasy, and there are dark flakes of mascara under my eyes.

"Get your shit together," I mutter at my reflection, scraping my hair back from my face with both hands. The girl in the mirror looks feral, and I bare my teeth before shak-

ing my head at myself, laughing softly.
And then the knocking starts again.

25

When I used to walk dogs in the neighborhood, I sometimes thought about where people like Campbell, Emily, and Caroline went during the day, when they pulled out of Thornfield Estates in their oversized SUVs.

Not far, apparently. Today, we're at Roasted, for a meeting of the Neighborhood Beautification Committee. Campbell and Emily are both wearing athleisure, but I've dressed a little nicer, pairing a gray pencil skirt with a pink blouse and matching heels. I'm still not quite as tan or as glossy of hair as they both are, but I can see myself reflected in Emily's giant sunglasses, and I know I look a lot more like both of them than I did just a few months ago.

Making a mental note to ask Emily where she gets her hair done, I reach down into my bag — another new purchase, this massive leather purse that could probably hold

Adele — and pull out the binder I've carefully labeled *TENBC* in a pretty, swirly font.

"Look at yooooouuuuu," Emily says, reaching out to playfully shove at my arm. "So organized!"

I smile, not mentioning that I was up until 1 A.M. working on this and that it took a stupid amount of concealer to cover the circles under my eyes.

Or that while I sat on the floor of the living room, cutting pictures out of magazines and sliding them into the binder's plastic folders, I'd heard those thumps from upstairs again, the weird sounds Eddie had said not to worry about.

Just a couple, and faint enough that I hadn't jumped or shrieked this time, but I'd still made a mental note to call an exterminator.

Now, though, I'm all smiles as I lay the binder out on the table, my ring flashing in the sunlight.

Campbell leans forward to look more closely at the ring, just like I'd hoped she would.

"When's the wedding?" she asks, and Emily perks up a little, too.

Gossip as currency, yet again.

I look down at the binder, flipping through its pages. "Honestly, we're not sure. It was going to be fairly soon — something small, you know? Casual, at home . . ."

"I'm sure all of this with Tripp has made planning a wedding hard," Emily says, sympathetic, and I look up.

"We're mostly trying not to think about it," I say, which is true.

Both women hum in agreement, and then Campbell sighs, turning my binder to face her. She flips through the pictures, but I can tell she's not really looking at them.

"I found a couple of ideas from *Southern Living*," I say. "For the flower beds in the front of the neighborhood? On that fourth page —"

"Did you know the police found out Tripp was at the lake?"

Emily says it in almost a whisper, and I jerk my head up, surprised. That's new.

But I'm not as shocked as Campbell, apparently. She sits up so abruptly that she kicks the table, rattling the wrought iron.

"Are you fucking kidding me?" Campbell whips off her sunglasses, her blue eyes wide. "He was down there? Seriously?"

Emily nods, and I slide my binder back across the table to me. "That's what the police said. I think someone saw him? Or there are receipts? Like, the actual kind, not the Kardashian kind."

I laugh a little at that — who knew Emily had jokes? — but Campbell is still looking at both of us, her sunglasses dangling from her fingers.

"So . . . he really did it. He killed them."

"Of course, he did," I say, more sharply than I mean to, and they both turn to look at me.

Fuck.

Clearing my throat, I flip through the binder some more. "I just mean . . . the police are doing their jobs. They wouldn't have charged him if they weren't confident he did it."

Emily nods, but Campbell still looks unsure, chewing her lower lip, her leg jiggling. "It's just so weird," she says. "Tripp could be an asshole when he drank, don't get me wrong, but he wasn't . . . violent. And he loved Blanche."

I'd thought so, too, but now, I wonder if him falling to pieces after she died, him wandering the house and drinking all day wasn't grief, but guilt.

And Emily pipes up, "They *were* having some issues though, Cam. You know that."

They both glance at me, quickly, then at each other, and I know what this is about.

"Tripp told me," I tell them, "that there were rumors about Eddie and Blanche."

Another shared glance, and I think they might try to bullshit me, but then Emily shrugs and says, "I mean. They were spending a lot of time together. And Bea was never around."

"Never," Campbell says, shaking her head. "That company was her whole life. Especially in those last few months. We barely ever saw her."

"That's true," Emily adds. "When we first moved into the neighborhood, Bea definitely spent more time with us." She smiles, tapping my binder. "She did stuff like this. But last spring, she was missing meetings, passing on parties . . ."

"But do you think . . ." I let the question dangle, and I see them look at each other again.

"No," Emily finally says. "But Bea and Blanche were kind of weird right before all of it happened."

Campbell sucks in a breath, sitting back in her chair, her gaze again darting to Emily.

"What?" Emily asks her, sipping her coffee. "It's true, and they're both dead. It's not like it can hurt anyone now to acknowledge it. Besides," she adds, waving a hand, rings throwing off showers of sparks, "it wasn't anything juicy. I think it had to do with Bea's mom or something. Back before Eddie was even in the picture."

I can see where that kind of gossip isn't interesting to them, but damn, do I wish I knew more about it. Hearing that Bea and Blanche had some kind of tension isn't new — Tripp had said the same thing — but why, exactly? I know there is something in that friendship that I am missing, and I can't shake the thought that figuring it out is key to understanding Eddie. I try another angle. "Did Bea have a temper?"

Both women laugh, shaking their heads as Campbell takes the lid off her coffee to drain the cup.

"Oh my god, no," Emily says. "She was sweet as pie. Tough, sure, ambitious and all that. But a real doll. I never saw her get mad at anybody. Not even when that catering company she hired completely screwed up her and Eddie's anniversary party. It was supposed to be Hawaiian luau-themed, but they brought, I don't remember, what was it, Cam?"

"Finger food," she replies. "Like it was a tea party. Little cucumber sandwiches, petit fours, that kind of thing. Bea just laughed it off. Eddie was the one who —"

She stops abruptly, glancing at me, then shrugs it off. "Anyway, no, Bea never even got mildly irritated as far as I could tell."

Silence descends, hanging awkwardly between us for a moment before Emily asks brightly, "So, are we all going to the country club tomorrow night?"

Oh, right. Another fundraiser, another thing stuck on my fridge because I'm one of these women now, the kind who goes to fundraisers at country clubs.

I smile at them.

"Wouldn't miss it."

As we stand up to leave, Campbell's eyes slide down my body. "Wow," she says. "You look . . . great, Jane. Really."

"Doesn't she?" Emily says, giving me another pat on the arm. "I think she might wear pencil skirts even better than Bea, and that was, like, her entire thing."

She's still smiling, but something about the comment bugs me. I hadn't consciously been emulating Bea, but I see now how I must look like I put on a Bea costume for this meeting. Me and my pencil skirt and binder, like some kind of pale imitation.

The ghost of Bea.

The thought unsettles me all the way home, and when I come in, I look at myself in the hall mirror.

My hair brushes my shoulders in the same long bob Bea wore. The earrings I'm wearing remind me of ones I've seen in pictures of her.

I'm even wearing the same shade of red lipstick.

Turning away, I pick up my purse, taking the binder back out.

She did stuff like this.

Do I want to be the new Bea to these people? Or do I want them to accept me as Jane?

I don't know anymore.

My phone buzzes, and I sigh, reaching into my bag to fish it out.

It's a text from John.

Hey, friendo, it starts, and fuck me, I hate him so much.

Little short on cash this week. Another $500 should cover it. You can mail it again. Cash. Xo

My fingers hover over the keys.

I could tell him to fuck off.

I could text Eddie.

And then I reach into my purse and pull out the folded sheet of paper, the one Eddie gave me with the Phoenix number scrawled across it.

Or I could find out who's looking for me. What they actually want. What they know.

And finally put this all to rest, so that I

can move on with my life.

Fingers trembling, I start to dial.

26

The Baptist church where John works isn't one of the bigger congregations in the area. In the South, I've noticed, some churches take up entire blocks.

John's hardly looks like a church at all. It's a squat, ugly brick building, and only the stained-glass window of Jesus surrounded by lambs tips you off to the fact that it's a house of worship.

I've dressed in one of my best outfits today, a blue pleated skirt with a white boatneck blouse, paired with blue-and-white-striped ballet flats and silver jewelry. When I'd looked in the mirror this morning, I almost hadn't recognized myself. I didn't look like the Jane I'd been two months ago, but I also didn't look like I was trying to copy Emily or Campbell.

Or Bea.

I looked like . . . me.

Whoever that was turning out to be.

My shoulders are back as I open the door, my head high, and when I step inside, the girl sitting at the desk gives me a bright smile.

She probably thinks I'm here to donate money.

She's half-right.

"Hiiiiii," I drawl, sliding my sunglasses up on my head. "Is John Rivers here?"

I don't miss it, the way her smile droops just the littlest bit.

I feel you, girl.

"He's in the music room," she says, pointing down the hall, and I thank her.

The church smells like burnt coffee and old paper, the linoleum squeaking under my shoes as I make my way to a room at the end of the hall where I can already hear jangling guitar chords.

John is sitting on a riser in the middle of the room, a music stand in front of him. I can see the cover of his sheet music book. *Praise Songs for Joyful Hearts.*

Appropriate, because my heart is pretty fucking joyful right now.

His fingers slide on the strings as he looks up and sees me there, and I register that beat, the fractional moment before he recognizes me.

He's wearing his navy polo today, the one

with the church's logo on the chest, and his hair has been combed back from his face. He's also wearing an awfully nice new pair of sneakers, and if I doubted it before, I now know that not all of Eddie's money went to a new sound system.

"Jane." John gets up, putting the guitar down, and I hold a hand up.

"I won't be here long," I tell him. "I just dropped in to let you know that I finally talked with your mysterious Phoenix contact."

The blood literally drains from his face. I watch it, the way his cheeks fade from ruddy pink to a sickly sort of gray, and it almost makes the shit he put me through worth it.

But not quite.

"You know, he was actually kind of a nice guy. Especially when I explained to him that anything you had told him was bullshit."

I can still feel the shock, the sheer fucking *relief* that had coursed through me as the voice on the other end of that mysterious phone number told me that he was employed by a Georgie Smith, who was looking for her sister, Liz. That Georgie thought Liz had had a daughter who had ended up in foster care in Arizona, that she might have gone by the name Helen Burns, and that Georgie would like to meet her.

I'd made myself sound regretful, almost a little wistful as I'd confirmed that I'd been in foster care with Helen, but that last I heard, she'd gotten involved in drugs, and I thought she might have headed even further west, Seattle, maybe? No, Portland. One of those. But in any case, I hadn't heard from her or seen her in years, and — a lowered voice here, a conspiratorial whisper — I wouldn't bother talking to John Rivers any further. John Rivers had a history of conning older women like Mrs. Smith — he'd string her along, promise he knew her niece, then he'd never deliver. The private investigator didn't sound surprised, just said he knew the type and thanked me for my time.

When I'd hung up the phone, I'd waited for real regret, knowing I'd just snipped the one thin thread still holding me to any family. And a year ago, even a few months ago, knowing my mom had had a sister who was looking for me would've made me feel almost pathetically grateful. Aunt Georgie.

Now, it was just another loose end to tie up. I'd made my choice, made my family, and I was closing the door on all of it.

And most importantly, now I was certain: no one knew what had really happened in Phoenix.

I'd gotten away.

John is still staring at me, his throat working, and I wonder if this is how good he felt when he surprised me in the Home Depot parking lot.

If so, I almost don't blame him for doing it.

"Anyway, I made sure he knew you were shady as fuck, and, just for a little extra flavor, I might've implied you were also kind of pervy and obsessed with me, so he will definitely not be answering any more of your calls."

That part's not true, but it's too fun to watch him sweat.

Still, he's not totally beaten yet. "You did something, Jane," he says. "You ran from something. Or you never would've paid me." He steps forward. "You never would've come to live with me in the first place if you weren't on the run. We were in the same group home for what? Two months? You barely knew me. But you needed somewhere to hide. Tell me I'm wrong."

"I don't have to tell you shit," I say, and he glances at the door, wincing a little.

I look over my shoulder, remembering the girl at the desk, remembering where we are, and almost laugh. "Are you . . . worried about me swearing? In this conversation about you blackmailing me?"

312

I move closer, my new expensive handbag dangling in the crook of my elbow, Eddie's ring winking on my finger.

"You are smarter than I ever gave you credit for, I'll allow that," I tell him. "But *this* is over now. You don't call me, you don't call Eddie, you forget you ever knew me or that I ever existed."

His face is sullen, but he still says, "Forget you? Or forget Helen Burns?"

My heart still thuds heavily in my chest when I hear that name.

It's over.

She's gone now.

"Get fucked, John," I tell him sweetly, and then glance up at the picture on the wall, another portrait of Jesus, this time with a bunch of kids around his feet instead of lambs.

"Sorry," I mouth at him with an exaggerated grimace, and then I walk out.

As I pass the desk again, I see the girl watching me with obvious curiosity on her face, and I give her another smile as I pull a checkbook out of my purse.

"My fiancé and I had heard your church was in need of a new music system."

I leave the church several thousand dollars poorer, but a truckload smugger. Let John ever try shit like this again now that his boss, the Reverend Ellis, came out to shake my hand and thank me effusively for my generosity, promising me that both Eddie and I will be thanked in every church program from here on out.

I want John to see that every Sunday.

Mr. Edward Rochester, and his wife, Mrs. Jane Rochester.

Okay, maybe I jumped the gun a little with the wife bit, but we *are* getting married. Eddie *is* innocent. And I'm — free.

I get into the car, my hands wrapped around the steering wheel, and I take a deep breath.

It isn't like I killed Mr. Brock, after all. Killing someone and letting them die are two different things.

He deserved it.

He let Jane die. The real Jane, the one I loved, the one who was the best friend I ever had, my sister, even if we didn't share any blood. We'd shared a home, though. We'd shared a nightmare.

She was always puny, always small. Always getting whatever cold or stomach bug went around our school. Usually, I could help. Vitamin C, orange juice. Taking notes for her so she didn't get behind.

But that last time, she got sick and didn't get better. The cough got wetter, deeper.

Her fever ran higher.

You have to take her to the doctor, you have to, I'd begged the Brocks, but they'd make excuses, like they always had.

She's fine, she's faking, it's not that bad.

Jane died in my bed, huddled next to me, her body glowing so hot I could hardly hold her.

But I did hold her. I held her as she gasped for breath and shook and finally went still.

Pneumonia. It might have killed her even if the Brocks had gotten her to a hospital. She was so weak already.

I would never know.

So it had felt like a kind of poetic justice, that night that it was just me and Mr. Brock in the house. Mrs. Brock was at bingo, and by then, I was the only foster kid in their care.

He'd been watching TV, a baseball game, and some call had pissed him off. Sometimes that had meant one of us got hit, but that night, he'd just stood up, screaming at the television, his face red.

I'd been sitting at the kitchen table, filling out paperwork for a shitty fast-food job when he'd suddenly gasped, clutched his chest.

He'd had heart issues for a while. I never

knew what was actually wrong with him, but I'd assumed a diet of whiskey, fries, and Pure Fucking Evil hadn't helped.

He had pills for it. Big ones in an orange bottle, and he'd choked that word out as he turned to me, his face the color of old milk.

Pills.

I hadn't gotten them.

He'd hit his knees, his mouth opening and closing like a fish out of water, his eyes bugging out of his head.

Mr. Brock wasn't a big man, wasn't much bigger than me, really, but I still liked him there on his knees. I'd gotten up, stood over him while he stared at me, uncomprehending.

The word had come so easily to my lips.

Die.

I wanted him to die. For Jane.

So, I stood there, and watched him struggle and gasp, and when he tried to reach for his pills, just there on the little table between the two recliners, I'd taken them. Held them in front of him. Let him see that I had them.

And then I'd gone into the kitchen and poured them down the sink with shaking hands, turning on the garbage disposal for good measure.

I only left the house when I was sure he'd stopped breathing.

For the past five years, I've run from that night, from the knowledge that surely people remembered I was the only one at home when Mr. Brock dropped dead.

But I'd forgotten how disposable people like me really were. No one connected me leaving with him dying.

He had a heart condition, after all. And Helen had simply left town. She'd been just shy of her eighteenth birthday, a high school graduate, ageing out of the system already.

I'd left with Jane's ID in my purse. Jane, who looked enough like me to be my real sister.

And I'd started over.

Successfully, it turned out.

Smiling, I start the car and head home. My new home.

My real home.

27

"Which dress should I wear?" I ask, and Eddie glances at the options I've laid out on the bed.

There are three: a simple cream-colored sheath dress, a sexier black number, and then a dress I'd ordered off of Southern Manors. Deep plum purple, green leaves embroidered on the Peter Pan collar, the sleeves capped. It's way more twee than anything I'd usually wear, but I was curious what the dresses Bea had designed were like, and I wanted to see if Eddie would recognize it. And if he did, would he say anything?

But if the dress is familiar at all, he doesn't show it. He just nods at the cream one and says, "I like that."

So I head off to my first country club cocktail party feeling slightly like a sacrificial virgin. The dress that had looked so sophisticated on the hanger is actually a little too long for me, the hem hitting me below my knees, the high collar a little too high, nearly bumping my jaw and making my skin look sallow.

The Country Club of Birmingham is a beautiful, tasteful Tudor-style building set far back on a wide green lawn and surrounded by old-growth trees. As we walk up the drive, I take in the stone and wooden timbers, the lights spilling out from the windows, and move closer to Eddie. We've done fancy restaurants and the church function, but this feels like some new test, one I'm not sure I've studied enough for.

Even in the evening, the summer air is so hot and heavy it feels like trying to breathe directly over a humidifier, but the flowers in the heavy planters just outside the front door are bright pink, and everything feels so vital, so alive.

Everything except for the people currently filing into the room.

They're all clones of the people I've seen in the village, or at the Methodist church's silent auction: slightly florid men in suits, excellently dressed women in bright colors with hair that isn't just blond or brown, but a thousand different shades of both, created by an expensive hairdresser.

The cost of the jewelry in this one room is

probably the GNP of some small countries. Maybe even some not-so-small ones.

There are tables along the back wall loaded down with food, and waiters are circulating with trays of canapés, but no one seems to be eating.

Drinking, though? That, they're doing plenty of.

It doesn't surprise me that the bar is set up in the middle of the room, creating a hub for guests to mill around. And when I get close, I can see that there's nothing but top-shelf stuff on offer.

Eddie's hand is a warm weight on my lower back, reminding me that I belong there, and I smile up at him.

Yet it's situations like these — seeing him here amongst these other men, the husbands of the women I've been studying so intently for the last few months — that remind me how much he stands out. How different he seems.

"Drink?" he asks me, and I nod.

"White wine, please."

He makes his way through the crowd around the bar, leaving me to stand there awkwardly, my hands clasped in front of me.

"Jane!"

I see Emily smiling at me, gesturing with one elegant hand.

She places one skinny tanned arm around my shoulders and pulls me into the group standing there in their cocktail dresses, and I wait for the surge of triumph to come, the smugness that I've transformed myself from dog-walker to one of them in just a handful of months.

But I don't feel anything like that. Mostly, I just want to go home.

"Jaaane," Emily drawls tipsily, "you know everyone now, don't you?"

"Hi, girls," I say brightly, and they all smile in return.

I'm one of them now.

"Girl, that dress is *so* good," Landry says. She's wearing something similar, so maybe it's not so much a compliment to me as to herself.

She's also wearing a great bracelet, a slender gold bangle with a little charm dangling from it, and I am already wondering if there's any way to slip it from her wrist without her noticing.

Fuck, no, I remind myself. *You don't have to do that shit anymore, and if you did, it would basically be suicide, just ask her where she got it and go buy one just like it.*

But that idea doesn't hold nearly as much appeal, so instead I wave her compliment off. "Oh, thank you. I couldn't decide what to wear, just decided to go simple."

"Is Eddie here?" Emily asks, and I nod again, gesturing behind me.

"I left him in pursuit of Woodford Reserve," I say, and all five women give those weird fake laughs like I've said something funny.

Actually, Eddie has been drinking more lately, the recycling full of empty bottles. I resolved to keep a closer eye on him tonight, especially since he's driving.

Of course, I don't mention any of this to *the girls*.

But Caroline seems to pick up on something in my tone, because she says, rather pointedly, "I still just can't believe Tripp Ingraham could have killed his wife and her best friend."

Over her shoulder, I see a man dressed far more casually than anyone else here, camera lifted as he points and shoots. Where do photos like these even end up? Who wants to look at a bunch of housewives gossiping?

"I mean, he's still saying he had nothing to do with . . ." Caroline's voice drops to a whisper. "The murders. And there's definitely going to be a trial . . ." She pauses, then stares directly at me. "Well, the whole thing must be such a nightmare for the both of you."

It feels so infuriating and yet so . . . fucking *apt* that Tripp Ingraham might be the one to ruin this whole thing for me. It's what the Tripps of the world do, after all. Fuck shit up for people like me.

"We're praying over it," I finally say, and lo and behold, that shuts them right up. The women all nod firmly, Anna-Grace even murmuring, "Amen."

The party is still going full-swing when Eddie and I decide to leave around ten or so. People are getting drunker, the music is getting louder, and I'm tired of smiling for photos.

"Did you have a nice time?" Eddie asks, and I'm tired enough to tell the truth.

"Not really."

That makes him laugh as he loosens his tie. "I hear you. Those people are . . . something else."

We make our way to our car, feet crunching on the gravel.

"Have you thought more about leaving?" I ask, and then turn to look over my shoulder at him. "I mean, I know what you said about Bea wanting to keep Southern Manors an Alabama company. But you could sell it, couldn't you?" I pause, worrying for a moment that I've gone too far. "I just mean that neither of us are from here. We could start over somewhere new."

He stops then. "Would you want to?"

A few weeks ago, I would've said no, that Thornfield Estates was the dream. But now that I've seen some of the underbelly of what I thought was a perfect place, I'm not so sure.

"I could," I finally say. "If you wanted to."

Eddie tips his head back, looking at the sky. "It would be nice," he replies, but that's not really an answer.

Then he starts walking toward the car, only to pull up short again.

"You dropped something," he says, leaning down to pluck a gold bangle bracelet off the ground.

I take Landry's bracelet and slide it back into my handbag. "Oh that. Thanks."

28

"Are you worried?" I ask as the car winds down the steep hill from the country club. The three glasses of sauvignon blanc I drank on an empty stomach have loosened my tongue. The purr of the motor is quiet, and there's no traffic up here, no sound, really, except for the soft sigh Eddie gives as he places a hand on my knee.

"About Tripp? I mean, I'm not *not* worried, that's for damn sure."

He reaches up and unbuttons the top button of his shirt, and when I glance over, in the dim light from the dashboard, I can see the shadows underneath his eyes, the hollow of his cheekbones.

I reach over and place a hand on his leg. "It's going to be alright," I assure him. "Now that Tripp has been arrested —"

Scoffing, Eddie draws his own hand back, placing it on the wheel as he negotiates another turn. "That's not exactly an end to it," he says. "There's going to be a trial, there will be reporters, there will be more questions . . ."

Trailing off, he shakes his head. "It's a fucking mess."

I think about what Campbell had started to say the other day at coffee, about Eddie's temper. The caterer who screwed up, Bea laughing it off, but Eddie . . .

No.

No, I told myself I wasn't going to allow those kinds of thoughts anymore. He asked me to trust him, and I will.

"We've got each other," I remind him.

Eddie's expression softens slightly as he looks over at me. "Yeah, there is that, isn't there?"

He smiles, leaning over to lightly brush his lips over my cheek. He smells good, like he always does, but underneath the spicy, expensive scent of cologne is the smokier smell of bourbon, and for a minute, I'm reminded so viscerally of Tripp that I nearly jerk my head back.

But Eddie is nothing like Tripp, and we've just been at a party, for fuck's sake. Of course he smells a little like nice booze. I probably still smell like those glasses of sauvignon blanc Emily pushed on me.

The house is lit up as we pull into the

driveway, and I wonder if there will ever be a time when I get used to the idea that I live here. That this gorgeous house is all mine.

Well, mine and Eddie's.

I have another glass of wine when we get in while Eddie answers some late-night emails, and then I decide I'm going to take a bath. I can't get enough of that giant tub, of being able to use it whenever I want.

Walking into the bathroom, I'm already shucking off my dress, letting it hit the marble floor without a care in the world even though it costs more than my rent at John's place did.

I'd brought a smaller clutch with me tonight, holding just my phone, lipstick, and some mints — and now, Landry's bracelet — and as I toss it to the counter, I hear my phone chirp.

Frowning, I pull it out of the bag, some little part of my mind wondering if someone noticed the bracelet, but when I see who the message is from, my stomach lurches.

We need to talk.

It's Tripp.

I sag back against the sink, staring at the screen as another text comes in.

I understand if you want to tell me to fuck off, but I didn't do this.

And for some reason, I feel like you might believe me.

I wait the space of three breaths, then four, and the last text comes in.

Which means you're in danger.

"Janie?"

I startle as Eddie appears in the doorway, his tie undone around his neck. "What's wrong?" he asks, then frowns. "You're pale."

Tell him, I think. *You lied to him about John and look how upset he got, don't lie about this.*

"Too much wine," I say, sheepish. "And Emily just texted me about some stuff for the NBC," I add, waggling my phone at him.

Eddie shakes his head. " 'The NBC.' For all that talk about moving, you're sounding like one of them."

His smile is fond, and I give him my best flirty one in response. "You know you love it."

"I love you," he counters, and my smile falters just a little, but thankfully, he's already turning away.

"Love you, too," I say.

And then I text Tripp.

Tell me when.

■ ■ ■ ■

PART VIII
BEA

■ ■ ■ ■

The party is held at the Tutweiler, an old hotel in Birmingham that Bea has always loved. Blanche had her wedding here just six months ago, and Bea had known then that she'd have to host some kind of event here herself.

The launch of the latest Southern Manors line plus the celebration of the company going public seems like the perfect occasion, and Bea spends months planning every detail. When the time finally arrives, the reception is even better than she'd hoped for.

The ballroom is decorated with Southern Manors items, each table holding a sterling silver apple, or a crystal pig, or a blown glass vase decorated with a gingham ribbon. It's classy and elegant, but warm and friendly, the exact brand Bea has worked to cultivate over the past few years.

She tries to be the embodiment of that brand herself, her dress beautifully made and outrageously expensive, but not overly dressy, her jewelry understated.

Blanche looks overdressed in a long black dress, her diamonds on display, and Bea enjoys that more than she should, enjoys Blanche seeming out of place in this space that was originally hers.

It's a perfect night, and Bea is the perfect hostess even though, as she looks at all the couples around the room, it occurs to her that she should probably pair herself up at some point. It's the one thing missing in her life, a partner, and as she watches Blanche slip her arm through Tripp's, she wonders why she hasn't given any thought to her romantic life before now.

She knows it's mostly because she had more important things to do, that Southern Manors has been her entire world since she graduated from college, but she suddenly feels the lack keenly and resolves to do something about it.

But not tonight.

Tonight is for her, for her success. For what she's made from nothing.

Her mother is there, wearing a mint-green dress that Bea picked out for her because she thought it would look pretty with the soft red of her mother's hair. But she sees now she chose wrong — it only brings out the yellow, jaundiced look of her skin, makes her seem tired and faded.

"Mama, do you want to go up to your room?" she asks quietly, leaning close as her mother sits at a table, a bottle of sparkling water by her elbow. Bea has given all the waitstaff strict instructions not to give her mother a drink, and so far, they seem to have been complying.

"No," Mama says softly, reaching up with a trembling hand to push her hair back. She's wearing her diamonds tonight, too. Not as ostentatious as Blanche's, and in dire need of a cleaning given how dully they attempt to glitter, and Bea can't believe she forgot to get Mama new accessories, something from Southern Manors.

"So proud of you, Bertha-Bear," Mama says, smiling, and Bea doesn't even correct the name. Tonight, she's finally put that past behind her, emerged shiny and new.

She circulates the rest of the night, and that was the mistake. She should've kept an eye on her mother, should've insisted she go on up to her room.

And, of course, she doesn't realize that mistake until she's on the dais, giving a speech, thanking everyone for coming, for making Southern Manors a success. For making *her* a success.

"Southern Manors is a family," she says, her

voice ringing over the sound system. "And the seed for this company started with my own family. With my mother's antiques. My grandmother's quilts. My father's love of a weighty bourbon glass."

The crowd laughs politely, and Bea clutches the edge of the podium, thinking that her father never gave a shit what he was drinking out of so long as the alcohol kept flowing. That she'd never met her grandmother, that anything of any value in her mother's home had been sold off before she'd even been born.

She knows these things are lies, but they're lies she's been telling for so long, it doesn't even occur to her Mama won't go along with the act. Why wouldn't she when it's these very lies that keep her in booze and Neiman Marcus?

Bea can see it playing out before it even happens, which is what makes it even worse when there's nothing she can do to stop it. She sees her mother rise from her seat, the stagger in her step, the way she sways even when she's standing still. Bea's throat clenches and her heart sinks somewhere near her knees.

"Bertha, what in god's name are you talking about?" Mama calls, her voice ringing out over the crowd even though the words are slurred.

A few heads turn her way, and Bea remembers that no one here, no one but Blanche knows it's her real name.

"Her daddy didn't know a bourbon glass from a beer bottle," Mama goes on cheerfully, like this is all some funny anecdote, like she's not punching holes in everything Bea has built.

Authenticity. It's one of the fucking buzzwords on all their marketing materials, and here her mother is, blowing it all to shit.

"And her Nana Frances died before —"

It seems to happen in slow motion. Mama turning to regale her tablemates, the waiter moving forward at the same time, tray of champagne glasses lifted high. Not just any glasses, of course, but Southern Manors' glasses, little champagne coupes shaped like peach halves, complete with glass leaves.

The collision is almost balletic, almost. Mama stepping on the hem of her dress, the waiter attempting to both catch her and somehow hang on to his tray.

Mama hits the ground to the sound of shattering glass, the waiter awkwardly crouched next to her, finally abandoning his tray to grip Mama's elbow.

And Mama is laughing.

There's a bloom of bright red blood on the heel of her hand, and she wipes it absentmindedly on her dress as Bea looks on, frozen.

335

"Whoopsy-daisy!" Mama calls out, laughing again, her face red, and still, Bea can't move, can't make herself cross the ballroom to see if she's okay or to help her to her feet.

It's Blanche who does that.

Years later, Bea will remember that so vividly, the way Blanche had helped Mama to her feet, babbling about these old carpets, about new shoes, giving Mama all the excuses she could want for what's just happened as if it isn't painfully clear just how drunk she is.

Only when Blanche glances over at her does Bea feel her limbs start to work again, and she makes her way over to the two of them, a rictus smile on her face as she takes her mother's other arm.

"Let's get you upstairs," she says, and her mother, still smiling and floating happily on her cloud of booze and god knows what else, lets herself be led from the room like a child.

Later, Bea and Blanche sit in the living room of Bea's suite. Blanche has a glass of wine, but Bea is drinking bottled water, unable to even stand the smell of alcohol right now.

"Why didn't you tell me it was this bad?" Blanche asks, and what can Bea say? That she didn't know it was this bad? That's a lie. That she didn't want anyone else to know how bad it really was?

That's closer to the truth, but it feels too hard

to admit, too shameful and big. Instead, she shrugs and says, "I've been so busy, I haven't spent much time with her lately. I always knew she liked her evening cocktail, but this . . ."

She lets her gaze go slightly vague as though she's never contemplated a world in which her mother gets drunk and embarrasses her, as if that hadn't been a regular part of her childhood.

"Maybe she needs some help," Blanche suggests. She tilts her wineglass up to drink more, then pauses, looks at the glass, and seems to realize that discussing rehab while guzzling pinot grigio might send a mixed message.

"I'll go back down to Calera," Bea finally says, setting her water bottle down on the bar with a thump. "Look after her a bit, get her back on the right path."

Blanche's brow wrinkles. "Are you sure —" she starts, but Bea cuts her off with a wave of her hand.

"I know what she needs." No one knew her mother like Bea.

January, Six Months after Blanche
Eddie didn't come back for nearly a week after we slept together.

I'd expected it, in a way. I knew I'd fucked up, hinting about how he could trust me, but as the days slid by, I'd started to wonder if maybe this was finally it. Maybe he was just going to let my supplies run out, let me starve to death up here.

I couldn't stop picturing it, my skeleton on this comfy bed with its white sheets, some new family moving in one day, finding me there. Maybe I'd become a ghost. Maybe I'd haunt this house forever, wailing away upstairs.

When I'd sold my mother's house, the one she died in, I'd wondered whether her spirit was still there, wandering the halls.

But then, today, Eddie came back.

He had supplies this time and more books, like he'd felt guilty. I tried to decide whether it was for the sex or for staying away, but I couldn't read him.

He just stood there for the longest time, looking at me as I sat on the bed, and I held my breath, waiting.

And then he crossed the room, scooping me up in his arms with this hungry sound, kissing me so hard I felt my teeth press against my lips, drawing the littlest bit of blood.

It had worked. Reminding him of what we were to each other. What we could be again. Even with my fuckup, he'd come back, and he still wanted me.

And I wanted him. Just as much, just as badly.

In spite of everything.

What the fuck am I going to do with that?

February, Seven Months after Blanche
Eddie was different today.

I couldn't tell you why or how, just that something seemed off. He was rumpled again, like he hadn't been sleeping well, and for the first time in weeks, we didn't have sex. He just dropped off the water and food, and said he had to go.

There was a drop of blood on his shirt. Just on the cuff. A scrape, too, there on his wrist.

I asked him what happened, but he said it was nothing.

He didn't look me in the eyes, though.

I hate this, feeling like I'm tracking his moods like the weather. Things were good, things were working, he had started to trust me. And now he's distant again, dropping off food, barely stopping to talk.

He looks better each time he comes in, too. More like himself.

Like the monster I witnessed on Smith Lake is slowly re-forming into the Eddie I fell for, the Eddie I married.

He's more confident in his skin now, and I wonder what has changed.

A girl.

Of course, there's a girl.

Eddie didn't tell me. I just know.

Today, when he came in, he was the closest to the Eddie I met in Hawaii that I've seen since that terrible night. Handsome. Competent. In control.

He couldn't pull off that kind of turnaround by himself. I know Eddie. He is at his best when he has someone to reflect off of, someone to be *someone* for.

I wondered who she was. Some woman from the neighborhood? Someone I knew? I try to imagine him with Emily or Campbell, with Landry Cole, but it's almost impossible. Eddie didn't like those women, always said they were boring compared to me.

At night, I lie on the bed, and I try to picture her, this new woman I know Eddie has in his thrall.

Is she younger than me? Prettier?

Does she know what he is?

When Eddie came up tonight, he was a little drunk.

That was a first.

He brought me a bottle of wine, too.

Okay, a small box of wine, the type that holds three glasses. No corkscrews or glass for me, I guess, but still, I hadn't had wine in so long, and the first sip went straight to my head.

Eddie sat on the bed next to me, his hand on my thigh, but he didn't make any move to take it further than that, even though I wanted him to.

I hated myself for it, but I still wanted him to.

"You're seeing someone, aren't you?" I asked.

I was drunk enough to say it.

He was drunk enough to answer.

"I am."

I'd been expecting that, but it still slammed into me, the words causing physical pain.

I felt like I couldn't breathe.

"Who?" I asked, and his eyes clouded over a little as he looked away, his hand sliding from my leg.

"No one you know."

That was all he would say.

He left right after that, brushing a kiss against my temple, and now I'm lying here, tears soaking my pillow.

They should be tears of fear. If Eddie has met someone, how much longer is he going to keep me in here? Surely, I'm a huge liability to him now.

But I'm not afraid.

I'm . . . angry.

Hurt.

Jealous.

Her name is Jane.

I got Eddie to tell me that much.

Today when he came in, I had just gotten out of the shower. That wasn't intentional — I never know when he'll show up, after all — but it still worked in my favor.

As soon as he saw me, standing there in a towel, his eyes went dark, hungry, and it was the easiest thing in the world to let the towel drop to the floor, to open my arms to him.

Afterward, he was like he always is after sex — looser, more vulnerable.

Easier.

"What she's like?" I asked, and almost without thinking, he replied, "Jane?"

Jane.

Her name is Jane. A simple one. A plain one. Is she a simple, plain girl?

"She's . . ." He trailed off, and I saw the guilt flicker across his face as he summoned her up in his mind even as he lay here in my bed.

"She's nothing like you," he finally said, and I wondered how he meant that.

But mostly, I wondered about her.

Was she downstairs in my house even now? Did she think about me, Eddie's poor dead wife?

Did she hate me?

I would hate me if I were someone else.

April, Nine Months after Blanche

It was stupid, the thing with the bed. I just wondered if she'd be able to hear it, *Jane,* somewhere below. I needed her to know that all of this — the house, the husband — is still mine.

Eddie asked me about it when he came

343

up later. "Were you making noise up here?"

I spread my hands wide, inviting him to take in the room, to take in me. "How could I?" I asked, and he shook his head.

"Right," he said, and turned to go.

I took his hand.

He didn't leave.

May, Ten Months after Blanche

The days are relentlessly ticking by and I feel sanity slipping from me again. How has it been so many months since Blanche and I disappeared? And why am I still up here?

Sometimes it feels like I have my husband back. Some mornings I wake up convinced that this is the day that he's going to tell me it's all over, that I can come out of hiding now — until I remember *her.*

I know a lot about Jane now. She was a foster kid, she lived in Arizona. Eddie met her because she was walking dogs in the neighborhood, but she lived in Center Point with some creep. She has brown hair, like me, but a few shades lighter. Apparently, she's funny.

And she's twenty-three.

Twenty-three.

There was a softness in Eddie's face when he talked about her. It wasn't a look I was familiar with. Eddie had looked at me with hunger, with anger, with admiration, but never softness.

What does that mean? Does he love her?

Does he still love me?

Because I think I still love him. In spite of it all.

June, Eleven Months after Blanche
I fucked up again.

Eddie came in today. He kissed me, he took me to the bed, he fucked me, and after it was over, I thought about him going back downstairs, back to Jane, and I said the thing that has been sitting inside me for weeks now.

"So is it hard, having a new girlfriend when you have a wife upstairs?"

He'd been getting dressed, and I saw the muscles in his back tense.

I shouldn't have said it.

I'd had to say it.

And then he looked at me and said, "Is that really a problem you want me to focus on, Bea? Do you really want me to think about how I might solve it?"

He left right after that.

FUCK.

Still no sign of him. It's been days. Is he just leaving me to die? That would certainly be an easy solution to his "problem."

For him.

Not so easy for me.

I've got my little hoard of food and water, some of it hidden under the bed, and I've started counting it obsessively, even though I know the counting is bad, and I shouldn't.

But I don't know what else to do. It's the only thing I feel in control of right now.

He came back today. Four days he left me on my own. I was so grateful to see him that I threw myself into his arms, breathing him in, and I felt his arms tighten around me, heard him murmur my name against my hair.

He'd missed me, too. But will it be enough?

July, a Year after Blanche

This is my last entry. Eddie is in the shower, and I have to hurry.

Jane, I know you'll find this. Eddie cares about you, respects you, and that means you're smart. I'm putting this book in the pocket of his blazer. It's too warm for him to put it back on when he goes downstairs, so I'm hoping he won't even feel that it's there.

Regardless, I have to risk it. For myself,

and for you, Jane. Please. Please find this. Please find me. I can't survive here any longer.

I'm upstairs. You have to walk to the end of the hall and go through a closet. I don't know the code to the door, but I think it might be the same as the code to the lake house, my birthday. Eddie isn't good with numbers.

Jane, I am begging you.

Save me. Save yourself.

Please.

Her childhood was so absurdly Southern gothic she sometimes thinks she must've made it up.

But no, she actually made her past blander and more boring, a pastel replica of Blanche's childhood. That was really for the best, though. No one wanted to know about the Too Big House in the middle of West Alabama. The dad who drank too much, whose fists were fast even when he was drunk. The mom who'd checked out on vodka and Klonopin so early in Bea's childhood that she couldn't remember her mother ever playing with or reading to her.

She hadn't been Bea then, of course. Back then, she was still Bertha. Bertha Lydia Mason. Bertha had been her dad's mother, Lydia her mother's, and she'd always thought they could've at least done her the courtesy of reversing the names. Being a Lydia would not have been as bad as being a Bertha.

But that was hardly the worst thing her

parents did.

She doesn't remember the first time her father hit her. It's as ingrained a part of her childhood as the canopy bed in her room, the place in her bathroom where the wallpaper never laid flat. Just there, like background noise. When he was drunk, when he was angry, sometimes, she thought, just when he was bored.

There had been money in her family at some point, close enough that her father remembered growing up with it and keenly felt the lack of it. It was money that had built the house, sometime in the twenties, but by Blanche's childhood, the house was practically sinking into the red Alabama dirt around it. There was no money for things like repairing the roof, and when a leak started, when the ceiling literally began to rot away in an upstairs bedroom, Bertha's parents just closed that door and pretended it wasn't happening.

Bertha learns to do that, too. It's easier, closing a door, creating a new reality.

She goes to the local public school because there isn't anything else in her tiny town. Not just a public school, a *county* school, which, for a reason she never really understands, bothers her father more than a city school would.

Her mother had gone to boarding school

near Birmingham. Ivy Ridge. She talks about it a lot, makes it seem like a paradise on earth, full of pretty girls in plaid skirts, redbrick buildings, tall, old trees.

Bertha looks it up on the computers at school, and it is even more beautiful than her mother had made it seem.

It is the easiest thing in the world to fill out an application.

Harder to get financial aid since her parents are supposed to apply for that, and they need tax returns and all sorts of other adult things Bertha doesn't really know anything about. But she's smart and resourceful, and one night after her father is passed out in what her mother still insists on calling the parlor, Bertha sneaks into his desk.

His papers are a mess but she finds what she needs, and by the time seventh grade is over, Bertha has an acceptance letter and a complete free ride to Ivy Ridge until she graduates so long as she maintains a high GPA.

It's the hardest her father ever hits her, the night he learns what she's done. Later, she'll lie in her bed, tongue probing the throbbing place in her mouth where her teeth feel loose, but the pain is nothing. The pain is worth it because she's built herself a life raft away from the sinking ship of her family.

It's really what starts it all, changes everything — Ivy Ridge introduces her to a new life, introduces her to Blanche, but more importantly, it introduces her to a new version of herself. The one she didn't know was there, the one who can make things happen.

The first day is so hot she can feel sweat pooling in her bra, slipping in a slimy trail down her back. Already, she can smell the powdery scent of her deodorant, and she suddenly has the horrible image of wet, yellowed spots under the arms of her brand-new white blouse.

She wants to check, but then what if someone sees her? And then she's not only carrying the heavy weight of being named *Bertha,* she's also the Bertha Who Looks at Her Own Armpits.

No, better to be sweaty than to be that freak.

The campus is gorgeous: brick buildings, violently green lawn, and even though her room isn't quite as fancy — lots of linoleum, plain twin beds with scarred wooden frames — it still feels like paradise, being away from home, being away from *them,* and she never wants to leave.

She meets Blanche that first day. They're not roommates — that comes later — but they live in the same dorm building, and Blanche has assigned herself as the unofficial greeter.

Blanche has the softest hair, and it falls down her back in a perfect smooth and shiny river, the color of coffee. Bertha's own hair is brown, too, but not this kind of brown, not this deep shade that makes you want to reach out and touch it.

"Bertha?" she asks, wrinkling her nose, and Bertha feels herself curl inward, shoulders rolling in, spine folding. It's a pose she's taken a thousand times. If she could just shrink into herself enough, her parents wouldn't notice her at all.

But Blanche puts a hand on her shoulder, keeping her from cringing. "No," she says. "That's not gonna fly. Don't you have a nickname?"

Bertha has never had a nickname because she's never had the kind of friends in her life who would give her one, and her parents barely call her anything at all.

Blanche smiles, teeth blindingly white in her tan face. "Bea," she proclaims. "That sounds better."

Bea.

It *does* sound better. It fits.

Bea. She sits up a little straighter, tries tucking her hair behind her ear with the same casual gesture she'd seen Blanche use earlier.

"Perfect."

And it is.

That spring break, Blanche invites Bea to her family's house in Orange Beach. Bea had actually never been to the beach before, but as soon as she sinks her toes into the sugar-white sands, she is in love, and this is the only place she ever wants to be, wind in her hair, salt water brushing her ankles.

Blanche laughs at her, wrapping an arm around Bea's waist. "Okay, it's pretty here, but it's just Orange Beach," she says, and suddenly Bea worries that she's been too effusive, gushing too much. Country come to town and all that.

But then Blanche splashes her and dashes off into the surf, leaving Bea standing alone.

Her father dies her junior year.

She doesn't go back for the funeral.

Later, there's a voice mail from her mother, and it's the most lucid she's ever sounded. Bea had braced herself for screaming, for slurred recriminations, but instead, her mother is kind. Sweet, even. Calls her "Bertha-Bear," a nickname Bea hates, but hasn't heard since she was a little girl. Wants her to come home for the summer. Wants to try to fix things now that Daddy is gone.

And she's shockingly tempted.

It's Blanche, though, who reminds her she doesn't owe Mama anything.

Bea hasn't told Blanche everything about her past, not wanting her friend to know just how shameful it all is, how dark. But Blanche isn't stupid, and Bea knows she's picked up some things. "You don't have to go," she tells Bea, and Bea sits on her bed, absentmindedly pulling at the loose plastic on her phone case.

"I have to go somewhere for the summer," Bea replies, and Blanche smiles, plucking the phone out of Bea's hand.

"Come home with me, then. We have the space, and it'll be fun!"

It's amazing to Bea that Blanche can make that offer, that she doesn't see it as the huge thing that it so clearly is. For Blanche, it's that easy. She can take Bea under her wing for an entire summer, and no one will mind, no one will think Bea takes up too much space.

So Bea says yes, and it's the best summer of her life.

Later, when her mother leaves her a voice mail, drunk and screeching about ungrateful daughters, Bea knows she made the right choice.

And if she hadn't known it then, she would have at the end of the summer, sitting on Blanche's massive canopy bed, the one with the lace trim and the pillows in all different shades of green.

Blanche is smiling as she fastens the necklace around Bea's neck. It's a sterling silver initial, a *B* on a delicate chain, and Blanche holds up her own identical charm to Bea's face.

"We match," she says, and Bea doesn't know why she suddenly feels like crying.

They're together their entire high school career, Bea and Blanche, Blanche and Bea.

Even "the Bs" occasionally. Bea loves that.

She sometimes thinks Blanche doesn't.

Bea's acceptance letter comes just a few days after Blanche's, and she's so excited that she can't help but leap off her bed as soon as Blanche comes in after class, squealing, "I got in!"

Blanche smiles at her, but her expression is a little confused and she asks, "Got in where?"

Bea laughs, nudging Blanche's shoulder. "Um, Birmingham-Southern, obvi," she says, and it actually takes her a moment to realize that Blanche's smile has slipped.

"Oh, wow," Blanche says, but it's faint, and suddenly Bea knows she's made a mistake, fucked this up somehow, but she's not sure how.

"I thought you'd be excited," she says. "I mean, it's not like we have to room together there, too."

Bea laughs to show how stupid that idea would be even though it's exactly what she'd been thinking they'd do.

Blanche laughs, too, but just like her smile, it's not real, and when she sits down on the edge of her bed, she says, "I guess I just thought you'd want to go to Randolph-Macon since you got in. And, like, hardly anyone here did. *I* didn't."

Which had been exactly why Bea didn't want to go to Randolph-Macon. She'd applied because Blanche had, but she hadn't thought she'd get in, and when she had and Blanche hadn't, Bea had dismissed it altogether.

But now she stares at Blanche and says, "So . . . you want me to go to Randolph-Macon?"

Sighing, Blanche starts brushing her hair. It's shorter now, just below her earlobes, and she's lightened it. It doesn't suit her as well as her dark hair did, but Bea had told her she loved it anyway.

"I just think maybe we should each have our own . . . things, you know?" Blanche says, and then she meets Bea's eyes in the mirror. "We can't be 'the Bs' forever."

For the first time, Bea realizes that Blanche isn't wearing her *B* necklace. Probably hasn't worn it in weeks, and Bea just hasn't noticed.

She feels her own pendant practically burning against her skin.

"Right," she says with a little laugh. "You're right. That would be stupid."

Blanche is clearly relieved, her smile brightening into something genuine as she puts her brush down and turns around.

"I knew you'd get it," she says.

So Blanche goes off to Birmingham-Southern, and Bea heads to Randolph-Macon, and they keep up on Facebook, through texts, but Bea doesn't go back to Birmingham. She gets an internship with an interior design firm her junior year, and then she's in Atlanta, and just two years after college, thanks to the contacts she's made, she's launching Southern Manors.

She doesn't see Blanche again until they're twenty-six, and finally, finally, Bea makes the trek back to Alabama, not even bothering to let her mother know she's there.

There's a mini-reunion in Five Points, some bar that's too loud, the drinks too expensive, but it's fun, being back in Birmingham, seeing the Ivy Ridge girls again. Seeing Blanche.

Whatever weirdness there's been between the two of them vanishes the second they see each other, Blanche squealing and throwing her arms out to hug Bea.

Her hair is shorter, almost severe, but it's pretty with her slightly elfin features, and Bea has a brief moment of wondering if she should try something similar. But no, what looks good on Blanche won't always look good on Bea, and besides, Bea is looking pretty good herself these days as Blanche immediately points out with a shrieked, "You bitch, look at you!"

The other girls also want to know what Bea's secret is, how she looks so great, who cuts her hair, all of that. The truth is so simple, though.

She's rich now.

When they'd known her at Ivy, she was lacking their patina of wealth and class, so of course she seems different to them now, of course she now looks prettier and better.

But Blanche is the real star of the show because she's getting married.

Blanche's engagement ring is huge, an emerald-cut diamond on a platinum band, and Bea has seen pictures of Blanche's fiancé on social media. He's blond and tall, and reminds Bea of the boys she'd met going to parties at Hampden-Sydney, the boys' college near Randolph-Macon. He looks older than twenty-eight and has probably looked like that since he was a teenager, earlier even. There's a certain type of boy who seems to be born with a golf club in his hand, and that's Tripp Ingraham.

"Richard Ingraham the Third," Blanche tells them, and Bea hides a smile behind her drink because of course Blanche is marrying a "the third," who's called Tripp.

The wedding is in the spring, and they're building a house, a big one, in a new neighborhood called Thornfield Estates.

Bea looks it up.

There's nothing to it, really. It's mostly a bunch of drawings of what it will look like one day, all manicured lawns and houses that are ostentatiously huge, but built like older, more modest houses. No white stucco here, just brick and tasteful navy shutters.

Houses start in the seven figures, but Bea is rich now, and why not settle in Birmingham again? Her business can be run from anywhere, and while she likes Atlanta, she hasn't really made a life there.

But buying a house that big in a neighborhood clearly meant for families feels silly and . . . obvious.

So she gets a town house in Mountain Brook, then an office in Homewood, and Southern Manors keeps growing even as she helps Blanche with her wedding plans.

"It's so good to have you back," Blanche says one night as they sit in Blanche and Tripp's living room, a bottle of white wine on the coffee table in front of them, their shoes off, bridal magazines all around them. "I've missed you."

Bea knows that she means it, and smiling, she reaches into her purse. "I'm glad you said that."

The necklace is silver, a little bee dangling from the chain, and Blanche laughs delightedly, clapping her hands. "Omigod," she says all in a rush. "The *cutest!*"

This time, Bea puts the necklace on Blanche, and later, when she asks if she can donate Southern Manors' décor for the reception, Blanche says yes easily, just like Bea had known she would.

It's good exposure for the company, which already does great business, but that's not enough for Bea. She wants it to matter *here,* in Birmingham.

She wants it to matter to Blanche.

And it does, in the end, but not in the way Bea had wanted.

The night of the benefit, of Bea's biggest triumph, Blanche rides with Bea and her mother in the car on the way over, and when they first get into the ballroom, once they've shown Bea's mother to her table, Blanche looks around at everything Bea has made.

"You know, I never realized how much of this stuff looks like it came straight from my house," Blanche says.

She's smiling when she says it, her fingers going to the little bee around her neck, but Bea sees her eyes.

Sees what she's thinking.

"Does it?" Bea says. "I never noticed."

■ ■ ■ ■

PART IX
JANE

■ ■ ■ ■

29

It must be the stupidest thing I've ever done, going to Tripp Ingraham's house. And that's really saying something for me.

He's been charged with murder. I am willingly going to an accused murderer's house.

I say that to myself over and over again as I jog down the street, trying to look like it's just a regular day, just regular Jane out for her morning run, certainly not about to do something so shit-stupid she might die.

His texts kept me up all night last night, and I can't explain it, but I need to hear what he says.

Because something in me tells me he's telling the truth.

Tripp is so many ugly things — a drunk, a lech, a Republican — but murderer still doesn't fit on him. I've known violent men. I've been around too many of them, and I learned how to sniff them out early. I had to.

Tripp just . . . doesn't smell right.

I hurry up his driveway, praying to god that no one catches a glimpse of me. His bushes are overgrown, dead leaves and flower petals strewn along the walk at the front of the house, and if I'd thought his place seemed dark and sad before, it's nothing compared to how it feels now.

After ringing the doorbell, I wait for so long that I think he's not going to answer, and I'm uncomfortably aware that anyone could come by and see me standing there. This neighborhood seemed to have eyes everywhere, and Tripp is not supposed to have visitors, not without it being cleared through the police first.

Like I was going to do that.

Just as I'm about to turn away, the door opens.

Tripp stares at me, wearing a plaid bathrobe tied loosely at the waist and a pair of matching pajama pants. His skin has gone grayish, his eyes nearly swallowed up by the hollows around them. Tripp looked rough before, but now, he looks half-dead, and I almost feel sorry for him.

"You came," he says, his voice low and flat. "I honestly didn't think you would. Don't just stand there. Come in."

He ushers me inside, and I'm hit with the

smell immediately. Old food, garbage that hasn't been taken out, and booze.

So much booze.

"Sorry I didn't clean up," he says, gesturing for me to head into the living room, but I shake my head, folding my arms over my chest.

"Whatever you have to say to me, go ahead and say it here. Say it fast."

He lowers his gaze back to mine, the corner of his mouth lifting slightly, and there it is again — a shadow version of that Tripp, sure, washed out and barely there, but still.

"Don't want to spend too much time in the murderer's lair. I get it."

I'd tell him not to be a dick, but that's like telling him not to breathe, so instead, I just glare at him, waiting, and eventually he sighs.

"You must've felt like you won the goddamn lottery when you met Eddie Rochester," he muses. "Rich, good-looking, charming as hell. But let me tell you something, Jane."

He leans in close, and I catch the ripe odor of him, the stink of unwashed skin and unbrushed teeth. "He's poison. His wife was poison, too, so at least they were well-matched in that."

Another smirk. "If I were you, I'd leave here, get whatever shit you can out of the house, and hit the road. Leave Eddie, Birmingham, all of it." He waves one hand, sagging back against the door. "Sure as fuck wish I'd listened when Blanche said we should move."

"Blanche wanted to *move*?" I ask incredulously, and he nods.

"Yeah. Two weeks before she died. Started talking about how she needed to be somewhere else, that she felt like Bea was suffocating her. Wasn't enough that Bea took her whole goddamn life, you know? She had to be right up under us all the time, too. And Eddie. Fucker was always over at the house, seemed like."

"But you said you didn't really think anything was happening there."

"Still didn't mean I liked it. Bea didn't like it, either. It's why she invited Blanche to the lake that weekend. To 'hash it out.' I asked Blanche what that meant, and she said they were at . . . I don't know. Like a crossroads or something. That she wasn't sure they could still be friends. And I thought maybe it was about . . ."

His throat moves, but he doesn't say anything, and when he reaches up to rub his unshaven jaw, I see his hands are shaking slightly.

"Things had been fucked up for a while," he finally says. "Between Blanche and Bea, between Bea and Eddie, me and Blanche. It was all just toxic by that point. Which is why I was confused as fuck when Bea called me and asked me to come up."

My blood turns cold. "What?"

Sighing, Tripp scrubs a hand over his face. "That weekend," he says, sounding tired. "Bea called me that Friday night, said she thought Blanche needed me. So I got in the car, drove up to the lake, and yes, we all had a lot to drink, but I passed out in the *house*. I was never on that goddamn boat. I woke up the next morning in the guest bedroom, feeling like someone had jammed a railroad spike through my skull, and neither Bea nor Blanche were there. I assumed they'd taken the boat out early, and I left. Drove back home."

His voice cracks and he takes a second to clear his throat, rubbing his face again. "I didn't know. I went home that morning, and I watched fucking golf on TV, and all that time, they were both . . . they were already dead. They were . . . rotting in that water . . ."

There are tears in his eyes now. "It wasn't until Monday, when she didn't come home and I couldn't get her on the phone that I even realized something was wrong."

His bleary eyes focus on my face, and now there are no smirks, no gross lines. "I swear to you, I had nothing to do with any of it. Yes, I was there, and yes, I should've told the cops that immediately, but I was afraid of . . ." He makes a strained sound that's too sad to be a laugh. "This. Fuck, I was afraid of this."

His hands clutch my shoulders, hard enough that I think I'll have bruises there. "I'm telling you, leave. I didn't get on that boat, but my fingerprints are on it. I didn't buy fucking rope and a hammer, but someone using my credit card did."

There's so much information coming at me at once that I barely know how to process it all, and I blink, trying to step out of Tripp's hold, trying to wrap my head around what he's implying.

"You're saying someone framed you?"

"I'm saying you still have the chance to walk away from these fuckers."

He lets me go, stepping back. "I wish to Christ I had."

I tear the house apart.

I don't know what I'm looking for, only that there has to be something, some proof that Eddie did this.

That's what Tripp was trying to tell me, I know it, and so here I am, opening up closets, yanking out drawers.

Adele rushes around my feet, barking frantically, and there are tears in my eyes as I survey my destruction.

Books off shelves, heedlessly tumbled to the floor. Cushions pulled off the sofa.

I pick up anything heavy, all those tchotchkes from Southern Manors, looking for drops of blood. I go through the pockets of Eddie's clothes. I push the mattress off our bed.

Something, something, there has to be something, you can't kill two people and not leave some sign of it, you can't. There are receipts, he's hidden a murder weapon, there will be clothes with blood, I will find something.

An hour later — no, two, almost two and a half — I'm sitting on the floor of the coat closet at the front of the house, my head in my hands. Adele has lost interest in me now, and sits in the hall facing me, her snout resting on her paws.

I've lost my fucking mind.

The house is a wreck, and I'm too exhausted to even think about putting it back together again.

Tripp is right. I should leave. Get out while I can because even if it wasn't Eddie, there's something going on here, something so fucked up that no amount of money can make it worth it.

I'm just getting up from the floor when I see a jacket in the corner of the closet. It must've fallen off a hanger while I was in here acting like a madwoman, but I don't remember seeing it.

I also don't remember the last time I saw Eddie wear it.

When I pick it up, I notice immediately that it feels a little heavier on one side than the other, and my breath catches in my throat as my fingers close around something in the pocket.

But when I pull it out, it's just a paperback book.

I imagine him, taking it to read somewhere, maybe at the office, maybe on his lunch break, and shoving it back in a pocket, forgetting about it.

I've seen Eddie reading plenty over the past few months, but always some boring military thriller. This is a romance novel, an older one with a pretty lurid cover, which doesn't strike me as Eddie's thing.

Maybe it was Bea's. A favorite read, something he kept close to him.

I open the cover.

It takes me a minute to realize what I'm seeing, the spill of words written over the typed pages confusing and messy to my eyes.

And then I see *Blanche* scrawled on a page, and feel like my heart stops beating.

Murdered my best friend.

Locked me away.

My shaking hands turn the pages so fast, I can hear paper tear.

And then there's my name.

Jane.

Bile floods my mouth, and I whimper, muscles seizing up.

Killed Blanche, locked me away, fucked him, Jane.

The words are blurring, and I'm so sure I'm going to be sick, but I can't be, I can't because Bea Rochester is not in that lake, rotting away like Tripp said, she's here, she's right over my head, and oh my god.

I rush out of the closet, my feet skidding on the marble floor in the hallway.

Adele looks up and barks once, sharp, as I run for the stairs, the book still in my hand.

A code, the same one as the lock at the lake house.

Another closet, this one smaller, one I've never even paid attention to because I hardly ever come upstairs, and oh god, oh god, the thumps, those noises, *transitional seasons,* that asshole, it was her, it was Bea —

My hands shake so badly I can barely open the panel at the back of the closet, but I manage it, punching in the numbers even as a part of me says she won't be in there. That this can't be fucking real.

A whirring sound, a click, and I push the door open.

At first, I'm just surprised to see what a big room is behind the door. Like a hotel room, almost, decorated, cozy despite the lack of natural light. A big bed in the center.

And next to that bed, a woman.

Now I really think I will be sick.

Bea Rochester didn't drown in the same accident that killed Blanche.

Bea Rochester never died at all.

Bea Rochester is standing right in front of me.

"Is he here?" she asks.

30

My head is spinning, and my stomach is still lurching.

Not *help me,* not *who are you,* but *is he here?*

I shake my head. "N-no. He's at work, he . . ."

"It doesn't matter," Bea says, and holds out her hands to me.

After so much time spent looking at her pictures, seeing her here, in front of me now, is almost too surreal to fathom, and maybe that's why I find myself crossing the space, putting my hands in hers.

"We have to get out of here before he gets back," she says, and I nod even as I say, "Tripp."

She frowns at me, confused.

"What?"

I shake my head, the shock turning my thoughts to a kind of thick, heavy sludge. "I talked to him today. Just a few hours ago, and he said he was there that night, that Eddie was there that night. It was him, wasn't it? Eddie killed Blanche. Oh my god."

The words come out a moan, and Bea grabs my shoulders. She's smaller than I thought she would be, somehow, but strong, especially for a woman who's spent so much time locked away.

Jesus, locked away. Locked up here. By Eddie.

"Jane," she says, and I think of Eddie telling her about me, telling her my name, and want to scream, but there's another sound.

The closet door opening.

■ ■ ■ ■

PART X
EDDIE

■ ■ ■ ■

31

Something has to give.

That's been the one thought spiraling through my mind for the past few weeks, and it was still there as I parked the car in the garage, turned it off, stared through the windshield.

Tripp charged with Blanche's murder, Bea locked away upstairs, and Jane . . .

Fuck, Jane.

Sighing, I opened the car door and headed into the house. It's late, and the weather is shit, and I should've come home earlier, but I was waiting out Jane, hoping she'd already gone to bed.

I wanted to talk to Bea.

Bea would know what to do here, how to fix this. Even though I snapped at her the last time for suggesting that the situation couldn't stand, I also knew she'd be the only one to get us out of it.

Opening the front door, the house felt too

quiet and a little too cold, especially after the heat of outside, but I didn't mind.

And then I saw it.

It looked like a goddamn tornado had torn through. Like it had been ransacked.

Jane.

I didn't even remember going up the stairs. Just that I was there at the closet, opening the door.

It actually took me a minute to realize what I was seeing. That the doors were open. That Jane was in there.

That she and Bea were standing there together.

It felt enough like a nightmare or some kind of stress-induced hallucination that I just stared at them for the longest time. Bea, her face pale, Jane, nearly gray, her eyes huge in her face.

And even as I looked at them, my brain was trying to whir into motion, trying to explain, to fix this.

Too late, I saw Jane reach for the silver pineapple on the table by the door. One of those knickknacks from Southern Manors I'd taken from somewhere else in the house to put up here, trying to make it look nicer.

As it swung toward me, Jane's face screwed up in fear and anger, I realized my mistake.

But Jane made a mistake, too.

The hit was too hard and badly aimed, crunching against the side of my face so that I immediately felt teeth break, tasted blood, the world just white-hot crushing pain.

Then darkness.

32

I really should've fucking known it.

My head ached, and as I opened my eyes, it seemed like they might explode out of my skull. There was a thick, heavy feeling in my stomach, and I turned my head to the side, suddenly afraid I was going to puke, but nothing happened. I just coughed and retched and wondered how the hell I didn't see this coming.

Bea was always too smart for this to be a permanent solution. Hell, *I* was too smart for this to be a permanent solution. But that first night, I'd been freaking out and panicking, and this had seemed . . . okay, it had seemed insane even then, but I was improvising. It's what I'd always done, made things up on the spot, adapted to my circumstances.

Usually it worked.

But this was Bea. This was *my wife.*

Of course it ended up like this, me on the

floor, bleeding, missing several teeth — and Bea out there, somewhere, with Jane.

The thought caused a quick surge of panic, and I tried to sit up, but that wasn't happening. I collapsed to the floor in the fetal position, staring blurrily at my own blood as somewhere downstairs, my wife and my fiancée . . . what, called the cops? Shared a glass of celebratory champagne?

Christ, I hoped it was one of those options, because anything else scared the fuck out of me.

It's not like I went to Hawaii with the express purpose of seducing and marrying Bea Mason. I hadn't known she'd be there — I'm not a stalker, for fuck's sake. But I'd gotten good at spotting opportunities over the years, and that's what seeing Bea Mason on that beach was.

Not just an opportunity.

The opportunity.

I hadn't known who she was, initially. I didn't exactly keep up with the home décor industry, but the girl I was traveling with, Charlie, did.

"Holy shit," she'd said as we'd been sitting by the pool.

I'd looked up from my phone to see a woman walking by in a deep purple one-piece, a flowered sarong around her waist. She was pretty and petite, and even from a distance, I caught the sparkle of diamonds in her ears, but I didn't think anything about her really warranted a "Holy shit."

"What?" I'd asked, and Charlie had thumped me with a rolled-up magazine.

"That's Bea Mason," she'd said, and when I'd just stared at her, she'd rolled her eyes and said, "She owns Southern Manors? It's, like, huge? I got that gingham skirt you like so much from there."

I had no idea what skirt she was talking about, but I smiled and nodded. "Oh, right. So, she's a big deal?"

"To women, yeah," Charlie said, then wrinkled her nose. "But I wonder why she's staying here? This isn't even the nicest resort on the island. If I had her money, I'd be at the Lanai."

And that's when Bea Mason suddenly got a lot more interesting to me.

Charlie had money. Lots of it. None of it was really hers, I guess, more her family's, but she was still comfortably loaded. Which meant that Bea Mason must have even more.

"It's her company?" I asked, looking back at my phone, keeping my tone casual.

"Oh yeah," Charlie said as she reached to

pick her daiquiri up off the nearby table. I could smell the sugary strawberry scent of it from my chair. "She's super inspiring. Built it up from this little internet business to a massive thing in like five years. Self-made multimillionaire. There was an interview with her in *Fortune* that my dad sent to me, and I was like, 'Goals.' "

I'd looked up from my phone then, and caught a glimpse of Bea walking away.

It wasn't just the money. The money was a big part of it, sure, but I liked that idea — that she'd made something out of nothing. And while Charlie ordered another drink and went back to her magazine, I'd done some googling.

The Southern Manors website had been charming, if a little cloying, and the pictures of Bea had proven that she was as attractive as I'd guessed. Not in the same showy way Charlie was, forever Instagram ready, but in a subtler, classier way.

Learning her net worth added a certain sheen to things, too, of course.

Two hundred million dollars. That's what Google said, although I knew those things weren't always accurate. Charlie's dad was supposed to be worth fifty million, but most of that was tied up in real estate and trusts. Charlie was even on an allowance. A generous one, definitely, but it wasn't exactly carte blanche.

"I'm gonna go up to the room for a bit," I'd told her, standing up from my chair and stretching, letting her gaze slide over my bare chest, my abs. I'd been up early to hit the gym, a chore, but a necessary one.

"Want company?" she'd purred, and I'd been sure to grin at her, chucking her underneath her chin.

"No, because I'm gonna nap, and I won't sleep if you're around."

She'd liked that, and caught my hand, pressing a kiss to the tips of my fingers before shooing me off. "I'll be up in a bit, then. Rest up."

I'd gone back to the room, but I hadn't napped. Instead, I'd thrown most of my things back in my bag.

I was good with people, figuring them out, predicting what they'd do, and I had a hunch Charlie was on to something with the Lanai. Bea Mason hadn't stopped to sit at our pool, after all, just walked through.

And I was right, I learned later. She'd just been checking out our pool area because she was trying to get an idea of what kind of bathing suit prints were popular among, as she put it, "normal women."

Looking back, that probably should've

been a hint, too.

At the time, I just patted myself on the back for guessing correctly.

I wish I could say there was some special trick to doing the kinds of things I do, some kind of secret code. But the fact of the matter is, I never really tried all that hard. All it took at the front desk of the Lanai was a chagrined smile to a pretty receptionist, a sheepish story about chasing my girlfriend all the way to Hawaii because I'd realized missing our vacation for work was the stupidest thing I could've done.

Not only did I get confirmation that Bea was there, I got a free glass of champagne for my troubles.

I'd asked the front desk to hold my things for me because obviously, I was hoping all would be forgiven and I'd be staying in my "girlfriend's" room that night.

Which wasn't quite how it turned out, but close enough.

My reasons for pursuing Bea might have started out a little mercenary, but I honestly did like her, right from the start. When I saw her sitting there on the beach, deep in thought, I was impressed. Most of the women I'd been spending time with were rich, but on someone else's dime. I liked that Bea had her own money, her own company. I liked the way she was always thinking about how to make it better rather than resting on her laurels.

And look, I'm not a total bastard. I sent Charlie a text, let her know that I'd had a sudden emergency and been called back to New York, but that I'd definitely give her a call next week.

She'd bought it, and I hadn't heard from her again until that email she sent after she saw that Bea and I were engaged.

And it's not like I'd read that all too closely, obviously. I hit delete as soon as I saw who it was from, although I did pick up a few key phrases before I hit the trash icon.

Motherfucker, that was there. *Manipulative, toxic, seriously psychotic,* nothing all that unexpected, although years later, when things with Bea started going wrong, I'd wondered if those words had been about me or my wife.

Well, the *motherfucker* was clearly me.

Talking to Bea that first day was so easy. Like it was meant to be. Honestly, I would've thought she would've had her guard up so much more.

Except Bea wasn't like that, not really. She wasn't always looking over her shoulder, she wasn't naturally suspicious. Later I'd work out that it was probably because she always knew she was the most dangerous thing in any room. Why should she have to look out for anyone else when she'd always win?

That probably sounds bitter, but I don't mean it that way. If anything, I was in awe of her. At first, at least. Before the murders.

33

I'd never seen anyone more determined to get what she wanted than Bea. Not even me. Like I said, I'd always been the type to seize on opportunities *that presented themselves,* rather than the person to go out and make those opportunities happen, which is what Bea did.

I think that's why I liked Jane so much right from the start. She was like me — always looking for an opening, then twisting to fit that opening. I'm sure she thought she was fooling me, thought I'd bought her whole act, but I recognized too much of myself in her not to see what she was doing. Whatever souls were made of, mine and Jane's were the same — or at least similar enough.

But Bea — Bea was a totally different beast.

My breathing sounded watery and thick, and I closed my eyes.

I should be thinking of what to do now, how to get the fuck out of here, but all I could think about was Bea.

Last year. That dinner. Blanche was flirting with me, I knew. What her intent was, though? No fucking clue. I wasn't from the South, but I'd lived here long enough to learn that flirting was like a second language with these people, or a casual hobby. Back home if someone had looked at me like Blanche was looking at me, I would've been sure they were ready to fuck me. Here, there was no telling.

Her hand was on my arm, her body close enough that I could feel the press of her breast against my bicep. I liked Blanche, definitely didn't like Tripp, and Bea was so focused on Southern Manors that I was beginning to feel like I never saw her anymore. But sleeping with her best friend seemed like more trouble than it was worth, and honestly, I liked Bea's money more than I liked sex anyway.

But that didn't mean that it wasn't a little fun, seeing Bea get jealous.

So, I didn't do anything, but I didn't try to avoid Blanche, either. I was in charge of her renovation, so it wasn't like I could brush her off. Lunches in the village to review architectural sketches and bathroom fixtures. Afternoons at her house to look at paint samples. Texts to confirm our next meeting. All of it seemed harmless to me, but god, Bea got pissed off.

And it wasn't like I hadn't known what Blanche was doing. I was just the latest prop in whatever cold war they'd been fighting since they were kids. But it had been nice, having Blanche pay that much attention to me. Bea was so busy building her empire, she'd stopped looking at me the way she used to.

The way Blanche did.

So maybe I encouraged it a little. Maybe I flirted back.

Maybe I left my phone unlocked so Bea could snoop to her heart's content.

Still, it would've just blown over eventually if it hadn't been for the shit about Bea's mom.

Another afternoon at Blanche's house, but this time, she went to kiss me, and yeah, I let her. Just for a little bit. I was curious to see how far she wanted to take it, and honestly curious to see if I was more interested than I thought, but strangely enough, I wasn't. Blanche was pretty, and clearly into me, but there was no real spark there, and after a little bit, I pushed her away, gently.

"We can't do this," I remember saying. "Bea doesn't deserve this."

And fuck me, but that had been the wrong thing to say.

I could still see Blanche's face twisting into something almost ugly. "Bea?" she'd all but sneered. "Do you even *know* Bea?"

The words were so angry that I wondered if she was drunk. But no, that was just sweet tea in her glass, and her gaze was sharp.

"Did you know her parents were both drunks?" she asked. "Did you know her name isn't even Bea?" Blanche poked herself in the chest with one finger. "I gave her that name. She was Bertha when I met her." A disbelieving snort. "Fucking *Bertha.*"

I'd known about the name thing and wasn't sure why Blanche was making such a big deal out of it. I didn't like going by "Edward," so I never had, and I didn't give a shit that Bea had felt the same about Bertha. But I didn't know that her parents were alcoholics, and I didn't like getting caught off guard.

"Did you know that they found her mother at the bottom of the stairs when Bea was the only person in the house?"

I saw in her face that she regretted the words the second they were out, saw the brief flaring of her nostrils and widening of her eyes that meant that even *she* thought she'd gone too far, but I kept my face carefully blank.

"You just said yourself that she was a drunk. Drunks have a tendency to fall," I replied woodenly.

"Yeah, well." Blanche hesitated, and I could practically see the gears turning behind her eyes. "This drunk fell about two weeks after she embarrassed Bea at her big reception for Southern Manors, so." She shrugged. "You do the math."

It was ridiculous to think that Bea would've had anything to do with that. Or so I tried to tell myself.

But then, I began to wonder.

There had been a secretary at my construction business, Anna. She'd been pretty and cute, right out of college, and Bea had wanted her gone from the second she'd met her. I hadn't done anything about it because Anna was a good worker, and hell, I had no intention of being the kind of creep who hit on someone who worked for him, so it wasn't like I was staring down daily temptation.

But then petty cash started disappearing, and one day when Bea was up at the office to bring me lunch, she'd opened Anna's desk drawer to grab a pen and there, shoved in the back, had been the missing money.

Anna had cried and sworn she hadn't taken it, but what could I do except fire her?

Nothing about it had ever sat right with me. Anna hadn't seemed like a thief, and Bea hadn't wanted her there, and it had been Bea who found the cash . . . it was all too neat.

I hadn't said anything, though, because I didn't even know what to say. I certainly didn't like thinking that my wife could be so manipulative.

And I shouldn't have said anything about her mom, but that night, the very same fucking day Blanche had told me about it, I'd opened my damn mouth.

"You didn't tell me your mom died in a fall."

Bea looked up from her laptop, her face bathed in the pale glow of the screen. She was wearing her glasses, her dark hair pulled up in a messy bun, and she looked so young all of a sudden, so different from the polished, poised Bea I was used to.

I liked it.

"Okay?" she said at last. "I did tell you she died suddenly."

"Right, but you said it was because she drank too much."

Bea turned her attention back to the

screen, her fingers clacking along the keyboard. "It was. She was drinking too much and she fell."

Frustrated now, I crossed the dining room and closed her computer, earning me a squawk of protest. "Right, but that's really different from what you led me to believe. I thought she had liver failure or something. Cirrhosis. I didn't realize it was an accident." My voice caught on the last word.

Flipping her laptop open with quick, jerky movements, Bea said, "Well, it was. She fell and I found her, which was obviously upsetting, so thanks for bringing it back up. So glad we could have this talk."

"Don't be like that."

Her gaze shot back to mine, red blotches climbing up her neck like they always did when she was pissed off. "Is there a reason you and Blanche were discussing my mother's death?" she asked, and shit. *Shit.* I should've seen that one coming, but I was so desperate to put these awful thoughts to rest that I hadn't stopped to think that she'd know exactly where I'd gotten that information.

"It came up today while I was over there," I said, and she let out a sarcastic laugh.

"Right, typical small talk, 'Hey, did you know how your wife's mom died?' "

"Don't be a bitch," I said, straightening up, but Bea didn't reply, even though I'd never spoken to her like that before. Her focus was on the laptop again, whatever email she felt had to be dealt with at 10 P.M. on a Friday night.

We didn't speak again that night, and later, I lay in bed next to her. She had her back to me, the curve of her ass against my hip, and for a moment, I thought about waking her up, trying to figure out if sex could fix this.

I didn't think it could.

And as I lay there, I tried not to think about her mother, lying at the bottom of the stairs, blood pooling around her.

Tried not to envision Bea at the top of those stairs, looking down at her. The picture was too clear though, too easy to see, and the more I pushed it away, the clearer it became, the more right it felt.

And I had no fucking idea what to do with that.

Was that the kind of person I'd married? Someone who could murder her own mother?

I truly hadn't believed it. Not until the night she killed Blanche.

34

I couldn't tell you why I went down to the lake.

Maybe it was because Tripp had stopped by, asking if I wanted a ride there, too, and I hadn't known Bea had invited him.

Tripp and I hadn't been friends or anything, but something about it, about the girls (*women,* I heard Jane say) going up there alone, then Bea texting Tripp to join them . . . something about it felt off.

I'd seen the way Tripp had been looking at Bea lately, with these sad puppy-dog eyes. I told myself it was because Blanche was making it so obvious that she was into me. He'd transferred affection or some shit.

But that didn't mean I had to like it.

So, it had bothered me, Bea inviting him, and long after Tripp left, I'd sat there in the living room, thinking about it, probing it like a sore tooth.

Why would Bea want him there? She

didn't even like Tripp, and this was supposed to be some kind of girls' bonding
weekend.

The house is dark and empty when Eddie gets there.

Or he thinks it's empty. After standing there in the living room, calling out to someone, he hears a snore from upstairs.

Tripp is in the guest room, passed out, his mouth open, his hand hanging off the bed. His snores are deep, congested, his breaths taking a while to come, and something about it strikes Eddie as weird. Unnatural.

But then again, Tripp is a drunk, maybe this is how they all sound.

The boat is gone, and there are signs they'd all three been there — Blanche's purse hanging up by the door, Tripp's keys on the counter, Bea's overnight bag on one of the bar chairs by the counter.

Standing there in the living room, Eddie tells himself he'd been a complete jackass, that the girls had taken the boat out and were having a great time, and he'd let Blanche get to him with all that shit about Bea's mom.

Then he looks out the back door and sees her.

Bea. Walking up the dock, soaking wet.

And Eddie knows.

And she had known he knew. He would remember the look on her face for the rest of his life, the way her jaw had clenched and her shoulders had gone back, head lifting as if to say, *Try it, motherfucker.*

And at first, Eddie makes the right decision. Taking her into his arms. Telling her he understands. Blanche knew this horrible thing about her, and she was telling people, what else could Bea do? She was protecting them, protecting everything they'd built, and wasn't she smart, getting Tripp down here to take the fall? He was so drunk, they would say. He and Blanche got into a fight, and he hit her, hit her so hard. Bea had tried to save her — Blanche was her best friend! — but she'd been drinking, too, and it was so dark. She'd been so brave, diving into the water, swimming away to get help.

Smiling at Eddie, Bea rises up on tiptoes and kisses him. "I knew you'd get it," she says.

Which is when Eddie grabs her, his arm cutting off her air, her feet scrabbling on the ground, fingers tearing a button off his shirt that he forgets about until days later, once

Bea was safe in the panic room.
Safe.
That's what he tells himself.

I couldn't turn her in, or let her go to prison. Not for a murder this calculated, not in a death-penalty state, not when they might start asking the same questions about her mother that I'd been asking.

(Not to mention that a trial would kill the business. No one wants charming knick-knacks from a murderer.)

But I also couldn't let her just *do* this, couldn't stomach the thought that the next time someone failed to fall in line with what Bea wanted, she'd just do away with them.

The panic room had been a solution.

Not the smartest, not the best, but fuck, what else could I have done?

Some of the pain was starting to recede now, or maybe I was just getting used to it. In any case, I could move more now, and even though my stomach roiled again, I was able to sit up.

Jane.

I didn't love her, not really. I knew that now.

I'd wanted to. So much. In the beginning, it had felt so easy. I could just love someone else. I could have a fresh start. I could put everything with Bea behind me, forget what she'd done, what I'd done, what we'd done, and start over with Jane. Smart, funny Jane who saw the good parts of me, never the bad.

Bea had learned the truth about my family eventually. That I hadn't spoken to my mom or my brother since I was eighteen even though they were both good people who hadn't done anything wrong. Their only crime was that they were a reminder of how thoroughly mediocre my beginnings had been.

Jane didn't know that, though. She didn't know that my mom still tried to email me through the public address I had at Southern Manors, or that I deleted them as soon as they came in. Or that when my brother had tried to send us a Christmas card, I'd sicced our lawyers on him, implying that he was harassing us.

With Jane, I was getting a blank slate.

But a part of me had always known it was never going to be that easy. I might've told myself that I hid Bea away to protect the business, that it was better the world think she was dead than a murderer, but the truth was . . . I couldn't bear to give her up.

It was that simple. That fucking terrifying. I still loved her.

That's what this had been, fucked up as it was. Love. Trying to save her from the outside world — and from herself.

"This is the best thing for you," I'd told her that first night when I'd put her in the panic room as she'd gaped at me, confused and angry, and maybe a little scared.

And I'd believed that. I still did. But Jesus, now she was loose, in the house with Jane, resilient Jane who I should've let go from the start. She didn't deserve this. I should never have proposed to her, not when I was still going into Bea's room, seeing her, talking to her, sleeping with her. But I'd wanted to give Jane the thing *she'd* wanted. I'd somehow, stupidly, thought this might work out. That there was a way out that ended with all of us getting what we wanted.

And I'd wanted both Jane and Bea. Hadn't been willing to give either of them up, keeping Bea upstairs, keeping Jane by promising to marry her, and now we were all fucked.

I should've known that Jane would figure this out. She kept getting so close, and for all that naïve young woman act, I knew she was as sharp as a drawer of fucking knives.

I, on the other hand? Curious, impulsive, greedy.

With a groan, I managed to get on my knees. I wasn't tied up or restrained in any way, just locked in an inescapable room.

Except that it had never been completely inescapable. There was one guaranteed way out. There always had been. I was just the only one who knew it because I was the one who'd built this fucking house.

It was dangerous, though. Stupid, even. And possibly deadly.

But I had to try.

■ ■ ■ ■

PART XI
JANE

■ ■ ■ ■

35

"You're nothing like he described."

I stand there in the hallway, my arm still aching from where I hit Eddie with that goddamn pineapple. I hit him too hard, I know that. And in a weird spot. I could still feel bone crunching, could see the teeth on the carpet. We had left him in there, closing and locking the doors behind us, and there's no sound, no sign that he's conscious or even alive in there.

And Bea Rochester is standing in front of me.

Alive.

Because Eddie had her locked in their *fucking* panic room. Oh, and apparently talked to her about me.

It's all so bizarre I can't even think how to reply, finally stuttering, "The p-police. We need to call —"

"What I need," Bea says, loudly sighing,

"is a fucking drink."

Bea moves down the stairs with the same confidence and focus I'd always imagined she'd have, her head high, her movements sure. I trail behind, arms wrapped around my middle, wishing I weren't still in my jogging gear from earlier this morning.

Bea is already in the kitchen when I get downstairs, going into the butler's closet. It's a narrow room between the kitchen and the laundry room with a little sink, wineglasses, and several bottles of wine, plus the whiskey Eddie likes.

I hang back as Bea opens a cabinet, her eyes moving over the bottles of wine in their little wooden cubbies. "Did the two of you drink the 2009 Mouton Rothschild?" she asks, glancing over her shoulder at me, and I stand there, my hands at my sides, arm still aching from the force I'd used in my hit to Eddie's head.

I feel like what I am — an imposter.

And I can't believe how . . . calm she is. How in control. I feel like the entire world has been turned on its head, and she's selecting wine.

But Bea only shakes her head, fingers dancing over the bottles. "The 2007 is still here. That'll do."

She plucks the bottle from its hiding place, then slides two glasses from the rack affixed under the counter, her movements smooth and sure.

And for the first time, I realize that this really was *her* house. It could never have been mine, and it sure as fuck wasn't Eddie's.

Pausing between the kitchen and the dining room, she glances at me again. "Grab the corkscrew, will you?"

That I can do, at least, and I open one of the drawers in the kitchen, pulling out the corkscrew before following Bea into the dining room.

She opens the wine, pouring us each a glass, then gestures for me to sit. She takes her own seat at the head of the table, and for a moment, I wonder if I'm supposed to sit at the other end, the two of us facing off like medieval queens.

Instead, I sit at her left, not in the chair closest to her, but one over, leaving some space between us, but not a football field length of oak table.

This is the same place where she posed for that *Southern Living* interview a few years ago, only now she's wearing wrinkled silk pajamas, her nails a ragged mess. But even though she looks like hell — pale, her hair longer, split ends fraying over her shoulders, dark circles beneath her eyes — underneath I can see the Bea Rochester I'd spent so much time imagining. The woman who built an empire out of gingham and bowls shaped like fruit, a brand modeled after a certain lifestyle she hadn't been born into but clawed her way toward just the same.

One of those bowls sits on the table now, filled with lemons, and she reaches out, pulling the bowl close to her before plucking a lemon free and rolling it in her hands as she thinks.

I pick up my glass now, taking a deep sip, the rich cabernet exploding on my tongue as Bea rolls that lemon back and forth between her palms.

Finally, she puts it back in the bowl and looks at me.

"So. Jane."

"So. Bea," I reply in the same tone and she smiles at me. Well, smirks, really, just one corner of her mouth lifting, and I realize I've seen that exact expression on Eddie's face before. Did she pick it up from him or vice versa?

Spreading her hands, she asks, "What do we do now?"

I like that word, *we*. And I like the way

Bea looks at me, like she's actually seeing me, not Jane-the-Dog-Walker, not the sad girl her asshole husband almost tricked into marrying him. The real me.

Lifting the wine bottle, I top off my glass. Hers is still full, so I set the bottle back on the table with a thump. Outside, a storm rages, rain splattering against the glass, thunder shaking the house every few minutes. There might also be the occasional thump from upstairs, but I can't tell.

I think of Eddie, sprawled on the floor of the panic room and wait to feel guilt, or regret, or . . . something.

Nothing comes except a queasy sort of relief. I was right. All those suspicions I had, all those bad feelings, they weren't lying to me. My instincts were as sharp as they'd ever been. And now Bea was safe.

"We need to call the police," I say again. "Tell them the whole story, all of it."

Bea nods, thinking that over. "The whole story. What do you think that is?"

Even though my mind has been reeling for the last few hours, ever since Tripp, ever since I found the diary, I've gotten good at thinking on my feet over the years and getting past shock as quickly as possible. That's been a necessary survival skill.

It serves me well now.

"I'm guessing Blanche is really dead," I say to Bea. "But it probably wasn't an accident like everyone thinks."

"They were having an affair," Bea answers, her voice mild, but a muscle quivers in her jaw, and she briefly clenches her teeth before continuing. "Eddie, of course, thought I'd never find out, but I knew almost from the start. He's never been as smart as he thinks he is."

I remember his story about "transitional seasons" and "raccoons in the attic," and snort, picking up my wine. The ground underneath my feet is starting to feel more solid now.

"But then Blanche had an attack of conscience, I guess. We'd been friends since we were kids, and maybe loyalty meant more to her than she thought. Or hell, maybe she just wanted to rub my face in it. Anyways, I knew the reason she'd invited me to the lake that weekend was to tell me."

She sips her wine delicately. "And I guess Eddie knew, too. And he'd rather kill Blanche than have me hear the truth."

Except that Bea invited Blanche. It was her lake house.

I frown a little, but don't say anything, and Bea goes on.

"Classic Eddie. Always wanted just one

more slice of cake, just one extra turn at bat. But he also knew that all of this" — she spreads her hands again, taking in the house, the neighborhood, probably their entire lives — "is mine. Couldn't have me divorcing him, now, could he?"

"So why not kill you, too, then?" I am doing a good job, I think, of sounding calm, but now my heart is racing because this isn't true. None of what she's saying is true.

She's a good liar, I'll give her that. Definitely better than Eddie. But I recognize this shit, and nothing she's saying is adding up.

Leaning forward, Bea folds her arms on the table, the sleeves of her pajama top riding up to reveal thin, elegant wrists. "I could never quite figure that out," she admits. "And trust me, I've had some time to mull it over. I think —"

"He loved you," I say, the words sour in my mouth. Because even though the story Bea is telling me doesn't make sense, somehow this explanation . . . does.

He loved her. Whatever happened here was fucked up and twisted, and Eddie could be ruthless. I remembered him with John. If he'd thought Bea was in his way, really in his way, I didn't doubt he could've killed her.

Instead, she was still here.

Bea looks at me, and for just a second, her confidence falters. She didn't expect that answer.

I watch her look down at the table, and then, after a beat, she lifts her head, shrugs. "Maybe. In any case, that's the story I can tell. He murdered Blanche, faked my death, then kept me locked away in this house like something out of a goddamn gothic novel while he seduced the naïve young woman who walked his dog."

She raises an eyebrow. "Thoughts?"

I take a long, deliberate sip of wine. "I guess that's a version of the truth."

"But you don't like it."

I don't. I don't want to be the tragic ingenue, the idiot who got duped by a handsome face and a huge bank account.

A victim.

I sit back in my chair, looking at Bea. Maybe it's the wine, but she's not looking quite so pale now, and even with her messy hair and pajamas, she looks almost . . . elegant.

"Why aren't you more freaked out?" I ask her now, and she meets my eyes across the table. She has pretty eyes, big and dark, her lashes thick without mascara.

"Why aren't you?" she counters. "You just

found out the man you love is a murderer and his dead wife is alive. A little screaming and crying wouldn't be unheard of."

I don't answer.

"Do you know what I think?" she continues. "I think there's a reason Eddie fell for both of us. No" — she holds up a hand, cutting off my attempt to demur — "he genuinely cares for you. He wouldn't have risked bringing you into his life if he didn't. But I think we're a lot alike, Jane."

"That's not my real name," I say, before I can stop myself, and she smiles.

"And Bea isn't mine."

"I knew that," I tell her. "Tripp."

She rolls her eyes. "Fucking Tripp."

I almost laugh at that because I know how she feels. But there's still something so . . . wrong about all this. She's too calm, too collected, too in control for a woman who just went through the most harrowing thing I can think of.

Then she leans forward and says, "Eddie said you were nothing like me. I don't think that's the case."

I look at her, sitting there like a queen, lying through her teeth, and I know they're the only truthful words she's uttered.

■ ■ ■ ■

PART XII
BEA

■ ■ ■ ■

36

He loved you.

I don't know why hearing those words out of Jane's mouth hit me like they do. Maybe because Jane, of all people, wouldn't want that to be true.

But Jane is a good liar.

I can tell, looking at her. I can also tell that she isn't at all the girl Eddie thought she was. A girl who would smash his face in with a silver pineapple, then sit here with his wife — who she'd been told was dead at the bottom of a lake — drinking wine.

I like this girl, so much that I almost feel sorry for Eddie that he couldn't see this side of her.

He might have liked it, too.

Or maybe he did. Maybe, as much as he hated to admit it, Eddie knew she was like me.

Knew that it was what had drawn him to her in the first place.

She takes another sip of her wine. She is petite, pale, her hair a color between blond and brown that isn't particularly flattering, and the clothes she's wearing look like muted imitations of the other women in this neighborhood. Maybe that was enough to fool Eddie, but he should have looked into her eyes.

Her eyes give it all away.

For example, she's nodding at me, sitting there calmly, but her eyes are almost fever-bright, and I'm sure she's not buying my story of what "really happened." The affair, Eddie killing Blanche, locking me away, framing Tripp. I'd counted on her thinking Eddie is smarter than he is, but that might have been a miscalculation.

In fact, looking at her now, she reminds me of Blanche. After the funeral.

"I'm so glad you're here." Bea hugs Blanche tightly, feeling just how thin she is in her black dress. Bea is not wearing black, going instead for the dark plum that will be a signature shade in this year's autumn line at Southern Manors.

Blanche hugs her back, says how sorry she is over and over again, but as she leaves, Bea thinks she catches something in Blanche's eyes. She's not suspicious, not exactly. Blanche would never make that big of a leap. But Bea can tell there's something about all of this that isn't sitting quite right for Blanche, even if she'd never say it, never even let herself think it.

Later that night, Bea sits in the wingback chair she'd had shipped from Mama's house, the only thing she'd wanted out of her god-awful childhood home, and finishes off the bottle of wine. It helps her to feel numb and fuzzy, helps to block out the picture of Mama's face right before she fell.

She had been high, that part was true, completely zonked out on whatever the current flavor of escape was. Klonopin, probably. Bea had watched her make her way down the hall like a woman much older than fifty-three, her footsteps slow and shuffling.

She had told Mama to get rid of that hall runner right there by the stairs, but of course she hadn't listened. Still, she'd only stumbled rather than fallen outright. She would've been fine.

Bea can't even say for sure why she pushed her. Only that she was there, and Mama tripped, and as she did, Bea's whole heart seemed to rise up joyfully in her chest, and it had felt like the most natural thing in the world to just reach out and . . . shove.

Her face didn't register fear or horror or shock. As always, Mama just looked vaguely confused as she fell.

It occurred to Bea at the funeral that she was lucky. If she'd just broken an ankle or fractured a collarbone, Bea would've had a lot of explaining to do. But she hit her head hard at the edge of the filial there at the bottom. Bea had heard the crack, seen the blood.

She didn't die right away, but when Bea had looked down at her, she'd seen that the injury was severe enough, the blood already pooling around her head.

Still, if she had called 911 right then instead of the next morning, if she'd pretended to hear a thud in the middle of the night rather than waking up to find her mother at the bottom of the stairs, Mama probably would've made it. It was the bleeding that did it in the end, after all.

Lying there all night alone at the foot of the stairs, blood gushing then slowly leaking onto the hardwood.

Bea had waited for months to feel bad about it, but in the end, all she'd felt was free.

And she'd put it out of her head, mostly, for years. Even Eddie didn't know the truth about how her Mama had died. She'd given him a vague story about Mama's drinking, and since Eddie was vague enough about his own past, he'd let it slide. It hadn't come up again until just a few months before Blanche died.

The two of them, having dinner at that same Mexican restaurant they'd gone to after Bea had met Eddie.

Things had been tense — this is after Bea catches Eddie and Blanche at lunch, after she fucks Tripp in the bathroom, not that Blanche knows about that — but Bea is still unprepared for how angry Blanche seems that night.

"He doesn't know, does he?" she asks, and Bea stares at her until she's the first to look away. "Eddie. That all your shit is fake. That this whole" — she waves one arm in the air — "Southern Manors thing was basically stolen from me."

"I know it's hard to believe the world doesn't revolve around you, Blanche, but I promise that's the case," Bea replies, her voice calm even as her pulse spikes.

Blanche takes another drink, sullen now. Was she always like this, or is this what being married to Tripp has done? Bea wonders.

She even looks like him now, her hair the same sandy shade as his, cut nearly as short. But her body is rail thin, unlike his, bangles jangling on her wrist as she plucks a chip from the basket. Bea can't help but inspect those bracelets, looking for something familiar, but no, not a one of them is from Southern Manors. They're all Kate Spade, and she wrinkles her nose.

Blanche sees. "What?" She's not eating the chip she's holding, just picking small pieces off of it, and Bea reaches over to wipe away the pile of crumbs.

"If you need bangles, we just did a new line," Bea says. "I'll send some over to you."

Blanche's lips part slightly, eyes wide, and after a moment, she gives a startled laugh that's too loud. "Are you fucking serious?" she asks, and Bea sees heads turn in their direction.

Frowning, she leans closer. "Lower your voice, please."

"No," she says, letting the remnant of her chip drop to the table. "No, I seriously want to know if you're pissed because I'm not wearing your stupid jewelry. I want to know if that's what's happening right now, *Bertha.*"

"Mature," Bea replies, and Blanche hoots with laughter, sitting back in the booth and crossing her arms over her chest.

"I'm asking you if your husband knows that everything about you is a lie. You're bitching about my bracelets, and I'm the immature one, okay."

Bea's hand shoots out, grabbing her wrist, the one covered in those goddamn bangles, and she squeezes so hard Blanche yelps.

"You're drunk," Bea tells her through clenched teeth. "And you're embarrassing yourself. Maybe leave that to Tripp."

Dinner ends early that night, and it's only two days later that Eddie is asking why Bea never told him her mother died in a fall.

Which is when Bea realizes there is no affair, when she realizes that even if Blanche had wanted to hurt her, Eddie did not. And because Blanche did not get what she wanted for once in her life, she's now acting out, firing the only ammunition she has left.

Bea shows up with coffee the next morning and breakfast pastries. She even gets Blanche one of those gluten-free abominations she likes.

"Peace offering," she says, and she can tell that a part of Blanche wants to believe it, that she wants things to go back to the way they were.

The lake trip is another peace offering. Another olive branch.

And Blanche grabs it with both hands.

Jane sits there, twirling the stem of her wineglass between her fingers, and I watch her mind work. I like not knowing exactly what she'll do, and it is oddly satisfying to see how shallow her loyalty to Eddie really is.

I hadn't lost him after all.

It surprises me how much that thrills me.

But maybe it shouldn't. Some of the things in the diary were for show, to cover my tracks — the majority of it, really — but the sex? The way I felt about Eddie?

That had all been real.

But then Jane sits up a little straighter and says, "We should call the police. Tell them what Eddie did. Let him pay the consequences."

Is she playing with me, or is that what she really wants? The ambiguity that I'd enjoyed so much just a moment ago is now irritating, and I wave one hand, finishing my wine.

"Later," I say. "Let me enjoy a few hours of being out of that room before I'm stuck answering a bunch of questions."

Looking around, I add, "You really didn't do anything new with the place, did you?"

Jane doesn't answer that, but leans closer, reaching for my hand. "Bea," she says. "We can't just sit here. Eddie murdered Blanche. He could've murdered you. We have to —"

"We don't have to do anything," I reply, yanking my hand out from under hers and standing up.

"The stressful part is always making the decision," Bea used to remind her employees. "Once you've made it, it's done, and you feel better."

That's how it was with Blanche.

Once Bea has decided that she has to die, it's easy enough, and the rest of the steps fall into place. She invites Blanche to the lake house, then texts Tripp at the last minute. She's going to need a fall guy this time, after all. One person dying in an accident while she's alone with them is one thing. Two would be harder to pull off.

So, Tripp.

Blanche is not happy when he shows up.

"I thought this was supposed to be a girls' trip," she says, and Tripp settles on the couch next to her, already drinking a vodka tonic.

"And I am a Girls' Tripp," he jokes, which is so terrible that for a moment Bea thinks maybe she should kill him, too.

But no, she needs Tripp to play a part in all this.

He does it well, too. Blanche is so irritated he's there that she drinks even more than Bea had hoped, glass after glass of wine, then the vodka Tripp is drinking.

And when Tripp passes out, as Bea had known he would thanks to the Xanax she'd put in his drink, Blanche actually laughs with Bea, the two of them dragging his limp body into the master bedroom, Bea pretending to be just as drunk as Blanche.

That's the thing she remembers the most about it all later. Blanche was happy that night. It had mostly been the booze, but still, Bea had given her that.

One last Girls' Night Out.

When they get onto the pontoon boat Bea bought for Eddie last year, Blanche is so unsteady, Bea has to guide her to her seat.

More drinks.

The sky overhead is dark, too, a new moon that night, nothing to illuminate what happens.

As with Mama, Bea doesn't have to do that much work, really.

When Blanche has slumped into unconsciousness, it's a simple matter of taking the hammer she'd bought, the heavy one, the one that looks exactly like the kind of unsubtle murder weapon a guy like Tripp would buy, and she brings it down.

Once. Twice. Three times. A sickening crunch giving way to a meaty, wet sound, and then she's rolling Blanche off the deck of the boat. It's dark, and her hair is the last thing Bea sees, sinking under the lake.

She stands there and waits to feel something.

Regret, horror. Anything, really. But again, once it's done, she's mostly just relieved and a little tired.

Swimming back to the house is something of a chore, her arms cutting through the warm water, her brain conjuring images of alligators, water moccasins. Below her, she knows there's a flooded forest, and it's hard not to imagine the dead branches reaching up for her like skeletal hands, to see her body drifting down with Blanche's to lay in that underwater wood.

Something brushes against her foot at one point, and she gives a choked scream that sounds too loud in the quiet night, lake water filling her mouth, tasting like minerals and something vaguely rotten, and she spits, keeps swimming.

The story is so simple. Girls' weekend. Tripp showing up unexpectedly. They went out on the boat, they drank too much. Bea fell asleep or passed out, to the sound of Tripp and

Blanche arguing. When she woke up, Blanche was gone, and Tripp was passed out. Bea panicked, dove in the water trying to save her best friend, and when she couldn't find her, swam back to the house.

Tripp had been so drunk he won't have any idea what happened, won't even remember he wasn't on the boat, and everyone knew he and Blanche were having problems. Maybe he'll luck out and they'll assume Blanche fell or jumped in of her own accord, never finding her body there at the bottom of the lake. Maybe they will find it, see that hole in her skull, and think he murdered her.

Either one works for Bea.

And it all would have been just that easy had Eddie not come along and fucked it all up.

He's in the house when Bea walks up the dock, his eyes going wide as he sees her. She doesn't even think about how she must look, soaking wet, shivering even though it's hot. All she can think is, *Why is he here?*

And that's it — the moment she loses it all.

She should've been paying more attention to just how weird it was that he was there, to that panicked look on his face. Eddie never had handled being surprised well, and like a lot of men, he always thought he was smarter than he actually was.

434

Bea had always believed that a man who overestimates his intelligence is a man who can be easily manipulated. Turns out, he's also a man who can be really dangerous.

Later, she wanted to tell him just how badly he'd fucked it all up, that she would've taken care of it, that she *had* taken care of it, just like she always did, but of course Eddie rushed in without thinking, just like always.

I stood there in the living room of the house Eddie built and I created, and I thought about that again, about what Jane had said.

He loved you.

That was it. That was the piece that made it all make sense. Why he didn't call the police that night, why he didn't just leave me to die upstairs. If all he wanted was the money, I had given him the perfect excuse to get rid of me and take it all. We hadn't signed any kind of prenup because I'd wanted to prove to the world — mostly to Blanche — that I trusted Eddie more than anything.

He could've taken what I'd given him.

But he hadn't.

And okay, yes, he'd met Jane, yes, he'd planned to marry her — but he still came up to my room, still talked to me, still made love to me.

All that time trying to figure out what the

secret was, the key to unlock all of this, and it was that simple.

He loved me.

Jane was in the doorway between the living room and the kitchen now, her phone in her hand. "Bea, I know you've been through something horrible, and you're probably in shock, but we have got to call the police. We can't wait any longer. This is crazy."

She looked back down at the phone, went to punch numbers in, and suddenly I was there, her wrist clutched in my hand, her bones so fragile underneath my fingers.

"Don't," I said, and in that moment, I saw the flash in her eyes that told me she understood what was really going on here.

I liked Jane, respected her even, but she was not going to fuck this up for me.

For us.

A thin, piercing alarm suddenly went off, startling both of us, and I dropped Jane's wrist, looking up at the ceiling.

"What —" she started, but I already knew.

It was a fire alarm.

Without thinking, I ran for the stairs.

You idiot, you fucking idiot, I thought as I ran, because this was another thing that was like Eddie. The panic room didn't open in case of fire because it was supposed to be a place you could go if there *was* a fire. Either

Eddie didn't know that, or he was betting that I would come and let him out.

And I was pretty sure it was the latter.

Jane was right behind me, yelling my name.

Upstairs, the smell of smoke was strong, gray wisps already snaking out beneath the door of the closet, and when I grabbed the doorknob, it was hot. So hot it burned, my skin stinging.

I yanked the door open to a blast of heat and smoke and pain, and somewhere behind me, Jane started to scream.

■ ■ ■ ■

PART XIII
JANE

■ ■ ■ ■

37

I haven't been in a hospital since I was fifteen, when I broke my elbow trying to impress a guy on a skateboard. I'd hated the experience then and it's not my favorite now.

I'm supposed to go home tomorrow, but where home is, I have no idea. The house in Thornfield Estates is gone, burned to the ground, and the new life I had tried to build is gone with it.

It probably says something about me that this is the part I'm fixated on, not the part where the man I was engaged to had locked his wife in a panic room for months. Weirdly, in a way, that part of the story was almost a relief. Everything that hadn't quite added up, everything that had triggered my fight-or-flight instincts made sense now. Everything was clear.

And I know that for the rest of my life, I'll see the look on Bea's face as she charged up the stairs to save Eddie. No matter what I felt for him, it was never that. It *never* could've been that.

Just like Eddie never could have loved me like he clearly loved Bea.

When Bea had opened the panic room door, there'd been a whooshing sound, crackling, a blaze of heat that had sent me stumbling back, and instinct kicked in.

I ran.

Down the stairs, out the door, onto the lawn, falling into the grass, choking and gasping.

In the end, I'd done the thing I'd been doing all my life — I saved myself.

Which meant I'd left Bea and Eddie to die.

Sighing, I unwrap the Popsicle my nurse had sneaked me. Banana.

I'm lucky. Everyone says so. No burns, just smoke inhalation, which makes my throat and chest still ache, but given that the house is literally ashes, I got out pretty lightly, all things considered.

Except for the part where I'm homeless and adrift now.

I'm about to settle even deeper into self-pity when there's a soft rapping at my door, and I turn to see Detective Laurent there.

"Knock-knock," she says, and my heart

leaps up into my throat, making me bite down on the Popsicle, the cold burning my teeth.

"Hi," I say, awkward, and she gestures toward the plastic chair near my bed.

"Can we have a quick chat?"

It's not like I can tell her no, and I'm guessing she knows that since she doesn't wait for me to answer before she sits down.

Crossing her legs, she smiles at me, like we're friends and this is just a fun bedside visit, and I try to make myself smile back until I remember that I'm supposed to be traumatized and upset.

The last few days have completely thrown me off my game.

I look down, fiddle with the wrapper of the Popsicle, and wait for her to say something.

"How are you feeling?" she asks, and I shrug, tucking my hair behind my ears.

"Better. Still raspy," I say, gesturing to my throat. "It all still seems so unreal, I guess."

Detective Laurent nods, the corners of her eyes crinkling as she gives me a sympathetic look, but there's something about the way she's watching me that I don't like. Something that makes me feel naked and exposed.

"I suppose you know by now that your

fiancé didn't make it out of the fire."

I press my lips together, closing my eyes briefly, but inside, my wind is whirring. Is this where she tells me they found two bodies in the ashes? What do I say? Do I tell her the truth about Bea and Eddie, about all of it?

"I do," I manage to croak out, fear sounding like sadness, which is good.

"And I imagine you also know that our working theory is that he burned the house down on purpose. That he wanted to kill himself and you as well."

No.

No, I did not know that, and my shock and confusion as I look at the detective isn't feigned. "On purpose?" I say, and she nods, sighing as she leans back in her chair.

"Jane, there is a very good chance Edward Rochester was involved in the murder of Blanche Ingraham and the disappearance of his wife."

"Oh my god," I say softly, pressing a hand to my mouth.

Detective Laurent shifts in her chair as outside, I hear the squeak of a wheelchair, the beep of various machines. "In looking into Tripp Ingraham's involvement, we found signs that Eddie had also been there that night. His car on the security camera at the Thornfield Estates entrance, one of your neighbors remembering that he also left home late the night his wife and Blanche had gone to the lake. Nothing concrete, and we were still in the process of gathering evidence, but now . . ."

She trails off, and I see her hand go to the badge at her waist for a second.

"What about Tripp?" I ask. "What happens now?"

It's weird and more than a little off-putting to feel any sympathy for Tripp Ingraham, and I'll eventually get over it, but now that I know the whole story, it's hard not to see him as a victim, too. Another person caught up in the shitstorm that was Eddie and Bea.

"He's been cleared of any suspicion," Detective Laurent says. "Truthfully, we never had as much on him as we let him think. We were hoping he'd crack, or bring down Eddie in the process."

Then she sighs. "Anyway, the fire was clearly set on purpose, which makes us think Eddie knew we were getting close."

Leaning over, she takes my hand. "I'm so sorry. I know this all must be a shock."

It is, but not in the way she thinks. They think Eddie killed himself because he killed Blanche and Bea. Which means they didn't find Bea's body in the fire.

Which means she's still out there.

"We may have some more questions later on," the detective says, patting my hand and standing up, "but I just wanted to let you know where things stood right now."

"Thank you," I say, and she smiles again.

"Take care of yourself, Jane."

As she heads for the door, I can't help but ask one more question.

"Did you . . . is Eddie's body . . ."

I make the words hesitant, like it's too horrible to even contemplate, and the detective's face creases.

"The fire burned with extraordinary heat," she says, gently. "There was nothing left. I believe they found . . ." She pauses, clears her throat. "I believe there were some teeth."

I see that stupid fucking pineapple in my hand, the way it crunched against Eddie's jaw.

The shards of white on the carpet.

"Thank you," I tell her, averting my eyes, letting her think I'm overwhelmed by the horror of it all.

I hear her leave and, after a moment, pick up my Popsicle again. It's partially melted, a sticky puddle of yellow on my tray, and I push one finger through it.

My ring still sparkles on my left hand. At

446

least I have that, and selling it will get me started on a new life at least. A smaller one than I'd planned for, but something.

Provided Bea lets me.

She's out there still, and she knows I know the truth. So, what's her next move?

"Sweetie?"

I glance up and see Emily standing in the doorway, frowning at me.

She looks over her shoulder for a second and then says, in a low voice, "I was just coming by to check on you, but there's a boy here who says he's your brother? And he's taking you home tomorrow? I didn't know you had a brother."

Fuck me, John.

"I don't," I say, and Emily's frown deepens as she steps more fully in, then smiles.

"Adele is already moved in, you might as well come, too."

Adele. I'd forgotten about the dog in all that had happened, and for whatever reason, that's the thing that finally makes tears spring to my eyes.

"She's okay?" I ask, and Emily nods. "Completely fine. Terrorizing Major and Colonel." Walking farther into the room, Emily takes my hand. "Come on, girl. Come home with me."

So I do.

38

The first few days at Emily's are nice. I get a pretty guest room and Emily orders takeout for me, brings me more ice cream for my throat, and this concoction she makes out of pineapple juice and sparkling water is actually pretty delicious. And it's nicer than I'd thought it would be, having Adele. She sleeps on the foot of my bed every night, her presence a warm, comforting weight.

So it's fine in the beginning.

Really, the shit doesn't start until the fifth day I've been there, when I'm up and walking around, basically recovered from the fire.

It's small at first.

Can I run into the village and pick up some croissants for her book club? Oh, and on my way back, can I run into Whole Foods? She has a list!

And now here I am, three weeks after I left the hospital, walking Major the shih tzu through the neighborhood.

As we walk, I wonder if I imagined the past six months. Maybe this was all just some kind of extended hallucination, and I never even met Eddie Rochester, never lived in the house set back from the road where, briefly, most of my dreams came true.

But our morning walk reminds me that no, it happened. There's only an empty lot where the house Eddie and Bea built used to stand. Ashes and crime scene tape, that's all that's left, but I take Major there anyway, waiting for . . . what? A sign? Bea to magically appear wearing a veiled hat and sunglasses, telling me it was all worth something?

That's not happening.

I'm just a girl who got caught up in other people's bullshit. Who got to taste a different life only to have it taken away, because that's how it always goes.

Still, it makes me sad to stand there, seeing the spot where the house used to be, remembering how I'd felt, cooking in that kitchen, sleeping in that bedroom, soaking in that bathtub.

Except that every time I think of that, I have to remember that Bea was always there, sharing the space with me. Waiting.

I've just turned to go back to Emily's

house, Major happily trotting along, when my phone buzzes in my pocket. It's not a number I recognize, but since it's a 205 number, which means Birmingham, I answer.

"Is this Jane Bell?" a man asks.

He sounds like what I'd imagine a basset hound would sound like if it could talk, his voice deep and drawling, and I tug at Major's leash as I say, "Yes?"

"I'm Richard Lloyd. Edward Rochester's lawyer."

I remember that name, remember Eddie handing Richard's business card to John, and my grip tightens on my phone.

"Okay," I say, and he sighs.

"Could you come down to my office this week? The sooner the better, really."

I want to tell him no. What good can come of meeting with lawyers?

But then I look back at the ruin of what was Eddie's house and remember that daydream I'd had, Bea striding out of the ashes to hand me something, some reward for everything I'd been through.

"Sure," I tell him. "I can be there tomorrow."

The office is exactly what I thought it would be. Expensive, masculine leather furniture, pictures of dogs with dead ducks in their mouths, magazines about hunting, fishing, and golf littering the coffee table in front of me.

And when a slightly florid-faced man in an ugly suit walks into the lobby and says, "Miss Bell?" he's exactly what I was expecting, too.

There was none of Tripp's air of dereliction around him, but they were clearly from the same genus, *Southernus drunkus.*

I imagine he walks over to the pub I saw on the corner for lunch every day, orders the same thing, has at least two beers before coming back to sexually harass the pretty college student currently answering phones.

But I make myself give him that tremulous smile Eddie had liked as I stand up, taking his proffered hand and shaking it. "Please," I say, "call me Jane."

"Jane," he repeats. "Don't meet many Janes these days."

I just keep the same insipid smile on my face and let him lead me to his private office.

More leather here, more pictures of hunting, only now they are photographs of this man, smiling broadly in a bright orange vest, holding up the head of a deer, its eyes glassy, its tongue lolling out.

451

Not for the first time, I think to myself that I am going to be relieved to get out of this place. The coddled bubble of Thornfield Estates has been nice, but everything else around here is pretty fucked.

"Now," he says as he settles behind his massive desk. "I have to admit, I was a little surprised when Eddie wanted to change his will so soon after getting engaged to you. Honestly, I actually tried to talk him out of it. No offense."

"None taken," I say, but I can hardly hear him over the ringing in my ears.

Eddie put me in his will.

Did he think Bea might get out one day? That she'd kill him? Was this his way of preemptively saying sorry, or was it just another play in their sick game? A way of putting her own fortune out of her reach, by giving it to me?

I'll never know.

"In any case, he had control over all of Bea's finances after she disappeared. Her shares in the company, all of that. And now," he says, handing a thick leather portfolio across the desk to me, "it's yours."

My fingers are numb as I place it in my lap, feeling the weight of it on my legs.

"The company is yours as well, of course," he goes on, writing something on a legal

452

pad. "Southern Manors. You can keep it, or
—"

"I can sell it, right?"

Mr. Lloyd's eyes meet mine across the desk, and his lips twitch slightly. "It's yours," he repeats.

I sit there, holding this, holding everything, and for a moment, I think about what it would be like to keep it. To run Southern Manors, to buy a new house in Thornfield Estates.

But no.

I see this for what it is — a gift. From Eddie. From Bea.

In exchange for keeping their secrets, they'll give me this.

And I will fucking take it.

I open the folder and stare at the paper in my hands. It's mostly legal jargon, and of course Jane Bell isn't even my real name, but none of that matters. All I'm looking at are the numbers.

It's all of it, I can tell. Bea's entire fortune, everything she built with Southern Manors, left to Eddie who then left it to me.

I'm rich.

Not just a little rich, either. This is millions. Hundreds of millions.

Signed over to me.

I raise my eyes to the lawyer's, and I don't

have to fake the tears. They're already there, but they're tears of relief, not sadness. Tears of fucking joy. Bea Rochester has handed a life to me. Not her life, not "Jane Bell's" life, but something new, something fresh.

Something I can make all mine.

"It's all been such a shock," I say quietly. "Everything with Eddie. I loved him, I really did, but I had no idea . . ."

I look back to my lap, my throat working. "I didn't know you could love someone, but also not know them at all."

"Honey, it seems like none of us knew Eddie Rochester," Mr. Lloyd says, reaching across the desk to pat my hand, his class ring heavy and cold.

When I walk outside, the wind has picked up, clouds moving quickly across the sky. The air feels thick and heavy with an impending late-summer storm, and I pull my umbrella from my purse even as I tilt my face toward the first few fat drops of rain.

The smile that spreads across my face hurts my cheeks. It probably looks stupid, too, a wide, childlike grin, but for the first time in a long time, I don't think about how other people might see me. I'm not tailoring my reaction for someone else.

I'm free.

Bea and her money have set me free.

Free to leave Alabama, free to use my real name again if I want to. Because the kind of money I have now is the perfect wall against the past.

I can be Helen Burns again if I want to. I can be Jane Bell forever if I want to.

I can be anyone.

EPILOGUE

I wonder about them sometimes. Eddie and Bea.

Once, as I was loading groceries into my trunk, I thought I saw them.

It couldn't have been them, of course. By then, I'd left Mountain Brook behind me. Left the whole state of Alabama. I'd used Bea's money to buy myself a little place — nothing as crazy as what I could've afforded, but still — my own small, cozy cabin in the mountains of North Carolina.

Turns out I liked the South.

But there was no way the woman in the sunglasses in the big SUV that cruised past the Ingles Market parking lot could've been Bea, no way the figure slumped in the passenger seat was Eddie. I couldn't even tell if it was a man, after all.

Adele had been in the car, and she'd given a short, sharp bark at the car as it passed, and I thought the person in the passenger seat had turned a little to look back, but they were too far away by then for me to be sure.

That was only a few months after the fire, though, so I'd been jumpier, primed to see ghosts everywhere.

I sometimes think I might always be looking over my shoulder.

I remind myself that when Bea opened the door to the panic room, there was a whoosh and a wall of flame. I remember the scent of burned hair, and a worse, darker scent, disturbingly like barbecue.

I remember that they found Eddie's teeth.

But I also remember those teeth flying out of his mouth when I hit him, and so . . .

I wonder.

I like to think that they both survived. That they're out there somewhere.

Maybe they've gone back to Hawaii. Or a more remote island, their own little beach somewhere.

I picture them on white sand, palm trees swaying overhead, just like I used to picture them when Bea was a ghost and Eddie was mine.

She sits there, smiling in the sunshine, her glossy hair pulled back from her face. Eddie is next to her. Not nearly as handsome as he once was.

I see Bea reach for his hand, see his fingers — thick with scars, raised red welts crisscrossing his skin — curl around hers.

We're together now, she'll say to him, *that's all that matters.* Not the money, not the life they'd built, not the house that's now just a black mark on all that green, green grass at Thornfield Estates.

And it won't be a lie when she says that they're better off now without all that, better off just the two of them, wherever they are.

It'll be the truth.

ACKNOWLEDGMENTS

I am always grateful to my agent, Holly Root, but especially grateful when it comes to this project. Holly, thank you for always seeing my potential and knowing my writerly heart better than I do sometimes.

Thanks also to Josh Bank, Joelle Hobeika, and Sara Shandler at Alloy Entertainment for this opportunity and for truly changing the way I write. It was such a joy to work with all of you!

To the entire team at St. Martin's including Sarah Bonamino, Sallie Lotz, Naureen Nashid, Marissa Sangiacomo, and Jessica Zimmerman. You're all rock stars, and Bea would snatch y'all up for Southern Manors in a heartbeat.

Obscene levels of thanks to Sarah Cantin for getting this book from the word go and then making it so, so much better! It's such a joy to work with someone who is both a razor-sharp editor and a wonderful advocate for the book, and I have appreciated it more than I can say.

As always, thanks to my family. None of this is any fun without y'all.

And lastly, thanks to every woman who ever got to the end of *Jane Eyre* and thought, "Honestly, Jane? You could do better."

You are my people, and I love you.

ABOUT THE AUTHOR

Rachel Hawkins is the *New York Times* bestselling author of multiple books for young readers, and her work has been translated in more than a dozen countries. She studied gender and sexuality in Victorian literature at Auburn University and currently lives in Alabama. *The Wife Upstairs* is her first adult novel.

CPSIA information can be obtained
at www.ICGtesting.com
Printed in the USA
BVHW040254121221
623793BV00019B/78